**Hide and Seek - Text copyright © Emmy Ellis 2020
Cover Art by Emmy Ellis @ studioenp.com © 2020**

All Rights Reserved

Hide and Seek is a work of fiction. All characters, places, and events are from the author's imagination. Any resemblance to persons, living or dead, events or places is purely coincidental.

The author respectfully recognises the use of any and all trademarks.

With the exception of quotes used in reviews, this book may not be reproduced or used in whole or in part by any means existing without written permission from the authors.

Warning: The unauthorised reproduction or distribution of this copyrighted work is illegal. No part of this book may be scanned, uploaded, or distributed via the Internet or any other means, electronic or print, without the author's written permission.

HIDE AND SEEK

EMMY ELLIS

PROLOGUE

Jolly19 waited by the fountain. *She'd* be here soon, the one he'd spoken to for so long. Heaven13. Blonde. Blue eyes. Eager to meet him. Teen girls had a thing about going out with older boys, so he'd discovered. It got them feeling all grown up, adults in a pubescent body, all of them naïve, none of them taking any notice of the dangers online, despite the warnings.

It wouldn't happen to them, that was what they thought.

Well, it had. And it would again. To Heaven13 anyway, and hopefully to the others he'd strike up conversations with in the future.

Silly cows.

The one he'd dumped during the night had lost the game. He'd found her—she hadn't hidden very well like he'd told her to. What she hadn't known was, her scent had given her away. The ripe stench of fear in the form of pungent sweat. She'd probably told herself she'd picked the right spot, wedged in the nook that had no purpose whatsoever, a slim waste of space in his cottage. At the back, she'd been, clothed in the shadows, but his head torch had sought her out, bathing her in its too-white glow, exposing her for the kid she was. Scared out of her wits and crapping it.

Teenagers thought they knew everything, didn't they, but she'd soon realised she hadn't. Her scream had delighted him, as had her eyes, wide, showing her terror—she knew what would happen next. He'd told her prior to the chase.

'Make sure you hide well, for if I seek and find, this is your fate.'

It had sounded so chilling, using a voice and words he wouldn't usually. Life got boring if you didn't try new things. He'd come so far from the old days, more mature, planning better.

A blast of sun warmed his face, and he snapped out of his thoughts, reprimanding himself for not being more present in the present. Perhaps last night's girl had thought about the past, too, in her final moments, her short, spoilt-brat life flashing in front of her bulging-from-being-suffocated eyes.

There he was again, slipping into what was, when he had what *is* right over there on the bench.

She'd followed his instructions, then, to sit there in a backwards baseball cap, a pink one, her wavy blonde hair in pigtails, just the sort of look he enjoyed. It reminded him of *her*, plus Francesca, a girl he'd once known. Her black vest top, spaghetti straps tight and pressing into her shoulders, gave both a young illusion but also an on-the-cusp-of-womanhood vibe, the way the material stretched across her chest. That was his thing, girls, those who teetered, walking the tightrope between a child and an adult. Budding breasts, hips on the brink of splaying, ready for having babies.

They were like *her*. Mum. She'd always looked young in body.

A hot breeze pushed through the bushes, wavering a leaf-drenched tree branch in front of him, temporarily obstructing his view. Annoying, that, when he'd been so enrapt. It broke that wonderful spell, the one he chased, that session of watching, her wondering when he'd turn up, or if he even would, leaving her sitting there alone, bereft, asking herself if all those words on her phone or laptop screen had meant anything.

They were the lure, those words, what he used to entice, so they meant *some*thing, just not in the way she probably imagined. No, he didn't think they had a future, the one he'd promised—two kids, a dog, and all the money she could spend. He didn't have a high-flying job, even at nineteen, because he was forty-seven, washed up in his profession, if it could be called that. And he didn't love her.

Her head, filled with dreams, had told her to meet him today. Her heart, filled with the yearning for an adult life now, before it was due, before she'd learnt the lessons all her teenage years would provide, had led her to that bench.

She was greedy to grow up.

Come tonight, she'd be wishing she was little again, safe at home, with none of the horrors he presented to her.

Tonight, she'd learn that all the things Mummy had told her were true. Predators lurked online. Men posed as young blokes.

Men lied.

Aroused, he pressed at his groin. It wouldn't do to message her yet, asking her to come into the bushes, her spotting the tent in his jeans. Besides, he needed to see how long she'd be willing to sit there. How important he was to her. How desperate she was to give him that kiss she'd promised.

So easy to coerce them to say these things.

She took her phone out, likely checking for a message from him.

She'd get the message all right.
Later.

While Dad was at work, Mum had her own way of making money.

John bunked school quite a bit and spent those hours in the shed torturing small animals. Rats, mice, those vole things. He went into the house only when thirst or hunger pushed him. Mum didn't give a toss about where he was or what he was doing. She had her own world, her own life, and if she had her way, it wouldn't include him.

John was desperate for her to love him, to show how much he meant to her. He was hoping for a miracle, that was the problem. Still, that desire was there all the same.

Dad worked shitloads of hours. He thought Mum grafted in a shop, like she'd told him with her lying mouth. She bloody didn't. She topped up Dad's earnings with her 'wages', and any extra she made, she obviously spent on her gin and bottles of tonic water.

The sodding lush.

Mum and Dad's bed squeaked. Grunts and various hoots of laughter drifted down the stairs. Each day the male voice was different, and over time, her gin bouts had become longer, one glass turning into many prior to these men's visits.

She was a pisshead. What, did she need to get on the sauce so she was drunk enough to go through what she did for a living? Giving herself to all those blokes?

Curiosity got the better of John, even though he had a fair idea of what was happening up there. He climbed the stairs, ears pricked to alert mode. Crept along the landing and paused to steady his breathing outside his parents' bedroom. The cries from inside grew louder. He put his palm on the handle. Turned it. Opened the door a bit. Peeked through the crack.

The man was on top of Mum, grunting. She had a pink baseball cap on. A school uniform. Short grey skirt that had ridden up and bunched around her waist. White blouse, open, revealing tits that spilled out of a black lacy bra. Her head whipped from side to side on the pillow, her sweat-soaked, blonde pigtails flicking through the air and landing across her face.

Images of the girls at school flitted through John's mind, and he imagined Mum was Francesca, who'd caught his attention years back when they'd been colouring in after playtime. Her white ankle socks were her main attraction, her slim calves seeming to grow out of them, flowers from the soil.

Mum opened her eyes and looked up at her customer, a laugh exploding from her.

John's breaths grew sharp. He ran to his room and fiddled with himself, replaying what he'd seen over and over, confused yet exhilarated. He wanted Mum to treat him like that.

He wanted her love.

CHAPTER ONE

Sweat drenched Elsa's armpits, to the point she worried it would transfer to her vest top. She moved her arms away from her sides, hoping the warm air would dry her skin. The thought of J knowing she was nervous didn't sit well. She wanted him to see her as the confident 'woman' she'd tried so hard to be while they'd chatted. The thing was, inside, nerves kept nipping at her, and doubts flourished—that was a word J had used, flourished, and she'd liked it so much she'd stolen it, used it in a conversation at school.

Everyone had laughed, taken the piss.

He was nice to her, if a bit rude sometimes. You know, sexual.

Those doubts wouldn't be quiet.

She thought about Mum sitting on the sofa, using her laptop to earn extra money from home. The poor thing had Chronic Fatigue Syndrome and could barely function some days. Dad did his best, working overtime and everything, but money was short, and luxuries were few and far between. J had said he had a fair amount of cash already, and she'd latched on to him even more because of it. Shallow, some might say, but if he could help her parents, as well as giving Elsa security, it couldn't be a bad thing, could it?

She was doing this for all of them.

Still, it wasn't right to use him, even though she thought she might love him a bit. She'd told her Best Friend Forever, Sasha, about J, and she'd said it wasn't a good idea to meet him, that she ought to stop talking to him right away and forget it all. Sasha was frightened Elsa would get abducted or something silly, and Elsa had laughed. Now, though, those words swirled in Elsa's mind, the possibility of them containing the truth a sharp sword in the gut. Their friend, Catherine, had been missing for a few days now. It was all over the news, her face in the top-right of the TV screen, her latest school photo, one Catherine hated because she had a spot right in the middle of her forehead.

Panic came then, filling Elsa's body with cold and smothering her skin with goosebumps. Mum always said if something didn't feel right it probably wasn't, and you should walk away immediately once your guts went all dicky. Sasha had echoed much the same, minus the dicky bit.

So why was Elsa still sitting here then?

She stood, legs shaky, and glanced around. She was alone. And also, why should she stay when it was clear he was a no-show? He was meant to be here over ten minutes ago and had stressed how much *she* needed to be on time, so how come he wasn't?

Angry now, and, if she were honest, ashamed she'd fallen for his promises when they clearly weren't real, she headed for the alley that led to the shopping centre around the corner, eager to be near someone. Her isolated spot on the bench in the courtyard had given her the jitters when J had mentioned it anyway, what with that shrubbery nearby. Anyone could be hiding in there, one of those abductors Sasha had been so worried about.

Elsa's phone let off the message tone. She kept walking, afraid, sensing someone behind her. The hairs on the back of her neck prickled, and her pulse thudded hard in her throat. Everything she'd ever been taught came crashing in: *Don't talk to strangers on the internet; don't meet someone you don't really know; if you meet, take a friend and make sure it's a public place; if someone offers you the world, it's probably bullshit.*

"Fuck," she gasped out, running, her chest painful from her quick breaths.

She rounded the corner, rushing up the alley, and it seemed too long, too narrow, the grey stone bricks closing in on her, clunky arms that wanted to crush her whole. Silhouettes of people strode by across the end, and she ached to be closer to them, for them to glance in and see her, to know she was there.

No one did.

I'm here! Help me! Something's wrong!

"Oh God..."

Tears stung to the point she lost her vision for a split second. The horror of someone following her was so real now, as if they were *right there*, an inch away. Was it J? *Had* he turned weird like Sasha had said he would? The mouth of the alley got nearer, and her fear abated slightly, but she kept up her pace. She dared to glance back over her shoulder.

A wide man, presenting his back to her then walking the other way. A hood up, head bent.

"Shitting hell!"

She sped up, terrified. Someone *had* been following her, and as she was almost to safety, they'd turned and given up the chase. That was what she thought anyway, and it chilled her even more, in spite of the warm sun on her skin and the heat generated from her sprint. Who was it? The picture J had sent her showed a nineteen-year-old man, slim, not a short and fat person. Was J really J? Was he some kind of pervert instead? What had the guest speaker on internet safety told them in assembly the other day? Grooming, that was it. Men pretending to be younger, sucking you in.

She burst out into the high street, never so thankful to see people. They milled around, going about their business, laden with shopping bags from Primark, Superdrug, all sorts, and some came out of the three-storey gym, as red-faced as *she* must be after all that exercise.

Elsa slowed, walking backwards so she could keep her eye on the alley. The man was just rounding the corner into the courtyard. He swivelled his head, and for a millisecond their gazes connected, despite the distance between them, then he was gone.

She shivered, convinced she'd had a near-miss. With her nerves shredded, she turned around and jogged to the precinct doors, pushing one and letting the building swallow her up.

Sandra's balloon stall had Elsa thinking of the past, and her eyes stung again. When she'd been small and money not so tight, before Mum got ill, Dad used to buy her a balloon every so often. She kept them until all the helium had seeped out and they became crinkled shells, the ribbon scrunched from where she'd gripped it. Now they were folded in a drawer, just memories.

Her phone blipped again. Shit, was that J?

A wooden bench was by the stall, so she sat on it, opposite the butcher's, the one where the owner had been killed out the back in his yard. She quivered at that, thinking it could so easily have been her, dragged into those bushes, J or whoever the hell that man had been doing all sorts to her.

She took her phone out and, stomach cramping, accessed Messenger.

Jolly19: WHERE ARE YOU?

That must have been the message she'd ignored on her way to the alley.

Jolly19: I'M AT THE BENCH IN THE COURTYARD. YOU ON YOUR WAY?

What if J and the man who'd followed were different people? What if she'd got this so wrong? She bit her bottom lip, closed the message window, and opened another—the latest convo with Sasha.

Elsa (Heaven13): ARE YOU AROUND? I NEED TO TALK TO YOU.

Sasha: YEAH, IN B&M GETTING SOME OF THOSE LUSH SWEETS WE GOT BEFORE. I THOUGHT YOU WERE MEETING J?

Elsa (Heaven13): I WAS, BUT THERE WAS THIS MAN. HE FOLLOWED ME.

Sasha: SHIT. I TOLD YOU! WHERE ARE YOU?

That question gave her the jitters. J had said the same: *Where are you?*

Elsa (Heaven13): BY SANDRA'S BALLOONS.

Sasha: I'M COMING NOW.

Relief wasn't the word. Elsa stared past the stall. B&M was up that way, round the left corner. Sandra gave her a tentative smile, eyeing Elsa as if she sensed something was wrong. Elsa was desperate to tell someone, but what if J wasn't who he'd said he was? He knew her name, and she'd stupidly given him her address. Sasha didn't know that; J had said no one should know, it was their business, fuck everyone else and their need to find stuff out.

"You all right, love?" Sandra called. "You look a bit flustered."

Elsa nodded and got up, the urge to be near another human forcing her feet forward. "I'm…" She paused. "I'm waiting for my friend."

Sandra cocked her head. "That's nice, but you still don't seem okay."

Elsa rubbed her clammy arms. "I just ran here, that's all. Didn't want to be late." She peered past Sandra. "Ah, there she is now."

She smiled and walked away, concentrating her sights on Sasha with the idea that if she took her attention off her for one second, her BFF would disappear. Elsa hurried, getting funny glances off people, like she'd nicked something from New Look or whatever. She reached Sasha and flung herself at her, tears burning.

"Bloody hell, steady on." Sasha laughed. "What's been happening? I *knew* something was weird, that's why I came into town so I was close." She eased back and held the tops of Elsa's arms. "We'll go into Costa so we can talk."

Elsa trailed her into the shop. Sasha, who had rich parents, ordered them a fancy Ruby Hot Chocolate, which was oddly pink instead of brown, and the barista put multi-coloured sprinkles on the squirty cream. They sat in a corner, facing the door so Elsa could see out into the precinct. J might come searching for her, and she wanted to spot him first.

"Tell me everything." Sasha raised one of the plates off the tray and plonked a salted caramel muffin in front of Elsa.

"I can't afford this," Elsa mumbled.

"My treat."

"But you keep paying for stuff."

"So what? Just eat it, will you? I won't even moan if you speak with your mouth full, and you know how much that gets on my nerves."

Elsa smiled, her stomach in knots. She sipped some of her drink and prepared herself to go through what had just gone on. "Look, J might be a nice person, okay, not one of those grooming ones like you said, but I got a weird feeling. I had to meet him at the bench in the courtyard, the one by the fountain. No one else was there, which made it worse, and I was just sitting on my own, waiting. Then I thought about what you'd said, you know, that he could be a weirdo, and I got worried and decided to leave."

"Good. Then what?"

"I got a message and panicked in case it was him. By that point, I reckoned someone was following me, so I ran down the alley. I turned back, and this bloke was walking off, back the way I'd come. He was short and fat, nothing like J, so I was right to leave, wasn't I? He had a hoody on."

"Why would a man in a hoody follow you then go back if it wasn't suss?" Sasha raised her eyebrows. "He was probably hiding in the bushes, the paedo." She bit a lump off her Belgian bun.

"It was horrible. Like I knew something was wrong, yet all the time we'd been speaking on Messenger, it was right." That was a lie; she hadn't felt totally comfortable even then. The rude stuff was a bit much. "All right, I had *some* worries, but nothing like I felt on that bench."

"It was stupid to even start talking to him. Who the hell just randomly pops up like he did? He wasn't even on your friend list at the time. If you remember, his message went into that other folder." Sasha spooned off some cream from her drink and ate it. "Okay, he said he knew a few of us, said he was someone or other's cousin, but how would we know? The cousin moved away and isn't on Facebook anymore."

True. I should have checked properly. "He knows my address," she blurted and blushed, her throat tightening.

"What?" Sasha dropped her spoon on the table and glanced round at the other customers, then leant forward and glared at Elsa. "Are you fucking me about?"

Elsa shook her head. "I know. You don't have to say it. I'm bloody stupid."

"Why did you tell him?"

"He said it was so he could put it in his satnav for when he dropped me home later."

"That is *more* than stupid." Sasha continued to stare at her. "You *know* the sort of shit that happens. Shadwell isn't exactly the safest place to live either."

"What, you think J's a killer?"

Sasha shrugged. "Who knows? We've had enough of them here lately. Then there's Catherine going missing." She stuffed more bun in her mouth.

Else chewed on her muffin, hating herself for being such a twat. The sponge clumped on her tongue.

"Listen." Sasha sipped some hot chocolate. "Even if J *is* who he says he is, you still shouldn't have anything to do with him. He's nineteen, you're thirteen. Why would a bloke want to be with a kid? And before you say anything, that's what we are. Think about that for a minute. A bit weird much? Did you…did you talk about sex?"

Elsa nodded.

Sasha sighed. "See, that's where it gets odd. Men shouldn't be talking about that with teenagers."

"He's still a teenager."

"You're making excuses. You're underage. He's wrong to do it."

Elsa knew that, but still… "He messaged to say he was there, at the meeting place. My phone went off as I walked away." She thought about where she'd been at the time—still within sight of the fountain. "Why didn't he just call out to me when I didn't answer my phone?"

"Because he was the fat bloke." Sasha pursed her lips. "I'm telling you, he was in those bloody bushes."

Another chill spread over Elsa's back. Her instincts had been warning her, even down to the sweat in her armpits. She'd known, this morning even, while dressing in the vest top he'd asked her to put on, and the pink cap, and when she did the pigtails. Yeah, she'd known. "What if he comes to my house?" The idea of Mum opening the door to a weirdo had Elsa sick to her stomach.

"I doubt he will. I mean, come on. If it's the fat man, is he going to risk your dad answering? Sorry, but I wouldn't knock on your door if I didn't know your dad was soft as shit."

Elsa's father was big, muscled, and he appeared 'rough and ready', as Mum called him. He was the opposite, though, like Sasha had said. Soft. Although, if the fat man came to the door and Dad suspected he was a paedo, Dad would flatten him.

"Okay, I feel better now." Elsa did, marginally, but—

Her phone jangled.

"Bet that's the supposed J," Sasha said. "You ought to block him."

"Should I read it?"

"May as well."

Elsa opened Messenger.

Jolly19: I REALISE YOU'RE FRIGHTENED OF MEETING ME FOR THE FIRST TIME. I GET IT. MAYBE WE COULD TRY AGAIN ANOTHER DAY? OR EVEN NOW. I'LL WAIT A BIT LONGER.

She showed Sasha.

"Now block," her friend said.

A part of Elsa didn't want to, the 'what-if' part: *What if he's nineteen and the same as the picture he sent? What if he really does love me and wants to give me a better life? What if he's genuine?* And the other part: *He could be the fat man, a groomer. He could have been speaking to me all this time, then planned to abduct me today. Is that what's happened to Catherine?*

She blocked him on Messenger and Facebook.

"That's that then." Sasha gulped some hot chocolate. "Now forget about it."

"I would if he didn't know where I live." Nerves gnawed at Elsa's tummy. "I can't believe I was so stupid. I thought…"

"You thought what?"

"Doesn't matter." She'd been about to say 'I loved him', but she'd had this convo with Sasha before and, ever practical, Sasha had said they didn't know what love was at their age.

Elsa gazed out into the precinct. A man stood outside Lloyds bank opposite. He had a dark hoody on and stared over. Elsa's guts rolled, and she reckoned she'd be sick if she didn't get out of there.

"We should go," she said, eyes burning.

"I haven't finished my cake," Sasha said, "and you've hardly touched yours, look."

"The fat man…" Elsa kept her arm low and pointed in his direction.

"Oh my God…" Sasha grabbed Elsa's other hand under the table. "That's him?"

Elsa bobbed her head, shaking all over. "I think so."

"Then we should tell someone." Sasha made to get up.

"No, leave it. What if he gets arrested for following me? He'll know it was me and come round my house after." She wanted a wee, and her mouth went dry. "Let's just wait until he goes away."

"But what if he stays there all afternoon?"

"Then we'll go to Sandra and ask her to walk us to the bus stop."

Sasha let Elsa's hand go. "Yeah, she'd do that if we told her there was a nutter about."

Elsa swallowed, her throat seeming to crackle.

They sat there for an hour, drinking a second hot chocolate, then the man walked off. Why had he come after her if he wasn't J? Why had he arrived at the precinct? How had he known she was there?

Then she remembered the tracker app. J had suggested they add each other to it so they could see where they were at all times.

Only J would know she was in Costa.

Her stomach bottomed out, and she puked all over the remains of her salted caramel muffin.

CHAPTER TWO

Jolly19 was beyond angry. The stupid cow had run, just as he'd been about to message her, asking her to come into the bushes. He'd planned to give her some excuse as to why he hid in there, but it had been moot anyway. She'd fucked off, heading for the alley, then town. He'd messaged to tell her he was there, but she'd ignored it and kept walking. What was *wrong* with her? Why the sudden bolt? He'd been sure she was ready to meet, his words of love securing the fact they'd get together, but something had gone awry.

She'd got scared.

Maybe it hadn't been such a good idea, hiding, making her wait, him wanting to know if she properly cared or not. Maybe he should have stepped out of the bushes straight away. But then she'd have seen him, realised he wasn't who he'd said he was, and she'd have run anyway, screaming, most likely.

He sat in his dad's old car at the multi-storey, seething at having to stand there for an hour while she was in Costa. It hadn't looked like she'd be coming out anytime soon, and an hour was all he'd give her. She'd also blocked him on Messenger, and her Facebook page was no longer visible. The tracker app wasn't showing her either. It'd be that little bitch she was with, Sasha, the one who commented on Heaven13's posts all the time. She'd have told her to do it.

Calmer, he took stock of the situation. He had two choices, one of them double-pronged. A: Walk away, pick someone else. B: Make a new profile and friend Heaven13—then off that Sasha cowbag so she didn't influence Heaven13 anymore. He'd start again, be someone else, one without a silly handle. An ordinary name with pictures uploaded, images he'd stolen from other people's albums. That was how he always did it. Views of places he'd supposedly been, on holiday and at home.

Photos of his dinner, cooked by his supposed mum, the one he wished he'd had. And he'd be sixteen this time. While nineteen had worked with the other two, them eating out of his hand, Elsa was seemingly wise to what he was doing now.

All the more reason to let her walk away.

Towards the end of John's tenth year, he'd seen many of Mum's sexual encounters. Dad had become well subdued, melancholy, depressed, and once, John even caught him crying.

"Never be ashamed to cry, John," was all he said on that occasion, wiping away his tears with the back of his hand.

Dad's hair seemed a lighter shade of grey, his moustache near white. Thirty-five and old already. His shoulders slumped; he had the air of someone defeated. His shirt, ironed by himself, looked worn and the collar no longer crisp. The centre crease in his trousers had faded on the knees.

John left the room. What had happened to make Dad so different?

Mum seemed in a daze half of the time. When the men friends weren't there, she was bitchy and walked with a stagger from drinking the gin. If they visited, she was happy, and the house rang with the sound of her laughter.

Later, John lay in bed, nearly asleep. Mum and Dad's raised voices disturbed him and, with his eyes still closed, he listened, tummy rolling over. Life was so scary here sometimes.

"If you weren't such a useless prick, I wouldn't have to do it." Mum sounded so spiteful.

"What? I work as hard as I can, earn as much as I can. Why the fuck can't you go out to work in a shop like normal women do? Like I was led to believe you were doing?" Dad said, his voice hoarse.

Oh God, he knows…

Mum sighed. "Because someone has to be here for John."

But you're never there for me.

"From what I can gather, you spend the whole day on your back, or pissed, and John takes care of himself. What good are you to him? You're not fit to call yourself a mum. I should have taken him away from you years ago."

"Oh, fuck off, Henry. Just fuck off. What the hell do you know anyway?"

Ice cubes clinked. So she was drinking then. Probably why she was gobbing off. Gin gave her courage.

"Me fuck off?" Dad's barking laughter was hollow and frightening. "It's you who'll be doing that before long."

The gasp from Mum pierced the blackness. John drew the covers up to his chin. He reached for the down-filled scatter cushion and hugged it to him, like he always did when he was upset. It crackled from him squeezing it.

"You'd chuck me out when I'm pregnant?"
What?

"Damn right I will. I don't even know if it's mine, you filthy scrubber. In fact, we can be almost certain it isn't."

"You cheeky bastard!"

The resounding noise of a slap slammed into the back of John's skull.

He reached into his pyjama bottoms in search of his safety net.

Mum and Dad must have come to some form of stalemate. No men visited Mum—at least none that John ever saw. Soon after, they were skint. Mum stayed at home lounging on the sofa.

Rows erupted. Dad came in from work to no meal. John had taken to making a dinner of sorts for himself each day, usually bread, beans on toast, or a boiled egg. Today he was making a jam sandwich, same as he had for the past week, what with her not getting any shopping in. She watched him, her usual way of creating unease inside him. She was waiting for the kettle to boil.

Dad came home then, and John relaxed a bit.

"What have you been doing all day?" Dad put his briefcase on the cluttered kitchen table. He sounded weary, tired of this shit.

John knew that feeling.

Mum sighed, all dramatic. "I'm tired, Henry. This baby is taking it out of me." She put on a suitably trite face and stood with her hip leaning against the worktop.

Dad huffed out a laugh. A sour one. "You and me both, Paula. Don't forget..."

John shuffled his feet. He'd yet to be told officially that he had a new sibling on the way. He cut his sandwich in half.

Dad came over and put a hand on John's shoulder. "We, um, have something to tell you, son."

John wedged some bread into his mouth and mumbled, "I already know."

Mum offered a secret smile and turned to make her coffee, leaving Dad to explain the mess she'd created.

John hated her so much. He marched out of that house, fists clenched in temper, ready to explode. The family cat didn't come when he called him, which knobbed him off even more. Visiting Twinkle's usual haunts in the front garden proved fruitless. Where was the little fucker?

Mrs Drayton, the neighbour who received the animal carcasses over the fence when John was finished with killing them, puffed out her cheeks as he slammed the front garden gate.

"Puff all you want, you old biddy," he muttered and stormed past the wall she perched on.

"I beg your pardon, young man?" Her mouth dropped open.

"Fuck off! You heard me." His chest swelled, and he turned to scowl at her, staring at her with the eyes that gave his teachers the creeps. He'd overheard them saying that once.

"Oh!" She whimpered and patted her headscarf that hid her rollers, her cheeks stained crimson.

John walked once up and down the street. The cat wasn't anywhere. He was probably in the shed. He stomped down an alley between two houses, made his way to the end, and veered left. His rear garden was the fourth one along. He used the gate and quietly gained access. Mum's and Dad's voices, loud and sharp, rang out through the open kitchen window. He ignored what they said. Dad was hurting; John didn't need confirmation by listening to more.

He headed for the shed. His anger abated, simmering to a quiet bubble, but somehow it was more dangerous than his rage upon leaving the house.

He found Twinkle lying on his side on the shed roof, lounging in the sun. Fast asleep, the stupid animal didn't hear his approach until it was too late. John grabbed his fur into his fist and lifted him by the scruff of his neck, carrying him into the shed.

He kicked the door shut behind him.

John didn't feel an ounce of remorse for hurting the animal. Bashing Twinkle's teeth out had so easily sated the terrible anger. He decided to always go with his instincts and do whatever his mind and body instructed from now on.

It was less stressful that way.

CHAPTER THREE

Bethany swallowed the lump in her throat. Seeing a body was never pleasant, but one naked and belonging to a child had a specific ream of emotions linked to it. A life cut way too short. Parents devastated—once they'd been informed. Schoolchildren confused, trying to understand how someone their age could be missing, let alone dead. *Dead*, not coming back to class, never to go on school trips, laughing with the abandon freedom from parents brought—*we're away from home, isn't it ace?*

They were in an old car park, one no longer used, round the back of the big Tesco on the retail park. Weeds pushed through the fissures in the ancient tarmac, and all around the edge, the once pruned hedges had been left to grow in an unruly mess, branches clawing upwards, leaves in hotch-potch clumps. Tesco had bought the land for use as a petrol station but had yet to commence the build. An employee, who walked through here on his way to work, having tromped over the field next to the nearest housing estate, had discovered her around two this afternoon.

In the tent, Bethany sighed.

"I'd say this was her." Mike cleared his throat, as he always did in times of stress or if he was trying not to laugh. In this case, it was the former. Obviously.

Bethany nodded. Catherine Noble had been missing for days. Thirteen, too young for…this. They'd tried finding her, and it was just this morning Bethany had discussed things with her team, saying they may well have to scale back on the search if news didn't turn up within the next couple of weeks. Catherine could be a runaway, eager to get to another city, one where she could live however she wanted. Except she wasn't. Her parents, distraught at their daughter 'going off like that' and it being 'so unlike her', would have their world smashed to pieces today, completely, not just that chunk they currently dealt with, the one that still had blooms of hope in slightly cracked pots in the garden that was their life.

"Shit," she muttered. "This is so upsetting. She's been tied up somewhere." She nodded at the body.

"Hmm." Mike sniffed and used his protective suit sleeve to wipe his eyes.

Bethany pretended she hadn't noticed.

Restraint marks marred Catherine's wrists, possibly from fabric, strips of rag maybe, tied tight so it had dug deep and bruised. The skin was a dark stripe on the outer wrists, normal colour on the insides, although 'normal' wasn't correct when talking about the hue of a dead person. Pasty. Grey. Soft and spongy to look at. Playdoh. And normal wasn't stab marks by the veins, as if someone had poked her with the tip of a sharp knife—or she'd self-harmed recently.

"Going by how dirty she is, she hasn't been able to shower or anything," she said. "No facilities? Or was she denied them?"

Catherine must have been incarcerated in some kind of hovel—Bethany had already sent uniforms to check the old steel mill in case someone had decided to keep Catherine there. It had been used on a recent case to hold women who'd illegally bought babies in an adoption scam, and she was buggered if she'd get caught out again in not searching it sooner. Two officers had added it to their daily route, going inside every day, just in case.

No one there.

Filth caked the soles of the feet and between the toes, as if the floor or ground, wherever she'd been, was covered with damp mud. Dried streaks of it on the rest of her body indicated her maybe turning over, shifting in her sleep or struggling to get away. Had she been tied up just by the wrists and not to some kind of attachment on a wall? Did her abductor feel he could trust her enough that he knew she wouldn't lash out at him?

Of course, it could be a woman—she wouldn't discount that, as two of the adoption scam people had been female, one of them an abductor/killer.

"Did you notice on the digi forensics report that although Catherine had spoken to someone online a lot, their IP and whatever was hidden?" Bethany asked.

"I did, so, like with that Joseph Hunt fella from the Raven case, this person knows about the Dark Web?"

"Or just how to disguise himself well enough that we can't find anything."

"Digi will, eventually. They're looking on the surface at the minute. Wait until they go deeper."

"We may not have time to wait."

That rankled.

While digi were doing their best, these things took time, especially as they didn't have Catherine's phone and had gone through her Facebook and Messenger via her mother's laptop. Catherine, believe it or not, had never used the laptop, preferring her iPad, which had yet to be located. It still didn't stop Bethany wanting answers *now*, though. She wouldn't be human if it didn't bother her that some man had preyed on the girl.

She steeled herself to look at Catherine's head again. She'd found it too disturbing before, but the dirty body was at odds with her face. White makeup had been applied to clean skin, clown-like, with rosy cheeks in deep red, blue eyeshadow in thick swathes, and scarlet lipstick painted to resemble a pout or give the rosebud effect, the kind of mouth young children had.

It churned Bethany's stomach. She'd seen something like this before, again in another case. Entirely too much information was put in *The Shadwell Herald* by the crime reporter, Peter Uxbridge. Someone at the station had been passing him information for ages now, but to give out sensitive stuff, well, it meant weirdos who read it added the same kinds of things to their own agendas. Like now.

Isabelle Abbott, the lead SOCO, entered. She'd been busy outside with members of her team when Bethany and Mike had arrived, directing them inside so they could see what was what and digest it in private.

"So, what do you think?" she asked.

Bethany frowned. "Restrained in a dirty place. Face washed and makeup applied prior to her being dumped. Hair put in pigtails—so, prepared for show, as it were. Why not clean the rest of her, though?"

Isabelle *hmmed*. "My take on it is, she's clean and nice on the one hand, which says to me: *Look how pure she is*. On the other, with the dirt, it could imply she's filthy in more ways than one."

"A thirteen-year-old, filthy?" Mike harrumphed and shook his head. "Come on now. In *that* way?"

"In whatever way," Isabelle said. "Some teenagers are more sex savvy than we know. Or it could mean jack shit. It might be as simple as her being kept in an unsanitary place, she got her face washed, only time enough left to sort the makeup, then she got dumped." Isabelle pointed. "We'll hopefully be able to determine where that mud came from. I sent a sample in just before you got here. The sooner Aradul gets to work on it, the better it is for you. We need a lead here."

Bethany couldn't argue with that. All the usual questioning had been done after Catherine's disappearance, and none of her friends could help, nor could family members. She'd apparently been acting normally, the same as always, yet digi had unearthed a long conversation thread, spanning months, between Catherine and someone called ManBabe19, who claimed he knew her via someone else and Catherine just couldn't remember. In the end, it hadn't mattered, because she'd continued speaking to him anyway, and they'd formed a bond. It was so easy, once you knew how to spot it, to see she'd been groomed. While your average person might just think it was chatter between two people, albeit getting a little frisky later down the line, it was clear where

ManBabe19 had engineered the discussions so they ended up talking about sex.

What was most disturbing was his suggestion of a tracker app. Catherine had refused, saying she didn't like the idea of him knowing where she was all the time, it was creepy, and besides, she wasn't sure of him yet, so until they met, she'd decline.

ManBabe19 hadn't liked that. He'd wheedled, coerced, trying to get his way, acting like the young lad he was supposed to be—except digi and everyone else were convinced this was an older paedophile well-versed in how to manipulate.

They needed to find him. But how? With the IP address hidden for the moment, and possibly hidden forever if he knew steps to prevent himself from getting caught, they were up shit creek, their paddles on the bank.

Presley Zouche came in, drawing Bethany from her thoughts. The ME acknowledged them all with a brief nod and gave the body the once-over. He placed his bag on an evidence step.

Presley opened it and took out a clipboard.

The previous evening, they'd met up on a rare night out and discussed Catherine being missing. Presley didn't usually get involved with any gatherings, so it had been a nice surprise when he'd turned up. Another surprise was Aradul, Isabelle's boyfriend, being allowed into their circle at last. Isabelle usually preferred to keep her relationship separate. Bethany wondered if everyone else here had a hangover or whether she was just unfortunate in that department. It may be the afternoon, but her headache still hadn't fucked off.

Presley scribbled the ligature marks on the wrists of a body outline on the top page. There was no need for him to sketch her position. The girl had been placed exactly like the outline—on her back, arms by her sides, legs close together.

"So she wasn't a runaway then," Presley noted.

"No," Bethany said. "She's undoubtedly been kept somewhere all this time. While we searched, yet at the same time entertained ideas she may have gone to London, she existed in squalor."

"Not necessarily." Presley popped his clipboard away. "She could have got dirty in the killer's garden. From the colour of that dirt, it's peat or compost. Too dark for your average earth." He placed a small plastic sheet on the ground and knelt on it beside Catherine. "Suffocation—petechiae is present. No marks around the neck, so not strangulation. No handprint on the face either, so no palm covering the mouth and nose, unless that's been hidden by the makeup." He leant over her. "Ah, something up her nose." He took out a pair of tweezers and an evidence bag, then pulled out whatever he'd seen.

A small white feather, if a little clogged and stiff with dried mucous.

"Possibly death by pillow or duvet," Presley announced. "Hideous way to go if she was alive at the time." He lifted one of her hands to inspect the nails. "I'll do the body temp in a second. Slight rigor. There's nothing except dirt beneath her nails. Can't see any skin where she defended herself or tried to get the killer's hands off the pillow."

Bethany imagined that scenario. A young girl, fighting to breathe, a killer looming over her, pressing something on her face. Her lungs burning, the realisation that she was being murdered frightening her. Or had she been asleep? Or knocked unconscious previously? The latter was preferable. She may not even have known she was dying, lost in a dream instead, oblivious to what that person was doing to her.

Presley took the temperature. "She died around six yesterday, p.m. For her to be in this position, I'd say she was placed here prior to rigor, so, with a three to four-hour window after that, she'd have to have been put here between six and ten."

"It's still light out at the moment in the evenings," Mike said. "Starts getting dark about ten."

"Obviously wasn't fazed at being seen leaving a body," Bethany said. "But look where we are. No one comes here these days. The estate's a fair way off. Anyone nosing out of their windows may not necessarily have seen anything but a blur of movement. They could even have thought someone was dumping rubbish."

She was uncomfortable at the fact that while they'd all been enjoying themselves, having a meal and a few drinks in The Flapping Crow at the top of the high street, Catherine had been going through hell, and a killer had been here, leaving her on the ground as if she didn't matter. She consoled herself that none of them had known, but it still didn't erase the guilt.

"CCTV isn't facing this way," Isabelle said. "It's on the other side of Tesco, at the front, pointing to the retail park."

"And there'll be nothing on the road leading out of the estate." Bethany sighed. "You can bet this bastard drove here and home again, unseen." She sent Fran a message, asking her to get officers to call on the people in the houses lining the field on the off chance someone saw something. Plus, she wanted Leona on CCTV to see whether vehicles in this area went through town to get home. "Okay, we're going to have to visit Catherine's parents."

She sighed again. Having spent a few hours last week with Debbie and Victor Noble once it was clear their daughter wasn't coming home, Bethany had got the sense they were a normal working-class family who were understandably upset their child had walked out. Catherine wasn't the type to run away, Debbie had been adamant. Bethany had dropped the bombshell that Catherine *was* the type to talk to a stranger online, though. It hadn't gone down well. Despite the proof printed out on A4, Debbie wasn't having any of it. While Victor had been floored by the news, he'd been angry at ManBabe19, not Catherine. Quite rightly, he'd said she was a child, a trusting one at that, and didn't know any better, whereas ManBabe19 knew exactly what he was doing.

Grooming.

"I'm dreading that," Mike said. "Debbie convinced herself yesterday that ManBabe19 has her holed up in his house, and Catherine would get away somehow."

"Well, she didn't," Isabelle said. "She got suffocated instead."

"Uh…" Presley drew their attention. "From what I can see, Catherine had sex recently."

Bethany closed her eyes for a moment then looked at the body. Presley had widened the legs.

"I'll know if it was consensual later, during the PM," he said.

"I think we'll leave that information out when we speak to the parents," Bethany said. "It's bad enough they'll be finding out she's dead. Maybe tomorrow they can be told. I'm worried too much information at once will send Debbie over the edge. She's strung tight enough as it is, and the poor cow hasn't slept for longer than an hour at a time since Catherine went missing."

"Shall we check if Alice is still there?" Mike asked.

Alice Jacobs, the Family Liaison Officer, had been spending time with Debbie and Victor. One, to give them support, and two, to keep an eye on them. Sadly, too often, the people who were supposed to love children the most were the ones who did away with them. Alice was watching them for signs of culpability, but if they'd done this, they were bloody good actors. To Bethany's eye, the parents were genuine, but looks and actions had been deceptive in the past.

She nodded. "Yep, we could do with her being present when the parents are told. She's got to know them a bit so will know when Debbie's likely to lose her shit. I'll phone her now."

Bethany stepped out of the tent. SOCO were on hands and knees, scouring the ground. Over the other side of the car park, some were using poles to part the long grass at the edge. Others were in the field, the grass cut low there, probably by the council. It was a shame it wasn't long all over—they'd have had clear evidence then that the killer had perhaps driven over it. Tyre furrows would have been left behind, and they'd know exactly which direction the vehicle had come from.

No such luck.

She dialled Alice. "Hi, are you with the Nobles?"

"Just got here. They wanted some time alone last night, so I left them to it about five."

Bethany's stomach rolled over. "Did they now."

"What's that mean?"

"Are you in the house?"

"No, still in the car outside. Peter Uxbridge from *The Herald* is parked opposite, the wanker."

"Wonderful. Okay, stay there until we arrive. The reason I said 'did they now' is because we've found Catherine."

"Oh, good news?" Alice's voice held hope.

"No. She's been left in the old car park behind Tesco, the one they're going to build a petrol station on. Estimated time of death, six p.m. yesterday."

"Oh no. Christ." A pause. A sniff. "But I see where your mind went." Alice let out a long breath. "I left at five. They were just about to eat dinner. Victor made a chilli—I was there while he cooked it."

"Dinner can be reheated."

"Well, I'd say it isn't them, but I understand why you'd go along the lines you are. But remember, their house was cleared—nowhere Catherine could be kept."

"I know. I don't think its them either, but it gave me the willies when you said they wanted to be alone, that's all. Anyway, we'll be there shortly. Like I said, hold off going inside. I want us all to watch how they behave when we see them for the first time today. With three of us observing them, we'll pick anything up if they're acting oddly."

"I guarantee, all we're going to see is broken parents."

"I hope so."

CHAPTER FOUR

Tom16: Hey, we've got mutual friends. Do I know you?
Karly: Um, IDK?
Tom16: Your name's familiar. Were you at Jessica's house party last month?
Karly: Yeah.

Tom16: That's it then. I knew I recognised your face.

Karly: I don't remember seeing you. [frown emoji]

Tom16: I stayed out of the way in the living room. Not much into drinking and smoking weed like the other lads.

Karly: Ah, I was in the kitchen. I don't like drink or drugs either. What school are you at?

Tom16: I left.

Karly: How did you get away with that? We're meant to stay until we're eighteen.

Tom16: Special circumstances. My mum's ill. She's got CFS.

Karly: What's that?

Tom16: Chronic Fatigue Syndrome.

Tom16 laughed. Amazing how much he'd found out about that illness from Heaven13. Talking to her hadn't been a waste of time after all.

Mum had gone into the hospital to have the baby, letting John stay by himself. He was used to it, what with her not really being present in the correct sense when he was home.

Dad came back, looking tired.

"She's had it then?" A question John didn't need to ask, but he didn't know what else to say.

"Yes, she's had it." Dad sighed, a deep exhalation that had him blowing the air through pursed lips. He sat on the sofa edge, legs bent, elbows resting on his knees, and rubbed his eyes.

Again, not knowing what to say, John managed, "What did she have?" Did he even want to know? Did it matter if the kid wasn't Dad's? Should he love it anyway if Mum didn't?

Letting his hands flop between his open knees, Dad stared at John with red-rimmed, bloodshot eyes. Maybe he'd rubbed them too hard. "A boy."

Oh. Would Mum hate it as much as she hated John?

"When will she be bringing it home?"

"I don't know, and I don't care." Dad took a deep breath. "I know you don't understand, being young an' all that, but that baby is no son of mine, that much is obvious. It's just you and me now, kid."

John's belly contracted, but at the same time, he couldn't help but get excited if what he thought Dad meant was true. He'd better check to be on the safe side. No point in getting his hopes up, was there. "What d'you mean, just you and me?"

"Exactly what I said. We'll be moving into the cottage by the stream. I'll rent it out for the two of us, and the place should suit us nicely. We'll take Twinkle with us, mind you."

Twinkle had got over being toothless. Mum and Dad, with their own problems to deal with, had barely taken the time to wonder why the family cat walked round all gums.

"Oh," John said. "Right." He'd always liked that cottage. There was the stream at the bottom of it where he fished with Dad, mainly to get away from Mum when she was in one of her nastier moods. He thought someone already lived there, but maybe they'd moved out.

As Mum was to stay in the hospital for at least ten days—she'd had a difficult birth and a caesarean section; good, John hoped it hurt—Dad put the house up for sale and explained that Mum could live there until it was sold. They wouldn't be going back, he said.

John had other ideas.

The cottage had two bedrooms, a living area, kitchen/dining room, bathroom, and this weird little slot between walls, like some kind of internal alley. Dad said maybe it was used for hanging coats and storing shoes, but there was a little area for that behind a door in the hallway. There was a cellar as well, but they wouldn't bother using it. Too cold and damp.

At last life was going to run smoothly. The rent was low because of repairs that needed doing. Dad assured the landlord he'd carry them out himself if the rent stayed at its reasonable price. The winters would be cold, only having the one fireplace in the main living area, no radiators or anything, but Dad said he could get some plug-in heaters off a mate.

That first week at the cottage, Dad had the week off work, and he fixed tiles on the roof, holes in the walls, and put cupboard doors back on their hinges. A busy seven days fixing the mess the previous tenants had left behind. They'd been kicked out for it.

The cottage offered a cosy retreat. A place to lick their wounds and start afresh, creating an even stronger bond than had previously existed. Dad was a good man, and he didn't deserve to be treated like shit by Mum.

John detested her. One day, she'd pay for everything, especially for not loving him.

Two weeks later, John spotted her walking down the high street pushing a pram. She looked tired. A few grey hairs had appeared amongst the blonde, and she'd clipped it back with a hairband. Her face appeared pinched, her walk unsteady and slow. Maybe the operation scars were still healing. John hoped she was in loads of pain.

The pram she steered was John's, saved from all those years ago. Anger mixed with jealousy that this brat slept in something of his. The Silver Cross bounced on its wheels, an old-fashioned eyesore.

He trailed her through the town and its shops. She didn't buy very much; the shape of a milk flagon was evident through the carrier bag she placed in the pram's basket. She left the pram and its contents outside each shop she visited, like she wasn't bothered if anyone nicked the kid. Maybe she wasn't. Maybe she didn't love this child either. Her last stop was at the butcher's, run by that nice bloke called Dave.

As she left town, John followed to where she now lived. It wasn't Churchill Street but Wrathmore Road, aptly named, he reckoned. She always aimed her wrath at him. He'd come here again tomorrow, early, and watch the house.

He had a half-brother he wanted to meet.

That afternoon, John went back to the house in Churchill Street. It was still up for sale, the sign lurching a bit in the front garden. There was no reason for Mum to move out so soon, but she had, and it gave him a place to go this boring Saturday.

Amazingly, the key still hung by its string on the inside of the door, easily accessed via the letterbox. Mum had put it there so he could get in, probably so she could carry on shagging whatever bloke was in her bed without being disturbed.

John wandered through the house, still with many of their belongings in it. The three-piece suite was in the cottage, but the large dresser that ran along one wall in the lounge was here, huge and majestic without anything else in the room.

Dad had taken a few items from it. A couple of picture frames and a brass bird—a starling that John had played with a lot over the years, the only animal he hadn't been able to kill, its beak sharp and useful when stabbing at furry beasts—but everything else sat on display behind the glass doors. Mum obviously didn't want anything in it.

The kitchen table still remained, the wood scarred from John poking it with a fork at mealtimes, a groove cut out of the side where he'd sawed it with a knife. Signs of his anxiety, ones Mum didn't give a toss about, and Dad, he just thought John was being destructive.

It was difficult to stand there and take it all in, that they no longer lived as a threesome. That they'd branched out and separated. Only a quick, fleeting thought on that subject, then he told himself it was better this way. He'd wanted to get away from Mum for years, and now he had. His life was more ordered. He carried enormous hate for her, and one day he reckoned it'd rage out of control. Why couldn't she just love him like a mum should? That was all she'd had to do, and everything would have been okay.

He trudged upstairs and rooted around in her wardrobe for what he wanted. The short grey skirt. The white blouse. He couldn't find the pink cap, which was annoying. He stuffed them in his backpack and would hide them in the cellar at the cottage so Dad didn't know he had them.

The shed was so full of many memories, especially the brown bloodstain on the floor where Twinkle had so recently lay unconscious, bleeding from the gums. The smell in there gave him a sense of security, and he wished he could take the wooden building back to the garden at the cottage.

It was the only thing from Churchill Street he was sad to leave behind. His little safe haven in a stormy life where he'd spent time with defenceless animals.

Sunday morning dawned bright and warm. John packed his rucksack with some water in an old pop bottle and a jam sandwich tucked into the inner pocket. Dad would be fishing in the stream all day.

"You off?" Dad called out.

John came out of the cottage via the back door in the kitchen. "Yep. Going to go and play at the park." He squinted, the sun in his eyes.

"Good lad." Dad gave a quick wave and resumed his study of the opposite bank.

At the front of the cottage, John checked the contents of his bag again. He had a busy day planned. He walked the mile or so to Wrathmore Road and hid behind a fat tree trunk. Mum came out of her house around ten, strolling slowly with her brat in the pram. Her hips didn't sway as much as they once had, her legs stiff and straight, as if her knees couldn't bend. She seemed a little better in the face today. Maybe she'd had a night of undisturbed sleep. Who knew? But she did look more refreshed, her cheeks rosy and shining, perhaps from a recent wash.

John followed her into town and waited down the side of the small newsagents as she put the brake on the pram and went inside the shop alone.

He walked up to that pram and stared inside, and the reality and certainty of what he was about to do was born. He'd thought about it but hadn't reckoned he'd actually go through with it.

Lifting that bundle out of the pram, he clasped it to his chest and rushed away from the shop towards Churchill Street. The baby remained quiet, still fast asleep, swaddled tightly in a knitted white blanket, even though it was a hot day.

He entered the back garden and went inside the house via the back door, which he'd left unlocked on his last visit, pocketing the front key that had dangled from the string. In the living room, he placed the kid on the carpet and opened the blanket, resting on his haunches to inspect this child who was related to him.

The baby's arms flung outwards in a reflex action, its face that of Mum's, albeit in a smaller form, its hair blond like hers. It was easy to imagine this baby as her, and any guilt in stealing this fucker didn't bother him.

He undressed it. The kid's eyes opened widely, mouth forming a large circle. It screamed.

John panicked, not knowing how to shut it up. He raced to close the curtains, and he had the sudden urge to go to the loo. Dressing the baby again awkwardly, he wrapped him up. The thing quieted, and John walked up and down, pacing and rocking until the shitbag went back to sleep.

What was Mum doing now? Was she frantically screeching that her baby was gone, had been taken? Had she rung the police, the shop owner comforting her until the patrol car with its blue flashing lights came to her rescue?

John looked down at the child. Had Mum ever done this with him? Had he been wrapped in a blanket and treated as nicely as this baby evidently was? It was certainly clean and appeared cared for.

No. She'd hated John from the first, she'd said so. She'd left him squealing in hunger, fists balled, face red with anger, a lonely child who'd only gained comfort from his dad.

Fucking cow.

Time passed slowly. The light was fading a bit. He must have been in the house for ages. Why did the baby still sleep? Why hadn't it woken, expecting a bottle of milk?

John left the house and walked until the noise of the canal broke him out of his thoughts and into the now. The baby stirred. Wiggled inside the blanket. Strained against John's grip, his eyes open wide, face contorting. He screamed. And screamed. Kept screaming as John ran towards the water.

The noise was so piercing it hurt John's head.

He stood by the side of the canal, looked left, looked right.

No barges. No people.

He took the blanket off his brother, whose arms flailed, mouth squawking its hunger. There was silence for two seconds while the baby inhaled a deep breath, and John took that opportunity to drop it into the canal. It must have plunged like a stone because John stood for a full five minutes afterwards, and the kid never bobbed to the surface.

If Mum couldn't love John, then she couldn't love the baby either.

No remorse then. None whatsoever.

And the blanket? John didn't recall what happened to it.

CHAPTER FIVE

Bethany studied Victor Noble's face at the front door. No sign of anything but dread, but that could be from the fear of getting caught for offing his daughter, or the fear that they'd come here to tell them bad news. His brown eyes were hooded by puffy top lids, where he'd had little sleep and had cried more than he probably ever thought he would. His short brown hair needed a wash, a tad greasy, but who gave a shit about that when their child was missing? She disliked herself for even noticing it.

"We'll need to come in," Bethany said.

"Have you found her?" He stepped back.

"Let's all settle at the table with a cuppa, shall we?" Alice took control, going in first and ushering Victor down the hallway and into the kitchen.

Debbie sat at the table, eyes bloodshot. She jumped to her feet. "What's happened?"

"Sit down, Deb," Alice said. "I'll make us a drink." She bustled over to the kettle and touched it. "Shouldn't take long then, seeing as this is still hot." She flicked the switch.

Bethany sat opposite Debbie, who lowered to her seat, glancing at them all in turn. Victor plonked down beside her, all the fight seemingly gone out of him. Mike had his notebook and pen out, and he stood by the door.

"What's going on?" Debbie asked, her voice wavering.

Victor grabbed her hand and held it tight. "It's bad, isn't it?"

"I'm afraid so." Bethany hated saying those words. "A body we believe to be Catherine's was found at two o'clock today by a member of the public."

"What?" Debbie's face paled. "Body? That means…"

Victor put his arm around her and squeezed. "All right, darling. Deep breath." He looked at Bethany. "Where?"

She wasn't about to tell them the exact location in case they both got up and drove there. It wasn't a sight they needed to see and, much as she didn't like to think this, they'd mess the scene up if they traipsed all over it. "In a car park."

The news didn't appear to have sunk in with Debbie yet. "How do you know it's our Cathy? It could be anyone, couldn't it?"

"I made an identification, going by her face," Bethany said. "We're certain it's her. I'm so sorry."

"Did she kill herself then?" Debbie asked. "I mean, maybe she was going through something we didn't know about. Oh God, the poor thing. She could have talked to us about anything, and we'd have supported her. First she runs off, staying God knows where, and now she's…she's…" She bit her bottom lip.

"Catherine was murdered, Debbie." Bethany held her breath.

"Murdered?" Debbie gaped at Victor. "She can't have been. That doesn't make sense. Who'd want to do that to her?"

"It'll be that ManBabe bloke, sweetheart," he said. "You saw the conversation. She was meeting him. You can't kid yourself that wasn't her talking anymore. She met him, and *he* did this."

Debbie's face crumpled, and she let the tears go. "No, I won't believe she was up for having sex with him. Someone's written all that as a joke, using her phone when she wasn't looking. Cathy's thirteen. She doesn't know anything about sex. She's a good girl." She leant into her husband, closed her eyes, and cried.

Bethany turned her attention to Victor. "We're still staying with that line of enquiry. It's clear from the conversations she had with the man that he coerced her over a few months. Catherine would have undoubtedly thought he was nineteen. Having an older boy interested in her…she'd have perhaps felt special. We've had officers out at their meeting place. As you know from reading the transcript, that was in the field by the train track out of Shadwell. We know Catherine wasn't worried about seeing him for the first time in a secluded place—he'd gained her trust, plus, she knew, being thirteen, she might get told off for hanging around with a nineteen-year-old, hence why she never told anyone. And if she told her friends, they're saying she didn't and are keeping it quiet. Pinky swear or whatever they do nowadays. We'll be speaking to them again after we've left here to see if any of them have a change of heart once they know what's happened to Catherine."

Debbie cried on. "This…this is a…bloody…nightmare."

Victor squashed her closer to him. "What…how did she…?"

Bethany steeled herself. "She was suffocated." She paused to let the words settle. "We have yet to locate her clothing, shoes, phone, iPad, and bag."

"She's naked?" Victor choked out.

"Yes."

"Was she…?"

Not going there. "We don't know yet. Her post-mortem will be carried out later today or tomorrow morning, depending on when the body is released from the scene."

"What do you mean?" he asked. "She's still *there*?"

Alice placed cups of tea in the centre of the table then retreated to stand by the back door that led to a well-kept garden.

Bethany nodded. "There's a tent, so please don't worry that passersby will see her. No one but officers and the ME will. She has to remain in situ for some time while the scene is being assessed. Once forensics are happy they have all the evidence they can get, Catherine will be collected."

"Shit a brick." Victor shook his head. "This is really happening, isn't it."

"Sadly, it is, and I can't tell you how sorry we all are. We'd hoped for a good outcome, that Catherine had just gone off with an older boy and would return when she realised it wasn't all it's cracked up to be. I wish that were the case, I really do."

Debbie lifted her head. "How was she suffocated?" Her eyelashes were clumped into spikes by tears. "I need to know."

"Don't do this to yourself, love," Victor said. "Have a bit of your tea."

"Tea? Like it's going to fix this?" Debbie thumped the table. "I want to know how my child died. I'm her mother, I have the *right*."

Bethany resisted sighing. It seemed Debbie was intent on torturing herself, or maybe she needed the facts so she could determine whether Catherine suffered. While it was a shock if a loved one died unexpectedly, if they didn't have any pain or suffering, it somehow eased the path of grief a bit. Bethany's late husband had died from smoke inhalation in a fire, passing out before the lick of hot flames could bring him agony. A small mercy, one Bethany was grateful for, so she understood Debbie wanting answers.

"We think with a pillow or quilt. There was a down feather in her nostril."

Debbie opened her mouth to possibly wail.

Bethany quickly continued. "However, we don't think she would have known anything about it."

"What do you mean?" Victor asked.

"There was no skin that the ME could see beneath her fingernails where she could have acted in self-defence." Bethany decided against mentioning the mud being there instead, although she would mention it on Catherine's body in case they had any idea where she may have been kept. The meeting location by the train line had fields either side of it, hay-like stuff that had been recently cropped by the farmer prior to Catherine going there. But no mud that would have streaked her like that.

"So she just kind of fell asleep?" Debbie asked.

"Yes." Bethany took a sip of tea, hoping she hadn't just lied and they'd find out differently at the inquest, then accuse her of keeping the truth from them. "She was dirty, though. Her body. Do you know of anywhere she would have gone to get mud on her?"

Debbie whimpered.

"No," Victor said. "We already told you everywhere we thought she might go when she went missing, and that was to a mate's house or the bloody park because she still liked going on the swings. Oh, fucking hell, this is *hurting*. She's a kid, still naïve in so many ways. All right, she said things to that man I never thought she would until she was older, but he asked her stuff outright, did you see that? Asked her about her breasts and… If I get my hands on him…I swear to you, I won't be held accountable."

Bethany waited a few moments for him to compose himself. His breathing was heavy, his face red. He had so much rage and grief with no outlet. Plus, he seemed the type to hold it all inside so he could be there for his wife, strong, someone she could depend on to get her through this terrible time.

"Okay. I realise this is difficult, me asking questions, but if I don't, we won't find who did this. Unfortunately, we're still no further forward with an IP for ManBabe19, so catching him that way isn't an option at present, but digital forensics will keep digging. So, next one. Did Catherine take a makeup bag with her?" Bethany asked.

"She hasn't even *got* any makeup," Debbie said. "We said that before, and you've been in her room, seen everything. She didn't wear it. She wasn't that sort of girl. Why are you asking this?"

"She has makeup on. White foundation, blusher, blue eyeshadow, lipstick."

"Why would she wear that?" Debbie frowned. "I don't understand. She's funny about makeup. Doesn't like animal testing. She's a vegan. There's no way she'd put anything like that on."

"Thank you. That helps." Bethany smiled sadly.

"You're saying that ManBabe fucker put it on her, aren't you?" Victor clenched his jaw tight. "Or he made her do it, because like Deb said, Cathy wouldn't have put it on willingly."

"We're leaning in that direction, yes. With this murder, we're obviously going with an intent to abduct her under the guise of Catherine meeting him of her own accord. This next bit of information may be distressing." Bethany took a deep breath. "She has restraint marks on her wrists. I have to ask you again: Do you know of anyone who would want to do this to your daughter?"

"Absolutely not," Victor said. "You've met the rest of our family and friends already. You've seen how lovely they all are. Mad with worry over Cathy, and this is going to knock them for six."

"Would you like me to arrange for someone else to break the news to them?"

Debbie put her forehead on her arms on the table and cried. "I need this to stop. I can't do this."

"No." Victor rubbed his wife's back. "No, we'll do it. *I'll* do it."

Bethany nodded. "Now, I have a horrible question. Regardless, I have to ask it, okay? It doesn't mean I think you're involved, but where were you both after Alice left you yesterday at five?"

"Here, all evening." Victor inhaled through his nostrils. "I get why you're asking, I do, and I'm glad you did, because if you didn't, you wouldn't be doing your job properly, and that'd make me think you're not up to finding that fucker. Deb's mum came round at half five. She stayed for dinner. Went home about ten. I went on my phone at that point to find this ManBabe bastard, searching Google, Facebook. I was at it until about four this morning. Deb was on her phone doing the same because you lot have her laptop. Look at our search history and times." He pushed Debbie's phone across the table. "My phone's in the living room. You'll see we were here, and if that's not enough, I don't know how else to prove it."

Alice stepped forward and took the phone out of the room. "I'll give Debbie's mum a ring."

"Thank you for your cooperation and understanding," Bethany said. "Given that Catherine died around six p.m. yesterday, when Alice wasn't here, we had to check."

"So he's had her alive all this time?" Victor groaned. "We've been here worrying, and all the while, she's been somewhere, probably wanting to come home?"

65

Debbie sat up and scrubbed at her eyes. "She'd have wanted us, and we weren't there."

Bethany swallowed. For those with decent parents, when in a bad situation, the instinctual thought was: *I want my mum, I want my dad.* The thought of Catherine being incarcerated somewhere, praying she'd see them again, was an awful thought. Or had that only been yesterday? Had ManBabe19 treated her fine during the days she'd been missing? Was he really nineteen and not older, like they suspected, and Catherine had got on well with him, thinking she was with her 'boyfriend'? Had things only gone wrong yesterday, hence her being killed? Or had she been lured by an older man, and when she'd seen him for the first time, knowing he wasn't a young lad, she'd realised it had all been lies? Did she try to run?

The not knowing was hard for Bethany, but nothing compared to what Debbie and Victor were going through. So many questions, so many unknowns, and it may never become clear what happened.

We might not find him.

Alice came back in. "Debbie's mum confirms she was here. I'll have a look through the phones."

Bethany drank her semi-warm tea then stood. "We'll be going now. Alice will stay with you. She'll pass on any information, like when Catherine has been taken to the morgue and when you can see her. We still need a formal identification."

"So it might not be her?" Debbie asked.

Victor stroked her hand. "They wouldn't be here if they weren't sure, love."

"Oh." Debbie let out a shuddering sigh. "I just hoped…"

Bethany had to get out. This was wreaking havoc with her emotions. She was just grateful she *could* walk away from the house for now, away from the grief for a while. Debbie, Victor, and Alice weren't so lucky.

"We'll go and visit Catherine's friends again," she said. "Please don't pre-warn them or their parents. I'd like to get their genuine reactions. Bye for now."

She walked out with Mike, cringing at the sound of Debbie crying again.

"We need to find this ManBabe fucker," she said to him in the car.

"I know." He rubbed his temples. "Those poor parents."

"I can't even imagine."

"Me neither."

She drove away, towards the home of a Gina Frost, Catherine's best friend. Their previous chat with her had thrown up nothing but Gina displaying shock, confusion, and hurt that Catherine hadn't confided in her about the chats. Bethany had believed the girl—she wasn't a teenager who seemed to want to grow up too quickly. But if Catherine had kept ManBabe19 a secret, behaving differently with him than she had with her parents, who was to say Gina wasn't doing the same?

Best friends had your back. Best friends didn't tell on you.

CHAPTER SIX

John felt manly beneath the balaclava and with his hood up. He'd looked at himself in the full-length mirror in his bedroom earlier, just to see what *they'd* see. If he wasn't him, and someone stood in front of him in this get-up, he'd be worried.

She was worried, the shape of her eyes said so, all round and wide, her mouth stretched around the sock he'd stuffed in there, which partially hung out. Too much fabric for the size of her gob, but what the hell. He'd tied her wrists behind her back, and she sat on the floor, naked, filthy from the many bags of compost he'd spread there. He wanted her to grow out of the soil, to flourish, like he'd imagined Francesca's shins doing from her ankle socks back when he was a kid.

"Are you going to do what I want yet?" he asked, voice menacing. He loved becoming this person, the one who had control. Such a contrast to his childhood, when his life had been defined by Mum, her resentment of him, her behaviour with those men, the kid she'd had, the one who had fallen in the canal because John wasn't able to hold him tight enough.

The girl, Tanya, didn't answer. He'd collected her after speaking for only a month. The plan was to watch her and Catherine flourish together, but of course, that didn't happen. They'd both glared at him, and he imagined they cried and whispered to each other when he locked them in and went upstairs. Perhaps he'd go and get Elsa in a month or two after all and put her here with the new girl he was chatting up. Karly—things were going okay there.

Tom16 was a winner.

A few weeks, and she'd be ready. If he left Elsa alone in the meantime, she'd relax, think he wasn't going to contact her again, then when he snatched her right from outside her house or while she walked to school, she'd realise he'd just been biding his time.

Jolly19 was on top form.

He thought of the first girl bar Francesca he'd ever become interested in, back when he'd been married, the one who'd shown him what his true predilections were. The one who'd sent him on this path now, where he chased young ladies, teenagers, ones with school uniforms, like Mum had dressed in with that man.

"Well?" he snapped. "*Are* you going to do what I want? What you told me you'd do? If you just look at the walls, you'll see our conversations if you need a reminder of what you agreed."

He gestured to the multiple pages of A4 he'd pasted up, which were alongside Catherine's and Elsa's. Them telling him they wanted kisses and more. He took the brass starling down from the shelf, the one from his childhood, and clutched it tight.

Tanya shook her head, snorting, letting out a strangled sound. She dug her feet into the soil, scrunching her toes.

"You're scared, aren't you?" he made the starling ask, tilting it this way and that as if it were alive. "Scared of Simon19." He squawked for a better effect.

He imagined her garbled noises were: *You're not Simon19. You're an old man. You're fat and gross, nothing like your picture. Why would anyone love you?*

"Ah, but *you're* nothing like you made out either, are you?" the starling said, all chittery and birdish. "Because if you were, you'd stick to your promises." He switched to his own voice. "You do realise, don't you, that if you don't give me what I want, I'll just take it anyway."

She released a muffled scream.

And it didn't matter, her being rowdy. This cottage didn't have anyone else nearby, and besides, they were beneath it, in the cellar. She could cry all she wanted. No one but him would hear her.

Just the way he liked it.

He advanced and whacked her face with the starling, the sharp brass beak piercing her cheek. That'd give her something to cry about.

The bird chuckled.

Dad was no longer fishing in the stream when John got back. He entered the cottage, looking for him in the kitchen. There was a crackling noise, and he jumped. John looked up and spun round to face the lounge doorway down the hall. Mrs Drayton, of all people, sat on the sofa scrunching up a Murray Mint wrapper after she'd popped the sweet into her lipsticked mouth.

"Hello, John."

Puzzled for a moment, he stared at her. Had she come to tell Dad she'd seen and heard John with the baby? More to the point...

"Where's my dad?" He marched in there and stood in the centre.

"Sit down, John." She moved the mint around in her mouth, and it bumped into her teeth.

"No. Not till you tell me where my dad is."

She shifted a little, probably making out she was getting more comfortable, but he reckoned she was scared of him. Why was she being nice when he'd always been so rude to her at the old house?

"Sit down, lad, and I'll tell you." She attempted to smile, her bright-pink lips quickly stretching and relaxing again.

John stayed standing.

"Your dad had the police contact me, asking if I'd watch you while he's at the station. There's been..." She glanced round, then at the ceiling, obviously trying to find the right words. "An occurrence."

"Is my dad all right? He was fishing by the stream. Did he...fall in or something?" It came so easy to play dumb. He let this scenario run through his mind, imagined Dad falling into the water and banging his head on a rock, and him drowning, dying. Tears fell without much effort. He loved Dad, wouldn't want anything to happen to him. No, never to him.

"No. Your dad's fine. Come and sit here." She patted the seat next to her and loudly swallowed spittle.

John sat.

"Someone stole your mum's baby. Took it away, they did. The police thought it was your dad. They came to ask him to go to the station. He needed…"

"No! My dad wouldn't have done that. I don't believe you."

"No, no, I know he wouldn't have done that. Your dad's a good man. No, he went down to sign a statement. He didn't do it, John, because you know the landlord for this place?"

John nodded, head bent. Reginald Button was a nice man. John looked at the carpet. An earwig made its way over the rough pile, and he stifled the urge to stamp on it.

"Well, he came over to collect the rent and spent some time fishing with your dad. It was very lucky that it was at the time your brother was taken."

John wanted to shout into her face that the baby wasn't his fucking brother, that he had nothing whatsoever to do with him, but he stopped himself.

"So," she continued. "They know it wasn't your dad. They just needed him to go and sign a bit of paper, stating what he was doing and who he was with. That's all. He'll be back shortly, and then I can go home. Sorry it's me you're stuck with, but your dad thought of me, and here I am. Now then, would you like a bit of something to eat?"

John thought of what he'd eaten that day, which was several hours ago, the jam sandwich he'd taken with him. He nodded, and she went off into the kitchen.

He decided he liked Mrs Drayton now and followed her. "Did you ring the police then? Did you see them with the baby?"

She turned from the cooker, where she was frying some eggs and bacon. "No, love. I'd only just got back from my daughter's when the police came to ask me if I'd seen anyone going into your old house."

Why would the police think anyone had gone to Churchill Street? Had John been seen?

Mrs Drayton splashed hot oil over the eggs then lifted the food out and put it on a plate. She walked to the pine table, and John went with her, listening to her prattle on.

"Turns out that the neighbours on the other side were out all day, too, and the people opposite are on holiday for the week, but one person did see someone going to the house, they just can't be sure who it was. Such a shame, poor baby. Still..."

John sat at the table. He rammed a whole bacon rasher into his mouth, quickly chewed and swallowed. "What do you mean, poor baby?"

"Oh!" Her cheeks reddened, and her hand flew up to her mouth to cover her quivering lips. "I'll let your dad tell you the rest. It's only right."

Dad had been cleared of any involvement in that baby's disappearance. The newspapers and local newsreaders shouted out the terrible crime, but after a week it was everyone's fish and chip wrappers.

The house on Churchill Street sold, and they moved on with their lives. John still spied on Mum, though. Spent at least one evening a week after school watching her in her kitchen at Wrathmore Road, washing up or preparing a meal.

She'd cut her hair short, almost into a soldier's crop, and now worked in a shop, as she should have bloody well done all those years ago. From his position in a tree opposite her house, John saw a few things he'd rather he didn't. She still supplemented her income with her prostitute ways, and more than once she swigged gin straight from the bottle. She pulled it out of her pocket while facing the window at the sink and necked it back, sometimes shaking her head after she'd swallowed.

Tanya kicked him when he moved closer to give her another beak stab. She looked just like Mum, with those pigtails, albeit bedraggled ones from where she'd sweated. His hair was also damp, what with the balaclava.

"Your kicks don't hurt," the starling said. "All you're doing is getting John's trousers dirty."

She seemed to growl.

"This will all be over if you just do what you said you would." He reached down and stroked her hair, tugging on a filthy pigtail.

She wrenched her head to the side to get away from him.

John spoke now, the bird going silent. "I bet your parents aren't even worried, are they? If you were telling the truth in our little chats, you being gone for a couple of days won't be noticed. How long, do you reckon, before they realise it was me sending them texts and your mate messages, not you?"

Tears seeped down her cheeks.

"John killed the other one," the starling chirped. "The one who was in here with you. Catherine." He switched to his own voice. "Her parents cared. They reported her missing straight away. It was on the news and everything. Mum and Dad doing a press conference: 'Please, if you have my baby, let her go.' I did. Just not in the way they wanted."

Tanya cried. Hard.

Good. She deserved to be punished.

Just like Mum.

John's fifteenth Christmas, Dad bought him a pair of binoculars.

On Boxing Day, John sat on the back doorstep, peering over at the bushes and trees that dotted the stream bank. Everything seemed so close through the lenses. The houses on the estate over there...he stared through someone's bedroom window and watched them get undressed.

Stiletto heels clip-clopped down the side of the cottage and stopped abruptly a pace away from him. John took the binoculars from his eyes and looked up.

She seemed the same, but of course, different. He hadn't seen her close up for years, but even if he hadn't been spying on her, he'd know her instantly.

"Hello, John." She smiled as if she were the kindest mum in the world. "Is your dad in?"

He didn't want to speak to her, didn't even want to associate with her, but he did just the same. That old need for her to like him, to love him, hadn't died yet. "No. He's out at the pub with Reg."

"Know when he's coming home?"

She spoke as if he'd only seen her yesterday, like years hadn't passed. He got up and walked into the kitchen, and she had the gall to follow. She leant her hip against the back doorjamb, her left knee bent, showing an expanse of cellulite-riddled leg through the slit in her long black skirt. She cocked her head, her stupid short, curly hair bobbing, and smiled.

"No." He tidied the worktops for something to do, grabbing stuff he'd left out when he'd made a ham sandwich.

"My," she said, her voice full of wonder. She used her hip to push away from the jamb and stepped over to him. "You've grown into a fine young man."

She stank of alcohol and moved to touch his arm, but he pulled out of her reach. Her hand came towards the binoculars hanging around his neck, and a kind of panic mixed with anger raced through him that she dared touch his stuff, that she was even here. What did she want Dad for?

He swatted her hand away, and she clasped his groin.

"A fine young man."

Everything she'd ever done to him played in his head, a lightning-fast film. Her leaving him to his own devices. Her telling him he was a piece of shit. Him desperate for Dad to come home from work so he'd get some good attention instead of the bad.

Inside a second, he had the tip of a knife off the worktop digging into the flesh beneath her chin.

Her hand dropped to her side, her eyes wide.

"Don't fucking touch me," he said. "You'll never fucking touch me again."

She stepped back, and the knife pricked her skin, drawing blood. He took it away, holding it pointing towards her. He'd stab her good and proper if she made another gesture like that, the sick bitch.

"Get out."

Walking in reverse, still maintaining eye contact, she made her way to the door, and only when she reached it did she turn and run. She passed the kitchen window, lifting her hand to cover her mouth.

Stupid woman. She should have left him alone.

John waited five minutes and followed her home. In the tree across the road from her house, he spied on her through the binoculars. She sat at a scarred wooden kitchen table, chin on her folded arms, gazing towards him. It was as if he were right there in the room, sitting nose to nose with her. He counted the pores on her face. Downy hairs, a soft gold, grew along her jaw.

She appeared worn out, defeated, upset he'd had the balls to stand up to her. He was glad, happy she was dejected, slumped in her squalid, seedy house. Had seeing him again brought her down? Had him ordering her out affected her this badly? It must have.

She'd had a screaming match with one of her customers five minutes ago. She'd struck him on the face, and rage had crossed his features as he'd stalked from her kitchen, from her house, and her life.

She lifted her head. A woman, who John presumed Mum shared her house and her profession with, stepped into the kitchen. Mum turned to her, hastily swiping at her tears, raising her sinful body from the chair and waggling her finger at her.

The woman left the room, slamming the door, and Mum walked to the sink and looked out of the window. She lit one of her many cigarettes and slung a gulp of gin down her throat.

The housemate had gone out, strutting along the road. Mum watched her. Sweat beaded her upper lip and across the bridge of her nose. John shivered at feeling so close to her.

Mum filled her glass with gin again and took a large knife from the wooden block. She sat at her table, tossed the drink back once more, squeezed her eyes shut. And then she toyed with the knife.

She ran the blade up and down the inside of her arm. Fresh tears spilled, but she left them unchecked. She placed the knife, sharpest side down, across her wrist.

John scrambled down from the tree. His jeans got caught on a branch, and he shook it free, then peered through the binoculars at her. She held the knife tightly while pressing the point on her wrist in almost jab-like motions.

He wanted to be there to watch her do it.

He ran across the small field, chest burning, adrenaline pumping fiercely. He checked for witnesses as he barrelled into Wrathmore Road and, no one there, he dashed down the side of Mum's house, into the back garden, hoping, praying there was some way he could get into the property. The back door opened when he turned the handle. Guessing the layout of the house, he walked through the lounge and into a hallway. Another door leading off it stood open. He stepped into the kitchen. Mum's short curls bobbed. And she was crying. Loud, racking sobs, shoulders shuddering.

"Go on. Do it, you old bag," John said.

She snatched in a breath, snapped her head up, moving it round slowly, and a weird smile twitched her lips. "You want me to do it? You'd stand and watch your mum slit her wrists?"

"Do the world a favour and just get on with it." He meant it an' all.

He moved to the table and stood to her right. She trailed the knife back and forth across her wrist, the blade not doing any damage at all, then she prodded again with the point, and it pierced the skin in several places, small trickles of blood oozing.

John stared at it, fascinated.

"You'd like that, wouldn't you, John? Just as you liked having your dad all to yourself. Before you came along, my life was wonderful. Then you ruined it. I've never forgiven you for that." She smiled her secret smile, yet this time it was somehow tinged with sadness.

"Didn't you love me at all?" He didn't know why he'd asked her that, it had just come out.

She sighed, pressed harder with the knife. "Oh, for a little while, yes, I think I did. But you were too cute, too cuddly, and your dad left me out." With those last few words, she stabbed at her wrists with the knife point, harder this time, and blood dripped from her arm onto the tabletop.

"You're doing it the wrong way, you silly bitch."

"You know things like that? You actually retain stuff in your head? Well now, and there was me thinking I'd given birth to a spaz."

John lunged forward, wanting to beat the shit out of her, reminding himself at the last minute not to touch her. "Go on, do it properly. Bloody kill yourself."

Mum peered up from beneath those long eyelashes, her eyes filled with tears, probably all for herself. The skin peeled back from either side of that blade while she drew it down her arm. Blood gushed, and she cried out in pain, maybe shock that she'd actually done it, and put her forehead on the table. The knife dropped from her hand, and her breaths became ragged.

John knew then. She'd never loved him. Never. If she could do this, allow him to watch her kill herself, she didn't care for him.

He walked out of that room and out of that house and ran back to the tree. There, he climbed onto his branch and stared through his binoculars to make sure she never raised her head again.

She didn't.
And he sobbed.

CHAPTER SEVEN

Elsa sat beside Gina Frost on the bed, while Sasha plopped down on the crushed velvet beanbag. After leaving Costa, Elsa and Sasha had rushed out of the precinct and caught the bus to their estate, Elsa worrying all the while that J was following them—or the fat man was. He was bound to have a car, being as old as he was. J had said he had a Porsche, and she felt all kinds of stupid now for believing him. What nineteen-year-old had one of those?

Sasha had been nice in their conversation on the top deck at the back. "He told you stuff you wanted to hear. It's okay to have believed him. All right, it isn't, but what I mean is, don't blame yourself for thinking he was telling the truth. Let's state the facts."

Elsa had almost rolled her eyes at that. Sasha liked breaking things down into 'manageable pieces' as she called it. Her mum had told her to do it, so it stopped her anxiety getting out of control. Sasha had a wild imagination, saw the frightening side of everything, which was why Elsa had ignored her warnings about J—they were what she'd expected. Seemed Sasha had been right this time, though.

Sasha had continued. "You thought he was nineteen, not some old man. You thought he had a good job because he was clever and passed all his exams. You believed him when he said he'd wait for you to grow up, and that meeting was just so you knew he was really who he said he was. You'd get to know each other, and when you were sixteen, you'd go further. I'd never have fallen for it, but I can see how you did."

Elsa could have been offended, but it was just Sasha's way.

"What if Catherine's in the same situation?" Elsa had glanced about in case the woman a few seats up was earwigging, even though they were whispering. Catherine's name had been all over the news.

"What?" Sasha had grabbed Elsa's arm. "You mean that J bloke's got her?" She'd shivered. "We should go and see Gina."

And there they were, in Catherine's best friend's bedroom. They were only allowed in for a bit, because Gina's mum was doing the dinner, so there wasn't much time to chat. Half an hour, tops.

"Listen…" Sasha glanced at the door like she thought Mrs Frost was listening behind it. "If Cathy told you anything, you need to tell the police."

Gina frowned. "She didn't. I'm not lying."

"Well, get this…" Sasha went on to tell Gina everything. "What do you think of *that* then?"

Gina went pale, and tears fell. "A man followed you?" She blinked at Elsa. "No, Cathy wouldn't have gone to meet some man, would she? Or even speak to one online if she didn't know him."

Sasha gave her a knowing look. "He made out to Elsa he knew her through someone else. And it makes sense now, what they're saying on the news."

"What's that?" Gina sniffed.

Sasha widened her eyes and nodded. "They want to know the whereabouts of someone calling themselves ManBabe19."

"What?" Elsa shrieked. "You didn't tell me that. Why didn't you say something before?"

"It was on the BBC," Sasha said, "I checked the news when we were on the bus. Your fella was Jolly19. Bit of a theme there, with the nineteen."

Gina, in bits, stared at them in turn. "Who's Man whatever?"

"Some bloke Cathy must have been speaking to," Sasha said. "Why else would they be mentioning him?"

"Oh God." Gina wiped her face and cuffed her nose on her sleeve. "What if it's the fat man you said about?"

"That's what I'm thinking." Sasha folded her arms. "Shall we tell your mum first or the police?"

The doorbell rang, and all three of them jumped and squealed. It showed their age, how silly they really were, and Elsa had never been gladder to have listened to her mum's advice: *If something doesn't feel right...*

She reckoned she'd had a mega lucky escape. Wherever Catherine was, Elsa could be there now, too, if she hadn't run.

She felt sick at the thought.

Gina's mother, Julie, was a friendly sort, if a bit worried at seeing Bethany and Mike again. She'd let them into her house, which smelt of dinner cooking and reminded Bethany they needed to eat at some point. Julie showed them into the living room and closed the door.

She wrung her hands. "What's going on? Gina's in a bit of a state over Cathy going missing as it is, so if something's happened, I don't think she can cope with much more."

"How has she been then?" Bethany wanted to know if Gina was acting shifty, like she hid a secret.

"Crying a lot. Her and Cathy went everywhere together. Stayed at each other's houses for sleepovers since they were about nine. The pair of them are so close."

"Yet Cathy never told Gina anything?"

"I believe her. She'd say if something weird was going on. I know my own child, and she'd have come to me."

That's what Debbie Noble thought as well. "Have you seen the latest news, about a male we want to talk to?"

Julie ran a hand through her long brown hair. "I've been busy today, so…?"

"It's come to light that Catherine had been speaking to a man, supposedly aged nineteen, for a few months prior to her going missing. On the day she didn't come home, she'd gone to meet him in a field by the train track."

"Oh God…"

"Unfortunately, Catherine's body was discovered this afternoon."

Julie dropped down onto a nearby chair. "Jesus Christ."

"She'd been kept alive all this time, until about six yesterday evening."

"Poor Debbie and Victor." She swiped at her tear-filled eyes. "How the hell am I going to tell Gina?"

"Do you want me to do it? I need to ask her again whether Catherine told her about the man. I want to do that before she finds out her friend is dead."

Julie nodded. "Okay." She blew out an unsteady breath. "Okay, but what about her friends?"

Bethany frowned. "What do you mean?"

"She has Elsa and Sasha up there. They came to see if she was okay."

"They all go to the same school, I take it."

"Yes. They're in the same class."

Bethany thought about the visit she'd made to the school with Mike, how they'd spoken to everyone in the assembly hall. She'd told them if they had any information, to come and speak to her afterwards or tell their teacher, a parent. No one had. "Can you get them down for me? I could do with talking to them."

Julie went out into the hallway. "Gina!" she called up the stairs. "Can you all come to the living room, please?"

Sets of footsteps tromped, and urgent whispers filtered in. Bethany raised her eyebrows at Mike. He did the same back.

Julie and the girls came in.

"Hi," Bethany said. "You probably remember us from the school safety awareness assembly. DI Bethany Smith and DS Mike Wilkins. Sasha and Elsa, please may we have your parents' phone numbers? We need to ask you some questions, and I'd rather have their permission."

They took their phones out and accessed the information.

Gina squeaked and went bright red. "Mum, there's something—"

"In a second, love," Julie said. "Let's just get the permission sorted first."

Sasha and Elsa gave Mike the numbers, and he left the room.

"But, Mum…" Gina looked at her friends. "There's something—"

"Wait, Gina," Julie snapped.

Bethany supposed the woman was nervous at how her daughter would react to the news. It was understandable, seeing as Julie would be the one coping with the fallout. There was an awkward silence for a while, the girls bowing their heads but glancing at each other. Something was off here.

Mike returned and nodded, standing by the door with his notebook and pen.

"Okay, girls, if you can just take a seat." Bethany indicated the sofa. She wanted them in a row so she could watch their reactions. "I've come to ask whether you've recalled anything about Catherine. Whether a secret you've forgotten about has suddenly been remembered."

Sasha and Elsa side-eyed each other.

Gina squirmed. "That's what I was trying to say. Cathy might have been taken by some man, the same one who's been talking to Elsa, and he wasn't nineteen but fat and old, and he followed her today."

Bethany's stomach filled with butterflies. "Elsa?"

The girl tapped her phone screen and handed the mobile to Bethany. She scrolled back through a hell of a lot of conversation between Elsa (Heaven13) and a Jolly19. The same patter from him as Catherine's conversations. And...oh, he'd convinced her to use the tracker app. There was too much to read now, but she got the gist. A male predator, contacting two girls at once.

"I'm going to have to take your phone, I'm afraid, Elsa. And you'll have to either come with us to your home for a statement or speak to us at the station. Either way, your parents need to be present. Can you get back on the tracker app so we can see where he is?"

Elsa shook her head. "I blocked him, then I went back on there earlier, just to see if he was on it, and he wasn't, so I deleted the app."

"Give me a few details about today. What was the man like?"

Elsa swallowed, and her eyes filled with tears. "I only saw his back and a quick look at his face. He was walking away from me when I turned—I felt like someone was following me. He was short, wide, like he's overweight. He had a black hoody on, and the hood was up. I went to the precinct and met Sasha, and when we were in Costa, he was watching us. That's when I saw his face."

Bethany's heartrate accelerated. "Where?"

"Outside Lloyds. He had the same hoody on, so it must have been him."

Mike walked out to alert the team.

"Okay, about Catherine. Gina, are you sure she didn't tell you anything?"

Gina shook her head. "No! I'd have told Mum if Cathy was messing with a boy."

Bethany took a deep breath and told them their friend wouldn't be coming home. They shrieked, grabbed one another, and cried. Julie rushed over and knelt in front of them, stretching her arms out to gather them all in a hug.

"She didn't tell me, Mum, I swear," Gina sobbed.

"It's all right. I believe you."

Bethany joined Mike in the kitchen.

"I've got hold of the blokes in the CCTV room at the precinct," he said. "They're finding the footage now, so it'll be ready for when we get there."

"Okay, ring Elsa's and Sasha's parents to let them know their kids are in bits and need picking up. Also that Elsa needs an interview. Leona can do that with a uniform. Glen's the best bet."

She went back into the living room, glad everyone had calmed down somewhat. She explained what was going to happen now and assured them they didn't have anything to worry about, but if they heard of anyone else being spoken to by a stranger online, they had to contact her immediately.

With Mike by her side, she left the house and drove them to the shopping precinct. A lead, at last.

But who was the hooded man?

Elsa shook from the news. Catherine was *dead*? Was J and that ManBabe bloke the same person? God, he'd taken Catherine, kept her for days, then *killed* her. She'd forgotten to tell the policewoman J knew her address. She'd tell the other one later, the one doing the interview.

Mum was going to worry so much when she found all this out. It'd set her back, she'd be more tired from the anxiety, and it was Elsa's fault.

Shit. What if the police showed her parents the conversations?

Shame and embarrassment burnt her cheeks.

How could she have been so stupid?

CHAPTER EIGHT

*M*um's funeral had come and gone. Dad attended out of respect for the woman he'd once thought she was. That was what he'd said anyway.

John didn't go.

Time passed again, John sticking to the animals for kills. He finished school and worked as a hospital *porter, still living with Dad in the cottage. Since witnessing Mum's death, something within him had stilled. The rage that was forever roiling in his guts, tainting his mind, faded, but it never went completely.*

Life was a manageable calm, the surface of his internal ocean flat, soft mental peaks lapping quietly.

Then he met Irena.

She was a nurse. He first noticed her when he'd been called to clean up a spill. A patient had been sick on the floor of the ward that Irena worked. It was his unfortunate duty to sanitise the floors. Sometimes he ferried patients to and from the operating theatres. Although the job didn't pay well, nor was it something he'd aspired to do, it was steady employment.

He saw her many times after that. It seemed wherever he went, there she was. Maybe she'd been there all along and he just hadn't noticed.

One day he sat enjoying a ham sandwich in the hospital canteen, while reading a book of poems Dad had given him at Christmas. Someone set a tray full of food down on the table and, rather than glance up, as John rarely wanted company, he continued chewing and reading.

"You don't mind, do you, if I sit here?"

They eased into conversation. Somehow, a date was set.

They met at seven p.m. in The Blue Star, where all the staff from the hospital went for drinks after work. It was on the nearest housing estate. John experienced a new world when he entered the pub. Popular music belted from hidden speakers, mixing with jovial voices and ribald laughter. Even though in an alien environment, he felt welcome, his past firmly cemented, hidden. He could begin again, start life afresh as if he'd never done any of those wicked things.

Though never ashamed of what he'd done, he wanted to be accepted by Irena, even at this early stage, not wanting any of his acts—that she'd undoubtedly consider horrendous—to come to her attention. Maybe she could give him the love Mum hadn't.

She sat to the left of the door on a carver chair. Her handbag by her feet, ankles crossed, she seemed so young, so fragile.

"Would you like another drink?" he asked.

Her smile really did reach her eyes, the corners crinkling. Her straight blonde hair fell onto her shoulders.

"Orange juice, please. Early start for me in the morning," she said.

With the bar relatively clear of people, being served took no time at all, and before John knew it, he was back at her table, dumbly holding two orange juices, unsure of where to sit. In the carver beside her, or opposite?

Opposite won.

The conversation was stilted at first. He fiddled with a beer mat, stripping the outer layer until no graphics remained, filling the unused ashtray with curly paper. In the end, they'd discussed the films they liked.

"Could we meet again?" he asked. "After work tomorrow? Or for lunch in the canteen?"

He must have sounded desperate, and the fact that she smiled and accepted the invitation blew him away.

Before they married, Irena moved into the cottage. Their wedding day dawned drab and wet, a quick registry office ceremony witnessed by Dad and Reg, followed by drinks at The Blue Star.

Irena's simple ivory suit complemented her figure, the small spray of red roses a vibrant splash against it, her cheeks flushed and shiny, her eyes sparkling.

Her parents, strict Catholics and aghast at their marriage, didn't attend. Irena rarely visited her folks. Over the first two years of them seeing each other, the family bond had eroded. Irena appeared not to mind, seemed happy living with Dad and John.

She'd said once, "All I need is you."

Soon, Irena announced her pregnancy. Everything considered bad lay dormant at that time. John didn't think of debase things, probably because he was settled in life, and he left the animals alone. Finally, he was loved, unconditionally, wholly.

Then two of them became three.

Edward was born in the place of their work with a lusty infant's yell at four twenty-two in the afternoon. Irena wasn't in labour long for a first birth, just six hours, and John went to the telephone booth to ring Dad.

"Take care of him, son."

John felt an affinity with Dad then, tangible even down the phone line.

Irena adored Edward. The relief that she wasn't like Mum was immense, and John really did feel lucky to be living the life he was. They moved from the cottage to a council house in Hubert Lane, a two-bedroom on the estate where The Blue Star was. Suburban life accepted John; he belonged somewhere. At fucking last.

Having a newborn in the home brought back memories from the past. John loved his son, doted on him, yet he'd been able to kill another baby. He had a confusing hour or two while cuddling Edward on the sofa one day, watching him while he slept, his tiny fingers unfurling. That he felt such love for this baby and none for the other one. That he'd never harm this child yet had no qualms about what he'd done to the brat.

The overcrowding thoughts got him angry. Was this what guilt felt like? There was no doubt his acts had felt right at the time, but now, with his own son in his arms, it seemed as if the killing of that baby had been committed by someone else.

Irena would think him hideous if she ever learnt the truth.

Unable to understand these feelings, John abruptly turned them off and concentrated on what he now had. A wife he adored. A son who was his world.

He wanted to forget the past and be the person he now was. Not that horrible monster who was driven by his thoughts to do such terrible things.

And for a time, he did.

John stroked the clothing on a hanger, which he'd hooked on a nail in the wall. Mum had put the outfit on often, then Catherine, and Elsa would have, too, had he brought her here. This was Tanya's first time, and she'd probably refuse to wear it, but she had no choice.

"See this?" he asked. "It's a bit like your school uniform, isn't it, what with the skirt that all but shows your arse cheeks. You're quite the flirt really, aren't you. I've been watching."

Tanya did that growly thing again, tears falling.

It was a bit tiresome, her keep crying. What was the problem putting on the uniform anyway? Mum hadn't had an aversion to it.

Strange, these young girls, how they gave promises then changed their minds once they saw him. It proved people judged a book by its cover, otherwise, they'd still love him when they knew he wasn't nineteen and 'fit', as they said these days.

Fucking bitches.

"So it's all right to go to school dressed like this, but not for John?" the starling asked. "What, do you want the boys there seeing everything?" John flipped voices. "I've seen you with your blouse buttons undone as low as you dare. You like them looking at your tits, don't you? Filthy girl."

Tanya snuffled on. He had the urge to hit her, to smack her for being so drippy, but that'd get her crying even more, and he couldn't be doing with that.

"Answer me," he shouted.

She stared downwards.

"Oh, you can't, can you." He put the starling on the shelf and stepped to her, whipping the sock out of her mouth. "*Now* fucking speak."

"I want to go home."

"I bet you do. Realised you can't handle a real man, have you? Seen that being with men isn't the same as the stupid dickheads at school?"

"I don't understand why you're doing this."

"It doesn't matter why, just that I am. Why is none of your business, and you'd do well to remember that." He poked at the air with a finger, wishing it was the starling and its nasty beak. "Now then, you're going to wear this get-up, and you'll smile an' all."

He snatched the blouse off the hanger—he'd previously cut the sides and the seams of the sleeves, then attached Velcro so he could get it on her without having to take the bindings off her wrists. The skirt was the same—saved her stepping into it while he held it out for her. She could knee him or anything, kick out. He'd tie her ankles, but then he couldn't do what he wanted if her legs were closed, could he.

He marched to Tanya and put the blouse on her, and she kicked him in the shins, as he knew she would. His temper frayed, so he slapped her face then poked his finger through the beak hole in her cheek, the end coming up against her gum.

"Stop it, just stop being so difficult. Mum wasn't. She enjoyed this sort of thing."

"I'm not your mum," she wailed.

He snatched his finger out. "Not until you have the skirt on, no."

John busied himself dressing her in that, too, asking himself why, if he hated Mum, he wanted to recreate her, and especially in this uniform. Why had seeing her on the bed in it done this to him? Why had it warped his mind?

He decided he didn't care. If he thought about it too much, he'd think of the other things he'd done in his life up until now. He hadn't felt guilty about it at the time, so why was he suddenly getting a conscience, same as he had when Edward had been born?

"Fucking cow!" He whacked her cheek again, harder. "Now, pack it in with the crying. You need a wash. There's your pink baseball cap and makeup to put on next."

CHAPTER NINE

Bethany and Mike stood in front of the monitors and small TVs in the precinct's CCTV room. They'd been here before during the Butcher case. Black Hair and Blond—she couldn't recall their names—had found all the footage, which was on the screen directly ahead.

They watched a short, wide man in a black hoody enter the precinct via the door that led to the attached multi-storey—so the fucker had a vehicle then. His face wasn't visible; he walked with his head down, staring at his phone until he got to Lloyds. Was he checking the tracker app to see where Elsa was?

He glared over at Costa. Thick beard—fake?—and large glasses, and he'd pulled some kind of drawstring on the hood so it hid the forehead and most of the cheeks. The bastard knew what he was doing, knew there were cameras.

"Can you fast-forward now, please," she asked Blond.

He whizzed it through for ages, stopping when Hoody appeared to stand more upright. He looked at his phone, tensed, and glared at Costa again. Was that the point he knew Elsa had blocked him? Switched the app off? It must have been, because he stormed off towards the multi-storey.

"We'll need to watch the car park footage now," she said.

Black Hair pressed PLAY on his screen. Hoody entered the car park on level one and got into a grey or silver Ford Fiesta, the old style, the rear number plate dirty on one half with thick streaks of mud, the other half illegible. Only one letter was visible: B. Or was that an eight? Or even a three? Mike got his phone out, undoubtedly to message Fran or Rob the details.

The suspect sat there for a while, then drove off.

"We checked where he went," Black Hair said, "and it was to the right, away from town."

"Can I see that, please?"

He switched to another camera. The car indeed went right, then out of sight.

"Do you have any more cameras that would have captured him after that?" she asked, desperate for some idea where Hoody might live.

"No, sorry."

She looked at Mike to silently ask him to pass on the direction the Fiesta had gone in. He nodded and tapped on his phone.

"Okay, can you send all the footage with our man on it to Fran at the station?"

They'd had to do this before for the Butcher debacle.

"And can I have a closeup shot of him while he's outside Lloyds, please. If you can send it to me via email, I can get it distributed faster." She handed him her card with her details on it.

While that was being done, she walked over to the door with Mike so they could talk quietly. His phone had beeped a couple of times, and she wanted to know what was going on. He held his phone out for her to read it.

Rob: NO HIT ON THE PLATE, SORRY.

"What?" she whispered. "No hit *at all*, even from the three possible options? That doesn't make sense." She read more.

Rob: OVER FIVE HUNDRED GREY OR SILVER FIESTAS. NO B, 8, OR 3 IN THAT POSITION ON THE PLATE. DOCTORED? HAVE SENT FRAN THE DETAILS.

"She's got a job on her hands, sifting through that as well as the CCTV," Mike said. "With Leona interviewing Elsa…"

"This is where uniforms come in handy. Let her know to nab one, give her a bit of help. What's His Face, the new lad. Jack? Moller, is it?"

"Yep." Mike got to work typing the message.

"She needs to get sightings of all those Fiestas from road CCTV, see where they were, and ring every man who owns one of them. Every woman as well, actually. A bloke could be borrowing his partner's car. Make it two uniforms to help her. Glen's out of the picture as he's with Leona. Also, ask her to see if there's CCTV of Elsa coming out of the alley. We might get a glimpse of him behind her."

"Okay."

Bethany turned to the CCTV men.

Blond handed her a printed image of Hoody outside Lloyds. "I've sent it via email, like you said, but thought you might want one to hand, too."

"Thank you." She folded it and put it in her pocket, then forwarded the email to Rob and asked him to do the usual with it. "Okay, you've been a massive help. Now, let's see the footage where the girls leave Costa."

Black Hair accessed the file. Elsa and Sasha left the coffee shop, glancing left and right, clutching each other, as young girls tended to do in times of trouble. They ran past Sandra's Balloons to the exit that led to the high street; they were spooked, and both peered back to where Hoody had stood watching them, faces showing their fear. Then they were gone, outside.

"Right, we'll be off then. I'll need that footage sent to Fran as well. Cheers once again."

She left with Mike, and they took the lift down into the precinct, walking through until they, too, were out in the high street. She checked where all the council cameras were, then spotted some on individual shops—if she didn't get what she wanted at the bus station, she'd come back here.

A quick walk to the station, taking the route the girls probably had, and Bethany went to the security office there and knocked on the door. A man in a guard suit opened it, frowning. Had they interrupted his tea break or something?

"Yes?" he asked.

She held up her ID. "We need to see some footage of two girls getting on a bus this morning, the Four A. Plus we'll need the actual footage of them on the bus."

"Gawd, what have they done? Been thieving, have they?"

"Not at all."

"Come in then. Len'll be here in a minute, the driver, so I'll get hold of him and ask him to miss his next route so you can do what you have to."

It was soon clear the girls had told the truth. The time they'd arrived here was in line with how long it would have taken to walk from the precinct. Len's camera showed them sitting at the back on the top deck, talking, only one other passenger present, a female. The lower deck camera, the one Bethany was most interested in, thankfully put her mind at rest. The bus hadn't been followed, as far as she could see, by a silver Fiesta.

Outside again, they walked back through the town.

"That's an hour of our lives we won't get back," Bethany said.

"Yep, but we needed to check just the same." Mike eyed Greggs. "My lunch didn't even touch the sides earlier. Want a baguette, seeing as it's creeping closer to dinnertime?"

"We might end up working late so may as well while we're here. And some Yum Yums. We'll get something for Fran and Leona as well."

Food purchased, they sat in the car in the multi-storey and talked while they ate, mulling everything over. The sticking point was the IP address being hidden somehow. Without it, they couldn't move forward to catch ManBabe19, and if her suspicions were correct, Jolly19. Bethany thought about an article she'd read recently, where some bloke had spoken to girls via Messenger on their birthdays. An easy way in, to wish them a happy day, get them talking while they were hyped up from receiving cards and presents, maybe excited at having a party, defences down.

Had Hoody got the idea from that? Catherine's conversation had him saying they knew each other via a mutual friend, so he'd used it as a link, something they had in common. A way to get her to trust him. After all, if they both knew the same person, it couldn't be sinister, could it—a crafty angle to dupe an innocent girl and one that had worked, unfortunately.

Teens, despite insisting they had, hadn't grown up enough to suspect foul play, to have alerts going off in their heads that a random, so-called mutual had chosen to chat with them. With Catherine it was exactly that. She was flattered, pleased he'd picked her, and her writing style was mature. Her parents, when Bethany and Mike had initially spoken to them, had said that wasn't her usual way of writing, so had the girl tried to act older because ManBabe was apparently nineteen? Had she wanted to impress him?

Bethany remembered the heady feeling she'd had with her first boyfriend and could understand how Catherine had been swept away by it all. The part of their chat where he'd asked to meet her was deftly done, segueing seamlessly with what they'd previously been talking about: what they liked to do. Catherine had mentioned she enjoyed train travel, and ManBabe had swooped.

ManBabe19: HEY, SAME AS ME! I'M A BIT OF A TRAINSPOTTER TO BE FAIR. I LIKE SITTING OUT IN THE FIELDS BY THE TRACK AND COUNTING THEM AS THEY GO PAST. WANT TO DO THAT WITH ME? WE COULD GO FOR A SPIN IN MY PORSCHE AFTER, IF YOU LIKE.

A Ford Fiesta was not a Porsche.

Bethany remembered she'd spotted a Porsche in Elsa's conversation, too, so ManBabe19 and Jolly19 *were* one and the same, they had to be. The man must have stuck to the tried and tested. It'd worked with Catherine, so why fix what wasn't broken?

Sick bastard.

She drove them to the police station. Mike could now give Fran, Jack, and any other uniforms some help with the CCTV. Bethany would watch Elsa's recorded interview if the actual chat was over by now, then she'd talk to Leona and ask what she thought.

Many heads were better than one.

As it happened, there had been a delay in Leona and Glen talking with Elsa—something about her dad having to travel back from work in London to be there with his daughter. Elsa's mother had CFS and could come in at a push, but she had no means of getting there and probably wouldn't be much use if she was, so she'd said. Her attention span was short now, her mind foggy more often than not, and she'd feel sleepy pretty quickly.

In the corridor outside Interview One, Bethany said to Leona, "I can do this now, if you like. There's CCTV upstairs that needs your expert eye on it."

Leona nodded, handing over a folder. "Good. I wasn't looking forward to talking to her, to be honest. The idea that she's been groomed…"

"I know, nasty business. Off you go then."

Leona walked away, and Bethany checked the folder contents. Copies of the months of conversation from Elsa's phone, plus a sheet where Leona had written things down that she wanted to ask, the top one being the tracker app.

Bethany entered the room, pleased Glen stood beside the door. Elsa sat with a man she resembled so greatly, it had to be her father. He was a beefy bugger, possibly one who used the gym. A little rough and ready, so she'd brace herself for a tough time.

"Hi, Elsa," she said. "Change of plan. I'm able to chat with you now."

Elsa appeared relieved, perhaps because she was familiar with Bethany.

"Nice to meet you, sir," she said to the father. "Although I wish it were under different circumstances, as must you."

He stood and reached over to shake her hand. "I'm Gary Masters, and yes, this is all a bit startling."

She accepted the greeting then sat. "I'm DI Bethany Smith. This is Glen Underby." She indicated the PC. "Now, we'd normally conduct this kind of interview in what we call the soft rooms, but they're occupied at the minute."

Leona had mentioned a sexual attack on a pensioner who was now in the process of giving her statement in the smaller room, and three young lads who'd seen a man expose himself to them through the school fence on Friday were in the larger one with their parents and the teaching assistant who'd also witnessed it.

The world was a shitty place.

"So," she continued, "I apologise for the more austere setting. Glad to see you have drinks." She turned to smile at Glen, assuming he'd provided them, and set the video to record. "Okay, have you been given the gist of things, Gary?"

"Yes, and Elsa's said a few bits and bobs. What I dislike about all of this is a man contacting young girls. I realise Elsa's said some stuff to him she may not want me to see, but that's not my concern, as in, she's young, she thought he was nineteen, and we've all had our first love, you know? I'm more bothered he's…well, he's a paedophile and a killer."

Thank goodness he wasn't about to give his daughter a hard time over what she'd said on chat. That would make this talk a lot easier.

"From what I saw, there isn't anything there that's too embarrassing for Elsa or you," Bethany said. "During the parts where the man tried to get her to discuss sex, she was reticent."

"It made me uncomfortable," Elsa said. "Like, I went bright red when I saw what he'd put. He said it was okay if I didn't want to speak about it, and that made me feel better, but then a day or so later, he did it again."

"Why did you go to meet him then, love?" Gary stroked the top of her head. "You know if you feel strange about anything, you can come to us."

"I know, but…" Elsa shrugged.

"It's difficult, isn't it, Elsa," Bethany said. "You're growing up and want some things private, but now you know what happened to Catherine, please make sure you never meet anyone online again, even as an adult, unless you're one hundred percent sure who it really is. And if you're not, meet in a public place with lots of people, and take a friend. However, this is advice for adults. I in no way recommend you do this at all at your age."

Elsa nodded. "He was just… I thought he was… I wanted a boyfriend, that's all."

Bethany smiled. "I get it, I promise, but pick a boy at school, okay?"

For the next hour or so, each of them had a copy of the conversations, all of them reading at the same speed and stopping to ask questions. At no point did Gary act as if Elsa was in the wrong, and she seemed to pick up on that and relax more. To be honest, as Bethany went through it all, Elsa's side of things was pretty silly and childlike, despite how she tried to act older, and from an adult's perspective, there wasn't anything there Bethany wouldn't have said herself in her youth. It was Jolly19 who was the problem.

Gary's cheeks flamed with anger at some points—she suspected he'd spotted the grooming techniques, the manipulation to steer the chat certain ways.

They came to a bit where Elsa had given him her address.

"Oh, sweetheart," Gary said.

"I know. I'm so sorry, Dad. I didn't think until after."

"Okay," Bethany said. "I need some info on what your homelife is like so I can work out what to do here. Your wife has CFS, yes? Where is she during the day?"

"Sometimes she stays in bed," Gary said. "Other times, she's up and about, or on the sofa. She can work from home on her laptop so has learnt to pace herself and only do what she can manage. Too much activity whacks her out, then she's fit for nothing for a few days after. Better to do little and often."

"Right, so would she be alone at times and answer the door if someone knocked—or would she leave it if it's too tiring?" Bethany asked.

Gary paled. "Oh God, you don't think he'll...?"

"I don't know." Bethany sighed. "Can you give her a ring for me now and tell her when she's by herself to not open the door until all this is over? She must also secure the house while she's inside—bolts, a chain on the front door, if you have them."

Elsa's tears came then. "I thought of him going home and hurting Mum and felt so bad for telling him where we lived."

"Don't worry, love, we'll sort it." Gary took his phone out.

While he rang his wife and explained, Bethany sent a message to Rob so patrol on that estate could go down Elsa's street a couple of times a day at random hours on their route. Police presence there, should Jolly19 be watching, may deter him from acting irrational. Then again, if he was still intent on meeting Elsa, he might do whatever it took.

Gary ended the call. "That's sorted."

"Thanks. Now, for the time being, Elsa, you need to walk to and from school with someone every day. They have to come and call for you so you're never by yourself."

Elsa glanced at her father.

"I'll take her," Gary said. "I was only in London today for an annual meeting; it's not a regular thing. I usually work in Shadwell and can easily nip out to pick her up as well."

"Good, with that covered, plus your wife ignoring the door and locking herself in, there's less chance of him deciding to come round. I've asked for a patrol car to go down there each day as well."

Gary let out a long breath. "Thank you."

"This is all my fault." Elsa cuffed her nose.

"No, it's the predator's fault," Bethany said. "*He* caused this, not you. Men like him are clever and know exactly how to twist a situation to their advantage. Don't blame yourself."

It was an easy thing to say. Might be difficult for Elsa to execute, though—blaming herself was a natural thing to do.

They chatted some more. With everything discussed, Elsa and Gary left, so Bethany went to the incident room.

"Did you get anything while I was gone?" She moved to the whiteboard to write up the basics of her time with Elsa.

"The footage of the alley," Leona said. "Same man as the one outside Lloyds if we're going by body size, height, and clothing."

"Right. Any cameras in the courtyard?"

Leona shook her head. "No. We've assumed he walked or drove to the precinct the back way, then went inside to watch Elsa in Costa. He may have parked initially near the courtyard, but with no cameras, we can't check where he came from."

Bethany grunted. "Right, we'll plod on for a few hours." She remembered she'd left the baguettes and Yum Yums in the car, and as uniforms were here now, the food wouldn't stretch to all of them. "I'll order a takeaway later. If we can just crack on with the CCTV and get that off our list, we can concentrate on other stuff tomorrow."

The uniforms looked at her hopefully.

"Yep, you lot as well," she said. "My shout."

Good job she had money on her credit card really, wasn't it.

CHAPTER TEN

John and his little family lived in Hubert Lane for thirteen years.

The evening had started the same as any other. He'd been stargazing, using the binoculars, plus the new telescope they'd purchased that year, plotting the stars on his chart. Irena was in the kitchen doing the ironing. Edward, a teenager now, stood *on the street corner where John could see him, talking to his friends, some of them girls. John knew them all, having lived there for so long.*

He didn't pay them too much heed. Their chatter rose through the open window, their laughter reminding him their childhoods couldn't be farther removed from his. The blonde girl offered Edward one of her cigarettes right in John's line of vision.

Bitch.

Later, once John had gone down into the living room, Edward came home in a strop.

"Lucy Berry's a right mean one." He slouched down on the sofa, chin hidden in the lapels of his coat, shoulders hunched.

"Why's that, son?" John asked.

Edward scowled. "I asked her if she'd be my girlfriend, and she laughed at me, like I was stupid or something."

John clenched his teeth, jaw muscles pumping. It was a typical girl response, yet it brought out such a rage in him, an ire he'd thought was gone, extinct, that it knocked him off balance. He fought to hold the anger back as it seemed alien now, and unnecessary. The amount of fury didn't gel with what had prompted it to erupt.

"Well," John began, not knowing what to say, "if she doesn't want to go out with you, that's her loss."

He hoped he'd used the right figure of speech. Edward was popular. Having bypassed that section of his own life, John was anxious to ensure he got his responses as a dad correct. Ridicule from his son would have cut deeply.

Edward's face brightened, and his head popped out from his jacket. "Yeah, I could ask Kerry out instead."

John frowned. Surely he didn't mean her*?* "Kerry? Kerry Thomas?"

Kerry, the daughter of the lane's resident scum. John kept his disbelief to himself. Edward would only chase Kerry even more if John opposed it.

"Yeah, she's nice."

John disguised his sigh of irritation with a yawn. "You do that."

He smiled and hoped it was convincing.

The anger that had surfaced seemed to float off again. Gone were the days of dark, violent thoughts and acts. They had no place in the life he led now. He didn't want them returning, messing up the stability he'd built around himself.

But inner demons could only be caged for so long before something or someone released them. It was Edward's cries coming through the dividing bedroom wall that did it.

John was in bed listening, the sound ripping him apart inside. Then it came, the inner rage, encompassing him. He gave in, embraced it.

The devil had returned.

John took to looking out of the bedroom window any chance he got, scoping the lane for any signs of Lucy Berry and spying on her through the binoculars. Hate festered from even the most subtle of slights, coiling round the heart and mind, a cobra squeezing a rat.

While observing the lane, he'd also let his anger reach out to other, unsuspecting residents. Amazing what you saw when watching, really watching, them unaware, going about their daily business. He kept tabs on them all, but especially Lucy Berry.

His inner voice had returned with some force, smashing into his carefully erected barriers. So much so that Irena asked if he was all right.

"Is anything bothering you, John?"

"I just feel a little out of sorts," was his standard response.

There was no way she could possibly understand. She adored their son just as John did, would even get why he felt as he did towards Lucy Berry. Irena had also been upset about the girl rejecting Edward. Her compassion overruled her indignation, though, considering how Lucy lived, what her life was like, and the incident was soon forgotten when it appeared that Edward had forgotten it himself.

But John's devil didn't allow him to forget, and he changed back to the sour person he once was, relishing terrible thoughts. Outwardly, he appeared relatively the same. But inside, a fire burned, and it wouldn't extinguish until he dealt with the arsonist who'd lit it.

Lucy's mum, or Bouncy Woman as he thought of her, had a spring in her step all the time, and he wanted to stop that spring. He needed to give her something to be so un-springy about, bounding along as she did, smile plastered on even when alone—he knew, because his telescope was his friend. She thought John fancied her. A quick slash across her face with a meat cleaver would wipe that grin away.

Lucy Berry was the one who needed to be taught a lesson first, though. She stood around with her friends, striking sexy poses, head cocked to the side, cigarette resting between lips too young to taste the smoke. And she flaunted herself, basking in the testosterone emanating from the young lads she hung out with, throwing her head back when she laughed. She was just asking for it. John would only have to follow her. Matching her footsteps would be enough of a scare. Whispered threats.

He knew her routine. He'd been watching Lucy and her mum on and off for the past month. Irena thought he'd taken up stargazing as a serious hobby now.

John followed and watched Lucy through his binoculars as she usually stood on the corner, to the left of their house, sitting on the street sign, obscuring the name of the road for visitors. Around seven each evening, she set up residence with Kerry Thomas, followed by a group of lads who walked up for their usual gathering. She dealt out cigarettes, her hot breath puffing into the air. One lad didn't take a cigarette. Edward.

She stayed there for a couple of hours. What must her mum be thinking, letting her go out in such a short skirt and a spaghetti-strap vest top, her tits on show?

John was appalled by Lucy yet also fascinated. Her hair, in pigtails, proved she hadn't grown up as much as she made out.

Pigtails.

A light drizzle fell. John angled the binoculars towards the left to watch her and got annoyed when she stepped out of view. He strained his neck against the wall to capture the scene, the plaster cold on his skin. She soon went back to her seat on the street sign.

She'd taken a hooded top from her bag and put it on, carefully placing the hood over her hair. She looked better covered up.

The light had faded, the streetlamps giving off their foggy orange glow. John moved away from the window, reaching for his black bomber jacket with the balaclava in the right-hand pocket, gloves in the left. He slipped the coat on, zipped it to the top, and left the bedroom, tripping lightly down the stairs with Bouncy Woman's spring in his step.

"Going to the pub for an hour, love!" he called.

"No stars out tonight then?"

Irena always replied the same way. He looked at her, took in her pretty face, the way her eyes softened as she gazed back.

"I just fancy a beer, that's all. Going to call Edward in on my way past."

"Oh, righty ho. See you in a while then." She seemed worried, her forehead ruffled. *"Will you be long?"*

"Not long, no."

He smiled at his wife, and she smiled back, probably uncertain of the change in him, unsure as to why he'd taken to going to The Blue Star alone. Perhaps she suspected him of having an affair. Knowing Irena, she'd be blaming herself, thinking he wanted to get away from her, that she'd done something wrong.

Regardless, his devil pushed him out of the house, and he approached the corner of the lane with the gang of kids adorning it.

"Hi, Mr Keagan," they chorused.

"Hi there, kids. Edward, time to go in, son."

John passed them, the darkness hidden within. He strode round the corner, across the main road, and into one of the small alleys that made up the estate's walkways. There, he waited. Lucy would walk some of the lads to their houses first, Kerry having gone in already, then come this way to go back home to the lane.

He put the balaclava on. Smoke-like breaths left his mouth; they dissipated into the wool, leaving a wet residue. He took the woollen gloves from the other pocket and slid them on over rough-skinned fingers. It was all the handwashing at the hospital that did it.

He looked inside himself and examined how he felt. A little nervous, perhaps a bit guilty—it being the first time he'd succumbed in years, the first time he'd been bad since he'd met Irena—and excited. His heart beat fast, seeming to rise into his throat. His nose ran, so he used his hand to stem the drip onto the facemask. Wool against wool created a squeaking noise, audible in the quiet hidey-hole. The bush he'd concealed himself in rustled and moved.

She's coming. Here she is.

She came across the main road, hands in her pockets, hood up and her head down. She'd made herself such an easy target that way. No hands free to protect herself should she fall. No eyes forward to see the danger. Perfect. She had less of a swagger now. Less self-assurance.

She strode past, her trainers squelching on the wet pavement, laces free and slapping at her bare legs, leaving muddy slash marks across her shins. Another unwise move on her part. She could trip on those laces. No common sense at all, that one. John counted fifteen paces and emerged from his hiding place and followed her. Lucy Berry had a way to go down the long alley, with no houses on either side, just wooden fencing and trees that bordered expansive fields. The streetlights here were few and far between. One at each end and two spaced out down the middle. Dark and ideal for his plan.

Lucy's shoulders tensed. She'd heard his deliberately heavy footsteps. She went a little faster, and he immediately matched her stride. Her head snapped upright, and John imagined she had her eyes trained on the end of the alleyway towards her escape, her ears tuned in to the movements behind her.

She upped her speed, slowly at first, as if she didn't want him to notice the change of step, then faster. Her breath trailed behind her as she puffed with terror and the unexpected exertion. He hoped her heart was beating harder, that her stomach had turned to mush, and the sound of her blood pounded in her head.

He matched her step again, and it was then she ran. She had three quarters of the alley to travel. John sprinted up behind her, closing the gap. She turned slightly, but with the hood on, her pigtail whipping in a thick strand across her face, it was impossible to see him clearly. The girl let out a strangled gasp, followed by a sob. She knew a man was gaining on her, so this should be enough to stop her from being so flirty, but his devil didn't listen. He wanted to take it a step further.

He was as close as he could get and slapped his palm over her mouth. She let out a muffled cry. He grabbed her left upper arm with his free hand and steered her, struggling, into the small copse that ran parallel to the fence. Branches snagged his balaclava, but he moved too quickly for them to tug his mask free. Her mouth wiggled under his hand. Oh, a feisty girl, trying to bite.

Keeping her facing away from him, and shoving her forward up against the fence, he adopted what he hoped was a menacing tone. His voice came out flat, without emotion.

"Do you want to live?"

She sobbed, nodding frantically, her eyes squeezed shut.

"Dirty girls like you deserve to be punished. Do you want me to punish you?"

She shook her head. John slid his hand down her left arm and gripped her wrist, folding her arm back on itself, between them. For fun, he stuck his thumb into the base of her spine, as if it were a knife, his fingers still around her wrist.

"I could stab you right now. No one would find you for days."

His exhalations came out in short, sharp bursts, as did hers. For a moment, he was fascinated that their clouds of breath merged into the night sky, floating upwards until they were nothing. She broke down then, and finally, he heard what he'd been waiting for. The soft pssst-hiss of her urine exiting.

He pushed her harder into the fence and jolted her upwards then back down again, enjoying the fact that the rough wooden surface probably broke her skin, maybe leaving splinters and drawing blood. Her face would show her ordeal and remind her of it for a while to come.

Muffled noises barked from her mouth.

"When I let you go, you dare turn around. You stay where you are for five minutes. I'll know if you move before then. If you do move and look at me, I'll kill you."

He let her go and took a step backwards. With her legs bent slightly at the knees, her feet around twelve inches apart, toes pointing inwards, she leant on the fence with her forehead for balance. Her arms hung loose and straight by her sides. Her hood half covered her face.

"Oh God, oh God. Mum...I want my mum."

John backed out of the trees, watching her, making sure she didn't turn to catch a glimpse of him. She didn't. Twisting round with speed, he ran, ripping off his mask, pulling off his gloves, ramming his fingers through his hair to tame the unruly mess the mask had made. Across the main road now, walking normally, upright, smiling.

He really hoped she'd learn, for her sake.

In The Blue Star, he drank a well-deserved pint. He replayed the events of the last twenty minutes or so, then returned home.

Irena asked, "Did you see anyone at the pub, John?"

"Not really, love. I had a pint or two, but the bar was pretty empty."

She seemed relieved.

CHAPTER ELEVEN

Tanya's legs wouldn't stop shaking. She stood in the compost, which crept up over her toes, cold and damp from the air in the manky cellar. That was what she felt the most, the cold. It had seeped into her bones, her muscles, which were stiff and seemed to creak if she moved. The strip of fabric around her wrists had sent her skin beyond sore now, numb, the previous discomfort not registering.

It was lonely here without Catherine.

"You need to go and hide," he said. "And if I find you, you're dead."

She shuddered and let out a muffled cry. Why was he doing this? What had she ever done to him to deserve being treated this way? He was mental, had to be. People didn't talk to you online, lying, saying they were a young lad when they were really old and fat. Why had he chosen her?

The makeup had dried, her skin tight with it. He'd used thick white stuff. She'd thought it was cream at first, the sort her mum used for wrinkles, but he'd said it was to match his mum's face when she'd gone all pale the day she'd died. The foundation had come through the hole in her cheek. It tasted funny, and the pain of the hole... God, it throbbed.

Tanya stared at him. Where could she hide? The cellar was about twenty by twenty, no nooks or crannies, just an open space with the hanger on the wall, the starling's shelf, and the silver door opposite. He stood in front of it, hands on his hips, a balaclava covering his features, just his fleshy lips and beady eyes on show through the holes. What was the point in it? She'd seen his face already.

She trembled at the memory of seeing him for the first time.

Tanya stood outside Wind Energy, being badgered by the woman in reception, who'd come out to see if she could help.

"I'm waiting for my boyfriend. He'll come and talk to you once he's here, about the tour he booked." It felt so cool to say that. Boyfriend.

"All right. Lovely. See you in a bit then." The receptionist went back inside.

Tanya's phone went off—maybe Simon was running late or something. He was supposed to have been here ten minutes ago.

Simon: MY CAR'S CONKED OUT ON THE MAIN ROAD. WALK DOWN AND MEET ME. I'M JUST GOING TO PUT SOME PETROL IN IT FROM THE CAN IN THE BOOT.

Tanya laughed, her stomach doing somersaults. She walked along the track that led to the road, slipping her phone in her jacket pocket. Halfway down, a car became visible behind the bushes planted at the edge of the property. It didn't look red, like he'd said it was, but silver.

She shrugged and continued.

Her phone went off again.

Simon: ALL SORTED. LET'S PLAY A GAME. COME ACROSS THE FIELD AND WAIT BEHIND THE BUSHES. WE'LL CROUCH SO WE DON'T SEE EACH OTHER, THEN AFTER THE COUNT OF THREE, WE CAN BOTH POP UP. FUN OR WHAT?

Tanya: LOL. OKAY.

She put her phone away again and ran across the field. At the bushes, she bent her knees and peered through a gap between bunches of leaves. Simon was getting out of a car, but she couldn't make his features out. His hood was up, and he seemed to have something covering his face. Her heart flickered, out of beat for a moment, and she went to rise, then—

A hand thrust through the bush and gripped her top. She let out a startled cry, then she was being dragged through, branches and leaves scratching her cheeks and tangling in her hair.

"What the fuck, Simon?" she shouted. Her attempts at getting him to loosen his hold proved pointless, as did her digging her feet into the ground to stop him yanking her through.

Why was he doing this? What had happened to the reveal game? Why didn't he have a red car?

She emerged on the other side, her pink baseball cap wonky. He hauled her to her feet, still grasping her top in his fist, and she jolted at how close he was. Oh God, he had a balaclava on. And it wasn't even Simon. This man was shorter and overweight, his eyes blue instead of brown, and they bulged while he huffed out heavy breaths, as if he wasn't fit.

"Who are you?" She ought to scream or something, but nothing would come out. She glanced left and right, but no cars were coming, no one out here to save her.

"Get in the fucking car."

He dragged her along the verge, and she struggled to get free, her chest hurting from the fear. She dug her nails in his wrists, but it had no effect, he kept on pulling her. Round the car. To the passenger side. He opened the door and tried to force her inside, but she fought him, hoping he'd stumble.

He didn't.

"Don't piss me about," he snarled. "Get in, or I swear to God, I'll bloody kill you."

He shoved her on the back, and her face landed on the driver's seat, the gear stick poking into her chest. Her legs were lifted; he crammed her in and shut the door. Tanya scrabbled to get the driver's door open, but she was too slow, and he was too quick coming round the front of the vehicle. He was there, knocking her cap off, fisting her hair and pushing her backwards to the other side. She sat at the same time he did, grabbed the handle, but he slammed his door and engaged the locks.

Her hair released, he punched her in the temple. She screamed, clutching her head with one hand, still tugging at the lock with the other.

"Now then, if you don't behave, I'll murder you right here, understand?"

She couldn't look at him. Couldn't stand to see the balaclava and his mad eyes. So she carried on screaming, bashing on the glass with both fists. She'd read about breaking a car window with the metal poles on a headrest, so she twisted to pull it free.

"You're going to be difficult, aren't you." He sighed and wrenched the headrest off, throwing it into the back seat. "Honestly, you girls..."

She swung a fist towards him. He caught her wrist, lowering her arm, and with his body, pressed her into the seat. The punches came again, several to her head, each one painful and hard.

She didn't see anything else except the blackness of oblivion.

Tanya came to but didn't dare open her eyes. Wherever she was, there was a chill to the air, and was that a brick wall at her back? She reached blindly behind and touched it. Was she outside? There was the smell of mud. She reached down and brushed her hands on the ground. Yes, mud, but fine, like the stuff Nan used in her hanging baskets.

Tanya's head ached. Then she remembered. Meeting Simon, except it wasn't Simon but some bloke in a balaclava. She quickly checked her pocket, but her phone was gone.

"Did you think I'd let you keep it?"

He didn't sound the same. The voice was high-pitched.

Her eyes snapped open. He stood there holding a golden bird ornament. Fear clawed at her insides, her throat closing up with it. He was there, that man, staring at her from across a room, leaning against a bare stone wall. And compost, loads of it in place of a carpet or lino. And some clothes hanging on the wall, a bit like her school uniform. Her baseball cap was on the floor.

She screamed.

"Really, that's such a boring racket." He walked over to her, jabbing the bird at the air.

She shut up, afraid, breathing heavily.

"And it's pointless. No one will hear you. Listen, I've got a proposition for you. Another game, seeing

as the last one didn't work out too well. We never did get to reveal ourselves over that hedge."

"Please, I want to go home."

"No." That weird voice again, and he moved the bird so it looked like its head was cocking one way, then the other. "We need to play. You hide, I seek."

She shook her head.

"Go on, up you get."

She ignored him, too scared to stand. He dropped the bird, lunged forward, and grabbed her wrist, swiftly draping something over it, then drawing her other across so they were joined behind her. He was tying them together with a strip of material. She tried to yank her hands away, but he held fast, so she kicked him, her heel hurting on his shin.

No shoes?

She glanced down.

No clothes.

And she was filthy, as if she'd rolled in the mud.

She screamed again, this whole thing a nightmare, and he let her go.

She raced for the door.

"That's it," he said. "Hide. I'll count to one hundred."

Tanya raced forward, up some stone steps that had a left-hand turn, a landing, then another left turn. She reached the top and was inside what seemed to be a coat cupboard, shoes on the floor and jackets hung up on pegs. There was another door to the right, and she pushed through, coming out into a hallway. She rushed into the kitchen to the back door, gripping the handle and pushing it down. She was locked inside, and panic flowed through her, sending her legs weak. A security light came on outside, a hedgehog or something snuffling in the grass, and there was a stream at the bottom of the garden, some trees, hedges, and then a field. Where was she? In the middle of nowhere?

She shouted for help, screaming in between, then bolted from the room into the hallway with a front door at the end. She got there, her legs gone to jelly, and fought to get free. It was locked like the other one, and she almost sank to the floor, defeated. But something urged her to keep trying, so she scooted into a lounge and made for the windows. None of them would open, the handles remaining in place, so she bashed on the glass with her palms.

"Help me! Someone, please, help me!"

Nothing out there but a front garden and a main road.

She darted around the ground floor and at last found somewhere to hide. A narrow kind of alleyway between the lounge and the kitchen, a space she wedged into, moving right to the back, letting the darkness there keep her safe. Her breathing jittery, she held her arms up to cover her bare chest, fists pressed to her mouth.

Why was she naked and dirty? What had he done to her while she'd slept? Taken her clothes off and rolled her in the compost? Fucking hell, this was mad, all of it. Had Simon arrived to do the Wind Energy tour and seen she wasn't there? Was his car down the road a bit, where he'd broken down, and she'd gone to the wrong vehicle, the wrong man?

She shivered, despite the house being warm, the chill of the cellar replaced by that of terror.

"Coming, ready or not!" *he called.*

"Oh God, oh God..." *She whimpered and closed her eyes, kept so still, praying, hoping he wouldn't be able to fit down into this space and get her.*

Footsteps on stone. Footsteps on carpet.

"The last one hid here an' all," *he said.*

Light came through her eyelids.

"Why couldn't you be more creative?" *he asked.* "There's a loft, you know."

She opened her eyes and squinted.

The light came closer—he was walking, walking towards her. She couldn't see him behind the beam, but the air changed with his presence. It went all crackly and thick.

She pissed herself.

"Dirty cow, just like that Berry bitch." *He clasped the top of her arm and tugged her back down the indoor alley.* "If you think I'm touching you while you're messy..." *He thrust her into another room.* "Get in that shower. And don't bother to dry yourself after. If you're damp, the compost will stick to you better, then there's something I want you to put on."

CHAPTER TWELVE

Back down in the cellar, after the piece de résistance of them getting together in *that* way, Tanya's whimpering reminded him of Lucy Berry, same as the piss had.

"You need to be quiet," he said. "Before I get annoyed."

He was already annoyed, disappointed, too, but hid it from her. She hadn't performed well in the uniform, nothing like Mum had with her customers, and John had the idea Tanya hadn't enjoyed it. Well, she shouldn't have acted all tarty during the chat then, should she. If you gave out the wrong signals, what was a bloke to think? Yes meant she wanted to do it, didn't it? Yet 'no' had been what she'd just said.

This girl was no better than Lucy and Catherine, flirting, asking for something she had no right to want at her age, and then when she'd got it, look how she'd behaved. Crying, screaming behind the gag, then going all wooden, unresponsive.

His suspicions were being proved correct— Mum was a slag who revelled in having sex with strangers. Lucy was a slapper in the making, what with the way she'd carried on with those lads— but why had she rejected Edward if she wanted sex? Wasn't he good enough?

John bristled at that. Lucy came from a rough family. Hadn't she known how lucky she was that Edward fancied her despite that? How nice he was that her scabbiness hadn't mattered to him? Catherine and Tanya, and probably Elsa, had she met John, were all just as bad as Lucy. They'd rejected him as soon as they'd seen he wasn't nineteen, good-looking, and made of money.

This thing he was doing, this experiment, had confirmed what he already knew deep down from years ago: outside appearances mattered to some females. Lucy had shown him that, and now, his maddened mind, his devil, had pushed him to prove it again and again by creating facades and luring girls in, only for them to retreat, want to run once they knew who he really was.

He should stop. The point had been made.

The devil may not allow that, though. John would just have to play it by ear.

He lunged at Tanya, irate at her responses to him since he'd collected her. "Get those clothes off. You're not fit to wear them. You're supposed to act like *her* when you've got them on, not like…not like someone who hates what I did. You saw how arsey I got with Catherine when she didn't do what I wanted, yet now you've done it."

He ripped at the blouse and skirt, the scratchy snap of the Velcro loud. She curled into a ball on the filthy floor, and he turned his back on her to hang the clothing up. Would there be a girl out there who liked him regardless and loved what he did when they had the uniform on? Should he keep going until he found one?

He faced her again and stared at her grimy shins. The compost wasn't doing anything to them. Rattled, he grabbed one of the new pairs of ankle socks he'd bought from the supermarket and slid them on her feet. *Now* maybe they'd grow out of the soil.

He thought of Francesca, how her slender legs had looked. Nothing like Tanya's.

"Why?" he shouted. "Why aren't you like them? *Her* and Francesca? Why?"

Tanya closed her eyes and sobbed.

He left her there, ran upstairs into the cottage proper and grabbed his cushion, the one he'd kept since he was a boy. The one he'd hugged in bed that night when Mum and Dad were arguing about her being pregnant. It still had the imprint of Catherine's makeup face on the fabric.

Back down in the cellar, he advanced on Tanya, who scrabbled into a sitting position and used her heels to push herself back against the wall. Stupid bint. She'd just made it easier for him. He stood at her side and held the middle of the squishy cushion in a tight fist.

"You're useless to me, you know that, don't you? Nothing like I wanted you to be." He laughed at that. "Ironic, because I'm nothing like *you* wanted *me* to be." A pause. "Dilemma." That was a lie. There was no dilemma here. Tanya had to go, just like Catherine.

He placed the cushion over her face and pressed.

Hard.

Tanya fitted well into the boot of the Fiesta. He'd placed her on top of a plastic sheet so she didn't pick up any fibres. Things had advanced since his old killing days, forensics so adept at catching criminals now. He'd been careful all the way so far in this project, right from when he'd paid that kid six months ago to do whatever to his laptop and phone to hide his IP address.

His careful planning didn't include washing the compost off the girls, though. He *wanted* people to see how they hadn't grown into what he expected them to be. How filthy they were because they'd rejected him on sight. What liars they'd been in life, making out they fancied him, then they didn't.

Bitches.

John had been meticulous regarding the compost on his trainers, though. The ones he'd worn in the cellar had been removed once he'd carried her into the kitchen, and he'd put her on the dining table while he'd slipped on a clean pair so he didn't leave any soil behind at their destination.

He'd refreshed her makeup after the cushion had done its magic, poking the thick foundation into the beak hole, filling it. She stared up at him with those sightless irises of hers, thick blue eyeshadow forming one-colour rainbows over the tops. The foundation was white—he'd found a tub of it on sale in the toy shop last year, buying it in preparation. Yes, he'd known what he was going to do, even back then. The thinking about it was maybe the best part. He'd coloured her lips with a bright-red hue, making a Cupid's bow with it.

She looked like Mum. The white signified how pale she'd gone after she'd killed herself. These small things mattered, clues as to why he was doing this, only ones he knew. It gave him a sense of superiority, something he'd experienced back in the day, married to Irena, his lovely life so quiet and peaceful until Lucy had come along and messed it all up.

That girl had a lot to answer for.

John stabbed Tanya's wrists with the point of a knife to mirror Mum's pathetic little jabs, then drove to the outskirts, away from any cameras. His number plates, covered—quite aptly, he reckoned—with wetted compost, would keep the nosy parkers of Shadwell from knowing who he was while he saw out his current plan. He'd formed a paste and smeared it on, leaving it to dry, then doing the same again until he'd built up a thick layer.

Resourceful was his middle name.

At the edge of one of the estates, he parked beside an old telephone box, now used as a free library. During their chats, Tanya had mentioned her love of reading, so it was a fitting place to leave her. He doubted anyone would be out at this time of night to find her, so someone up with the larks, eager for their next read, would find themselves smack bang in the middle of a thriller when they realised she wasn't a large doll or shop mannequin.

John got out and flexed his glove-covered fingers. Looked at the edge of the housing estate over the way. Minimal lights on—few people awake then.

He strode to the boot and opened it, staring down at the naked bitch who'd promised so much and given so little in the end. His chequered past seemed so distant now, another life entirely, lived by someone else. He'd killed various people, no pattern to it, no rhyme or reason other than they'd upset him at some point. But these girls, they were different. He'd consciously selected them to prove a point to himself, and even though that point had been confirmed and he should move on, try to forget it all, Elsa still played on his mind. And then there was the current chat with Karly going on.

Maybe he should leave Karly hanging *before* she hurt him.

As for Elsa... He'd see what the devil wanted. While John thought it best to leave her, the beast inside him might have other ideas.

He scooped Tanya up and carried her to the phone box, placing her down at the side on the grass, her legs pointing towards the footpath and the estate. If her eyes were closed, it'd look like she'd just decided to lie there for a nap, albeit with no clothes on, but she appeared innocent enough.

If only they knew how she wasn't.

He couldn't hang around and admire her, admire his work. Someone might come along in a car and spot him. Spot her. One other quick thing to do, then he was off, going to the cottage. On the way, he threw hers and Catherine's phones out onto the verge, plus Catherine's iPad, their clothes and bags. The mobiles were both off, SIMs removed, and those SIMs he dropped down a drain halfway home.

He couldn't wait to arrive. There was news to catch up on about Catherine that he'd missed while with Tanya, and he needed to check again to see if Tanya's parents had finally realised she was missing rather than staying at a friend's house, her usual habit, so she'd said when she'd promised they'd stay together for a couple of days and do all the things he wanted.

Funny how she'd changed her mind about that. How she hadn't wanted to do it, and all because he was overweight and much older than he'd told her. He'd be a dick if he didn't realise his body played a big part in that. He'd probably repulsed her as much as Bouncy Woman had repulsed him all those years ago.

At the cottage, he parked and walked down the side, entering via the back door. For a brief moment, it reminded him of coming home after that baby had gone into the canal, and oddly, he expected Mrs Drayton to be sucking a Murray Mint in the living room.

What's wrong with me?

He shook the vision off and locked the door, staring at the compost-freckled trainers on the floor. Would he wear them in the cellar again? Would he go and spy on Elsa, nab her, and bring her here?

"I don't bloody know, do I!" he shouted at the ceiling. "God!"

John stomped to the kettle and made a cup of tea. Irena used to do the same in times of stress. He calmed a little, then used his phone to access *The Shadwell Herald* app.

CATHERINE FOUND DEAD!

PETER UXBRIDGE – REGIONAL CRIME

Catherine Noble, thirteen, missing since last week, has been found today. Her body was discovered at two p.m. by a Tesco worker on his way to start his shift. She'd been left in the old car park, naked and dirty all over, except for her face, which was heavily made up in garish clown paint.

Her parents, Debbie and Victor, have been informed.

A close friend said, "They're devastated. No one thought this would happen. We all believed she'd run off to London and would come home when she realised running away wasn't fun. I can't believe this. It's so surreal. I mean, we're never going to see her again, and that's what I can't get my head around. How does a girl just disappear with a man like that?"

School friends of Catherine are also struggling. We have it on good authority that three of them have helped the police with their enquiries, coming forward with information. However, the man in question there is Jolly19, not ManBabe19, who lured Catherine to meet him. Authorities believe it is the same person.

Please warn your teenage daughters that if they're talking to anyone online, make sure they know them first. This person is saying he has a mutual friend with the girls, leading them to believe he's safe. He states he's nineteen, has a good job, earns lots of money, and owns a Porsche. Ask your daughters if anyone has said this to them and stop the contact, then call the police—before it's too late.

Police believe Catherine met ManBabe19 in the fields beside the railway track. Another girl, also thirteen, was asked to meet Jolly19 in the courtyard down the alley at the end of the high street. Both are secluded places. She arrived to find no one around and got scared. She left—only to be followed by a heavy-set man in a black hoody, who waited outside Lloyds bank, staring into Costa where the girl was with her friend. Police have found him on CCTV. Look at the image accompanying this article. Do YOU know this man? If you do, call us at *The Herald*, Shadwell police, or Crimestoppers. He must be apprehended immediately.

John sweated profusely. Elsa had gone and blabbed, or maybe it was that fucking Sasha. There was no way he could get to Elsa now—the police would be keeping an eye on her. He'd have to either concentrate on Karly or halt proceedings.

How would this latest snippet affect Karly? She was friends with Catherine, Elsa, and Tanya, so there was no doubt she'd hear about this. Thankfully, he hadn't mentioned the Porsche or any of his usual spiel yet, so maybe he could get away with just being a lad to her. But the paper had said three girls were helping with enquiries. Of course, one was Elsa, and he'd bet his last penny another was that Sasha bitch, but who was the third?

The devil decided he needed to find out.

Whoever she was, perhaps she had to be shut up, like Elsa and Sasha, but how could he do that now the police were poking their noses in?

He threw his cup. It hit the tiles above the cooker and smashed, pieces dropping onto the hob. He'd clean it up tomorrow. Too tired now. He'd had a busy evening, and a good night's sleep would clear any cobwebs. Tomorrow, he'd see how he felt, then decide what action to take, if any.

CHAPTER THIRTEEN

The story of Lucy Berry being attacked spread through the lane. In good neighbour mode, John held his hand to his mouth when her mum related the tale to him and Irena.

"Poor girl, she was just walking the lads home, you know? Wasn't even that late at night. I'd keep Edward in if I were you. Who knows, this madman

might like the boys, too." Not so bouncy now, Lucy's mum crossed her arms under her ample chest. Her cheeks, ruddy from indignation, inflated as she took in a breath and then let it out. She continued, totally ignoring Irena.

"Anyway, John, how are you?"

She gave him what she probably reckoned was a saucy wink. After living in the lane so long, he thought she'd know he wouldn't stray, that Irena and Edward meant the world to him. Still, he suspected she felt she could try, that even the most devoted of men could be swayed by her charms.

Not this man. Try this game again and you'll see what you get.

He stilled the inner rage, masked it so Irena and Bouncy didn't pick up on it. "I'm fine, thank you. More to the point, how is Lucy?"

"Oh, she'll be all right. She's a tough one, she is."

Irena took in a sharp breath, but Bouncy didn't appear to hear it. John suspected Irena would be thinking Lucy might need some support at this time, not this brush-it-off attitude. All Bouncy probably cared about was a few weeks' worth of gossip, chatting at doorsteps, and a good dose of much-craved attention the attack on her daughter brought her.

"What did the police say?" Irena was such a concerned person, always caring.

John was glad she'd asked that; he wanted to know, too.

"Police? Oh, I didn't bother them with this. No fear. Not with them stolen car stereos I've got

stashed in my spare room. Don't want them poking about, do I?" Bouncy let out a harsh laugh, almost a bark, her tits heaving along with her hilarity. "Anyway, all he did was scare her a bit. Made her piss her knickers an' all."

"Oh!" Irena turned with tears in her eyes and stepped back into the house. For her, this discussion was closed.

John should have followed Irena inside to give her some comfort, but instead, he said, "Your poor girl."

"Aww, John, you're so...nice."

Again the wink, this time accompanied with a brush of her fingers along his forearm. He backed away to the safety of his doorstep; they'd been standing in his front garden discussing the tragedy.

"Well, a little niceness doesn't hurt, does it?" he said.

"No, it most certainly doesn't." Her fulsome lips spread into a lascivious smile, showing yellow teeth.

"Well, I must be away now. Help Irena with the washing up. Sorry to hear about Lucy. I'm sure with a bit of special attention she'll be fine."

How easy it was to slip into being the normal bloke. Just as easy, too, to slide into his real self.

Bouncy walked towards the gate. Her hand on the latch, she turned back, looking at John in that leery way she had. "Irena is a lucky woman. Wish I'd met you first."

That wink. Again.

John smiled, waved, and went indoors, closing the door firmly to shut out that hateful woman and everything she represented.

Irena stood in the kitchen, her hands hidden by the bubbles in the sink. "You know, much as I don't like being spiteful, that woman really is awful. Nothing seems to faze her, and I'm sure, and have been for a while now, that she has her eye on you. I'd almost convinced myself, what with you going to the pub a lot recently, that you were seeing her." She laughed the laugh of the worried, hiding how she really felt, keeping suspicion at bay.

He placed his arms around her waist from behind, nuzzling his chin into her neck. "I love you, I love Edward, I love my dad, and no one else. No one."

He must have sounded abrupt; she tensed, her shoulders going rigid beneath his chin.

"You do believe me, don't you?" His tone was softer then. He'd let the devil part of himself bleed into the other. His hatred towards Bouncy had spilled out in his voice when talking to his wife.

He detested Bouncy even more for that.

Irena relaxed, her head falling back to rest against his cheek. "Yes, I do."

John had thought his devil would be quiet now Lucy had learnt the error of her ways. Unfortunately, scaring her wasn't enough. He'd let his bad side in once again, and now it wouldn't go away.

He'd watched Bouncy to refresh himself with her habits. On occasion, he followed her to where she worked, to the places she went to of an evening, just to get a better feel for her.

Although she had big heaving tits and a lardy arse that shuddered with each step, she still thought herself attractive and that others thought so, too. The idea of it had John coming out in a sweat.

She bounced past his front garden fence and stopped, her hand on one of the picket points, and stood, hip cocked.

"Hello, John." She beamed.

He'd been weeding, and so as not to appear rude, said hello back as he always did to anyone who passed the time of day.

"See anything you fancy, Mr Keagan?" she said.

Once again, anger seeped into his bones. What a ridiculous question. He couldn't be attracted to her, with her bright-orange blouse partially buttoned up, showing a low-cut, white top underneath, her ample melons jumping out. Her short black skirt revealed pitted thighs, straining beneath her tights, and the cellulite reminded him of the day Mum had come by the cottage. This woman had revolting blubbery lips, smothered in red lipstick that had collected itself in lumps in the corners of her mouth, and it sent him queasy. Her accent alone grated on his nerves.

"I beg your pardon, Ms Berry?"

He tried to sound like he was amused. She must have thought as much; she chuckled and walked off swinging her backside, reminding him of a pregnant cow.

Later, he watched her through the front bedroom window. Angled to the right this time, he had a clear view through the sides of her bay windows. Previously, she'd been in her lounge, and she must be in the shower now. Then she entered her bedroom, turning on the light, leaving her curtains open. As it was dark, he had the totally foul view of her towelling herself and applying talcum powder. Her thighs wobbled as she walked on tiptoes to a drawer. She stooped over, displaying her grotesque arse. She must be listening to music—she flung herself around, tights in hand, swaying.

She dressed, styled her hair, applied her makeup. She was going out then.

He'd have to follow, of course.

He glanced to his left. Edward stood on the corner, minus Lucy Berry. She hadn't been with the group of teenagers since John had taught her a lesson.

Bouncy came out of her house, approaching the group. John could hardly bear to watch her cannoning down the lane. She stopped and spoke to the teens, hip cocked yet again. Edward looked shocked, his mouth an 'O' of surprise. John waited for her to leave them and proceed down the alleyway, then he went to the front door and called Edward indoors.

"Yes, Dad?" Edward stood in the living room doorway, his face showing concern.

John smiled at him to alleviate his fears. "What did the Berry woman just say?"

Edward reddened, moving uncomfortably from foot to foot. "Oh, nothing much..."

"Edward, it's okay. You know I'm only being nosy. Come on, what did she say?"

"Oh, um, that she betted us boys wouldn't mind having a woman like her for a girlfriend. We just laughed, you know. She was only joking."

"Ha! What a strange woman. Let's hope she was joking, eh, else you'll have a worry on your hands. Go back out with your friends, son." John shook his head.

"Okay, see you." Edward dashed back outside.

White-hot anger belted through John's body. Hurriedly, he ran to his bedroom, collected his innocent-looking carrier bag from where he'd hidden it from Irena, slung on his coat, and headed down the stairs.

"Going out to the pub. Call Edward in later for me."

Roaring filled his ears. He waved to Edward and his friends, told them he was away to the pub for a spot of elbow exercise and he'd see him later.

He had to be sure Bouncy was going into town to the karaoke that was held in The Flapping Crow, something she did weekly on this night. She always walked through Southbourne—a series of fields and pathways with a small children's park in the centre, unlit by any street lighting, much to his advantage.

He warned himself to remain calm and not get out of breath. Mentally sorting out his mind, he'd been scanning the path ahead through Southbourne. There she was, just coming up to the bridge over the stream. His carrier bag would rustle, but if he was quick, by the time she heard it, it'd be too late.

He pulled a new balaclava over his head, slipped on gloves, and took out his weapon covered in a sock, then hastily shoved the bag, containing clean dry shoes and trousers, into a bush for his return.

The moon offered a dim light.

With no time to think, he dashed up behind her.

The bank beside the bridge was sludgy, but he'd known he'd get wet, so it didn't matter. He pushed her hard in the back, and she slid the short way down into the stream. She let out a small 'Oh!', but the sound of splashing water muffled it. She unceremoniously sat slumped in the cold water with her back to him.

Condensation had formed inside his mask, his lips and the skin surrounding them wet and slippery. He couldn't control his breathing like he had with Lucy.

He made his way down into the stream, carefully placing his weapon on the bank. He knelt behind her, putting his hand on those damn curls of hers, and drew her head back, gripping her so she couldn't move left nor right. He checked no one else was around. All seemed quiet, and thankfully, Bouncy hadn't uttered a single noise since he'd startled her.

She moved her eyes to her right then, trying to see him, and they widened when she realised it was a masked man. He patted the grass behind him until he touched the sock-encased weapon. John tugged the sock from it and stuffed it into her mouth.

She panicked. Her breaths came out in short, snotty blasts. He watched her for a second, amazed she'd chosen not to wallop him.

It was then he realised his mistake. He'd left the small reel of wire in the carrier bag. He couldn't go back for it.

"Get your tights off!"

She whimpered and, rocking from side to side, removed her tights. In the moonlight, her limbs looked like large blocks of cheese.

John shuddered.

She sat there, a suckling pig, mouth stuffed, and about to be trussed.

"Put your hands behind your back."

His armpits dripped sweat, and despite the cold evening, he was hot. Once she'd complied, he snatched the tights from her hand and let go of her hair. Roughly shoving her head forward, he bound her hands together, creating a figure of eight with the nylon, tying it tight.

"Lean back against the bank."

She did as she was told. John stood looking down at her, and she gawped up at him standing just to her right. He wondered if she'd recognise his clothes. Her snorting came again in earnest.

He straddled her. She rested so far back on the bank it'd be impossible for her to escape, her legs held fast by his position on top of her. He leant forward for his weapon. A meat cleaver, thick and heavy, sharp and menacing.

"Let out a sound, and I'll kill you. Got it?"

She nodded, head going in all directions.

He brought the cleaver up to her line of vision. She gagged on the sock, letting out retches. The wet mud had dirtied her hair on the ends.

He brought the blade to her right cheek. Pressed down to see if she'd scream, but she continued with her snotty emissions. He jerked his hand and sliced her cheek clean off. It fell into the stream and lodged itself with the current against her pitted thigh.

She fainted.

For a split second after he'd sliced, the wound resembled brawn. Curious, he picked up the pouch of cheek and examined it, then placed it in her hand. Not seeing anyone or anything untoward, he rinsed the cleaver in the water then lopped off her other cheek and put it in her free hand.

Her face was a nasty mess. Blood streamed from the wounds, down onto her hair, and made its way into the water. He'd read somewhere that if wounds bled, it meant the heart was still pumping. He wondered if the diluted blood would sail past Dad's cottage in the same stream there.

He couldn't have planned it better. He'd leave her in a dead faint against the bank, water taking away any evidence. Bouncy's face was far enough away from the water that she wouldn't drown.

He climbed out, keeping low as he came level with the bridge. Seeing no one around, he retrieved his bag, stuffed the cleaver in it, removed his gloves and mask, and walked off.

The Blue Star stood five minutes away. He'd go in through a back door used by employees. This led to a short corridor, then to the public toilets. He entered the men's, looked around, and slipped into a cubicle, changing his sodden trousers, socks, and shoes, placing them in his bag.

Dry from the waist down, he went to the bar to enquire if the billiards tournament was on that night. It wasn't, but he wanted to be seen asking.

He left the pub, dropping the cleaver and reel of wire down a drain, and walked the main road home, avoiding Southbourne.

"All right, love?"

Irena was so bloody caring.

"Yeah, I just need some things put through the washing machine."

Irena took the bag and removed the clothes from it. "These are soaked. What have you been doing?"

He didn't know what to say. His mind clammed up on him. He hadn't expected Irena to ask that. She was usually so quiet and accepting.

"I, um, fell over the bank a couple days ago on the way back from work, landing in the edge of the stream." His laugh sounded hollow.

Irena frowned. "So why didn't you stick the clothes in the washer then?" She bent to stuff the clothes in the machine.

His heart hammered. He was lying to his wife, and it didn't sit well. Yet he could hardly tell the poor woman what he'd been doing. His mind raced. "I'm sorry. I just forgot. Remembered the bag when I spotted it by the front door on my way in just now."

"By the front door? Are you messing with me, because that bag wasn't there earlier."

With stiff movements, he put some Ariel into the machine drawer, on dangerous ground with Irena. "It was in the bush."

She stared at him oddly. "Right... Edward was telling me what the Berry woman said to him outside earlier. With what she said to you last week, I think she's got a cheek, she has."

John nearly choked.

Cheek. She hasn't got any.

In the garden, he cut up his gloves and mask and created a tiny bonfire in a metal bucket.

Irena watched from the kitchen window.

Shit.

CHAPTER FOURTEEN

12:07 a.m.

Karly: HELLO? ARE YOU THERE?

12:15 a.m.

Karly: ARE YOU ASLEEP OR SOMETHING?

12:30 a.m.

Karly: LISTEN, MY MUM HAD A CHAT WITH ME EARLIER AFTER WHAT'S BEEN HAPPENING. CATHERINE, THAT GIRL IN THE NEWS? WELL, SHE'S ONE OF MY FRIENDS, AND SHE'S BEEN MURDERED. MY OTHER FRIEND IS ALSO INVOLVED. LONG STORY, BUT I'VE BEEN TOLD I CAN'T SPEAK TO ANYONE ON MESSENGER ANYMORE, SO IF YOU WANT TO CHAT, IT'LL HAVE TO BE ON MY FACEBOOK WALL. SORRY AND EVERYTHING, BUT I'M NOT SURE I KNOW YOU, EVEN IF YOU'RE TELLING THE TRUTH ABOUT BEING AT JESSICA'S PARTY. HUGS!

12:47 a.m.

Karly wanted to scream. She couldn't get to sleep. When her mum had told her about Catherine, Karly hadn't believed her at first. All right, she'd reasoned with herself as to why Mum would lie and say her mate was dead, telling herself Mum *so* wouldn't do that, but at the same time, it couldn't be real, could it?

Even everyone at school had thought she'd just gone off, you know, taken herself away for bit of a laugh, but to find out she'd been kidnapped, held somewhere for a week, then murdered?

Bloody hell.

She rolled over yet again, trying to get comfortable. Guilt was keeping her awake. She hadn't told mum about Tom16, and there was no chance she'd be telling Dad, not with the way he was. Mum had asked her if she'd been talking to anyone she didn't know, and instinct had told Karly to lie—there'd be a shitstorm to get through if she admitted it. And besides, they'd hardly said much to each other anyway, nothing about a job and a Porsche or whatever the hell Mum had banged on about.

Karly had stayed downstairs in the living room all evening, scared, to be honest, to go up to her room like she usually did. She'd checked Messenger to see if Tom had contacted her again, but there was nothing. Their convo had ended on him saying he had to go and help his mum with doing the washing, so maybe he'd been busy since then.

Either way, she'd avoid him now, whether he was genuine or not.

She didn't want to end up like Catherine.

CHAPTER FIFTEEN

John took his family to Chivenor, Devon. The sea air and change of scenery worked wonders for clearing John's mind after he'd chopped at Bouncy Woman. Irena relaxed, her smiles coming easily. Edward loved the holiday.

The surrounding towns were a joy to visit, and there were so many places to explore that were *close to the caravan park. The stress of home life faded. On the outside.*

Dad had paid for the break and given them spending money. He'd said John looked tired and stressed, that they should get away, forget about the daily grind. They were able to eat out instead of cooking in the caravan, pretending they were well-off.

Tonight, Irena had a headache, though. Curtains closed against the light, she rested on the bed, a hand over her eyes. "It's a migraine. I'll stay in the caravan; you and Edward go to the clubhouse. I'll be fine."

"Are you sure? I don't want to leave you if you're poorly."

"I'm sure. I need the quiet."

Irena turned away, her eyes squeezed shut. What was going through her mind? The wet clothes incident came back to him, and slight panic rushed through him that maybe Irena suspected him of something. No, surely not?

He closed the narrow door to their little room and made his way to the clubhouse with Edward. John put worrisome thoughts of Irena out of his head once they entered. A fancy-dress competition was well underway, children a riot of butterflies, complete with wings, fairies, princesses, and many a Batman or soldier. They flitted around on the dance floor.

John and Edward sat at a table near the front. The day before, Edward had made friends with a lad of his own age, who came bounding over.

"Want to go in the arcade, Ed?"

Edward looked at John.

"Go ahead, son. Be here by eleven, and we'll head back to the caravan."

John slipped him twenty pounds, and Edward raced off with the vigour that only the young possessed.

John sipped his pint of beer and watched the other holidaymakers. And then he saw her. His heart quickened, and, as sight sometimes played tricks, he momentarily thought it was Mum, gliding across the dance floor towards him.

Her walk was a carbon copy. Her features, not so much, but enough to startle him into thinking she'd somehow come back, or that her suicide was all in his mind, her funeral some macabre stunt someone had played.

Before he knew it, he was out of his seat, following the woman out of the clubhouse.

She seemed distressed, swiping at her cheeks with the cuff of her black suit jacket, her sniffles loud in the stillness. Darkness had come to visit while he'd been inside, a chill pervading the air.

She made her way to the farthest of the caravans then down the meandering pathway that led to the 'D' part of the site. D for Devil, D for Death. John pursued her, stifling a chuckle at how quickly he'd allowed his demon to overtake him when in the caravan he'd felt lost and afraid. One minute, ensconced in holiday harmony, the next, chilled with hate and the desire to harm.

The woman veered towards a clump of trees that bordered the park.

The poor cow resembled another, so his mind was twisted by the need to upset her in some way. Thoughts tormented him, Mum's voice jeering his incompetence, his uselessness to such a degree that he careened out of control. This person had a family out there; somewhere a person loved her. Regardless of his thoughts, he was prepared to snuff her out.

How would I feel if someone wanted to hurt Irena?

The thought pounded through his head. The urge to hurt this woman was stronger than his need to walk away. It was wrong, but it didn't feel wrong. The force within overpowered his weakness, while another little voice begged that no blood be shed. It'd be difficult to hide such mess, and he had no covering for his face. His pulse surged, bubbling, roaring in his ears until he could hardly walk straight.

Staggering up behind her, following in her wake as she moved into the woods, he tried to tread carefully. Bark pieces on the ground shuffled with each step. Fuck it. He didn't want to alert her until they were deeper into the woods.

Traffic sped by along the outskirts of the caravan park. His darkness took over him, and the other kind of darkness surrounding him enveloped them within its infinite chasm, and he lunged.

John used his right hand to yank her head back by her hair and his left to cover her mouth. Her eyes bulged in fear. Her arms flailed, windmill sails.

He stepped backwards, taking his hand from her mouth but still gripping her hair, and forced her to fall to the ground by kicking at the backs of her knees. Down she went like the proverbial sack of shit. She was winded, so, taking advantage of it, he dragged her along by her hair, farther into the woods before her brain realised she needed to scream.

The trees enclosed them from view, and she sobbed, trying to pull his hand from her hair. It hurt when your hair was pulled as hard as that. The last time Mum had wrenched John's, he had a sore head the next day.

He knelt behind her, putting his hand over her mouth. She whimpered. She wasn't daft—she knew it was her time. Her turn to be one of those women you read about in the papers over your bacon and eggs, your tea with two sugars.

He needed to adopt his scary voice, the one he'd used on Lucy Berry. "Shut the fuck up!"

She went silent, and her eyes grew larger, rounder.

He took his hand away from her mouth again.

"Is that you?" she whispered.

What the hell was she talking about? Maybe she thought he was the one who'd brought her to tears earlier, the one who'd upset her enough for her to walk out of the clubhouse and down this dangerous route.

He didn't bother to answer her and positioned her head on his knees.

In the moonlight filtering through the canopy of trees, he looked at her upside-down face while she looked up at his.

She remained silent.

With his free hand, he got out his penknife and flicked it open with relief, knowing this would be over soon, that he could go back as if nothing had happened, sit at his table, then when Edward appeared later, return to the caravan to see if Irena was all right, her migraine hopefully gone.

He smiled tightly and let this bitch see the knife, stroked her bare neck with it, sending her his message. Her eyes told him she knew it was over now, that she was just unlucky. The woman struggled then, flailing on the ground, arms and legs thrashing. He held on to her hair, his fist clenched tightly in it. There was a pause in her movements, and he seized his opportunity.

Her ivory neck gaped open all too quickly, a second pair of lips in a jolly smile. The wound filled with her blood, and it gushed and oozed, none of it getting on him or his clothing. He shuffled backwards, letting the liquid of her life trickle down the sides of her neck. He didn't want his trousers ruined.

He tossed her forward, and she slumped onto the ground. John got up, breathed in and out with short, sharp bursts, and leant against a large tree to gather his thoughts, to get himself into some sort of order.

Arcing his foot over the ground to level out any indentions or footprints, he wiped his knife and hand on the grass then casually made his way out of the woods.

Going back into that clubhouse, he had to look and act normal. That when the alarm was raised, when the woman was discovered, everyone would be racking his or her brains to remember anything just a little bit 'off' that evening. While he washed his hands in the men's, he visualised the police questioning people once her body was found. Had anyone seen him? Would anyone ask why he'd left his seat?

He shook the thoughts off, went into the main hall, and sat in his seat, which still, amazingly enough, had his half-finished beer on the table. The sheen of sweat on his face got him paranoid, something he hadn't experienced before, as if he had a spotlight on him and everyone could see it.

He smiled and said to those seated nearest his table, "Have you seen Edward, my son? I've been looking for him and got in a bit of a panic."

Hopefully, that'd answer any later questions.

"Yes, love." A rather blowsy woman, flouncy frills on her top bringing to mind Shakespearian times, said, "He came back about ten minutes ago, looking for you." Her cerise pink lips wobbled and, after taking a huge gulp from what appeared to be a gin and tonic, she continued, "Said to tell you he's gone to the bowling alley."

"Oh, thank goodness." John downed the dregs of his pint. *"Best be getting another drink then, now I know he's safe."*

He walked off, sure he'd acted innocent. He got a cold, fresh lager and returned to his seat, laughing at those in fancy dress, a crocodile line of freaks donned in their outrageous outfits. He applauded the winner and chatted as much as possible with his blowsy companion and her hangdog husband.

He was calmer, especially when Edward popped back for more money.

Ten o'clock came round, overall a pleasant evening, save for John's stomach playing him up. Nerves. But it would be fine.

An hour to go, and many people had seen him sitting there, enjoying an evening of albeit strange entertainment. A band belted out sixties music once the fancy-dress competition was over.

"Where d'you come from then?" Blowsy shouted over the din of Wild Thing *by The Troggs, poking John's shoulder with a hard index finger.*

He didn't want to give out too much information, didn't want to get too friendly with these people. The woman was the obvious force in the relationship, but the man seemed there just for the sake of it, happy it seemed, to bumble along with her as his life-long partner.

"Oh, up north a bit." John sipped his drink, *glancing away from her to watch the dancers, hoping she'd take the hint that he wasn't going to be too forthcoming.*

"We all come from up north somewhere, what with being down in Devon, mate."

"I suppose we do, yes." Claustrophobia paid him a visit, the sense of being cornered. His alibi was getting on his wick.

"Us, well, we come from London. Have a right old fucking laugh there, we do. Got a market stall, sell cleaning stuff. Brings the money in all right. What d'you do then?"

"I work in a hospital."

"Ooh, you look like the doctor type. I was saying to my George here, he looks like the type who's a doctor. You can tell, see, from the way you hold yourself. Upright and all that." She turned her jowly face to George, nudging the poor man in the ribs when he appeared not to have heard her, eyes glazed over, his only movement his arm going up and down to bring his glass to his lips.

"I was saying, weren't I, George, that I thought this bloke here was a doctor. I was right. What did I tell you, eh?"

This seemed to give her much pleasure, being right, and George smiled at John, tilting his glass slightly and returning his gaze to the dancers doing the Mashed Potato.

"Useless, him. No point trying to start a convo with that geezer. I tell you, I might as well be living with a bleedin' statue. I do all the work on the markets, but him, he just sits at home. Reckons he's disabled, gammy leg. My arse! I reckon he's just a lazy bastard meself."

She reminded John of Lucy Berry's mum. The surge twisted—no, he couldn't let it happen again. Not twice in one place. He tuned in to her once more as she related some incident from her days on her market stall.

"Well, I says to her, 'If you dare fucking look at me like that any time soon, missus, you'll have my fist to deal with.' Well, that soon shut her trap, didn't it? There was no way I was going to replace or refund on a used mop. Filthy dirty, it was. She reckoned it didn't do its job properly. I said, 'If you weren't so bleedin' minging, mate, the mop would've cleaned up good and proper.' Disgusting, she was. Looked like she needed a dip in the mop bucket an' all."

Some people annoyed John to the degree he could take whatever he had in his hand at the time and smash their faces with it. He gripped his pint glass so hard his knuckles bleached white.

"Anyway, she trots off, dirty mop in hand, and I says to meself, 'I bet she hasn't cleaned her floor in a month of Sundays judging by the state of it.' Black as the ace of spades, it was."

Her raucous laughter split the air. Even over the noise of the band, many heard her, and still George sat there, an elbow-bending zombie. Inebriated as she was by too many gin and tonics, she'd just keep on and on if John continued to give her an audience.

Edward came back, out of breath from excitement, having won four quid on a fruit machine that at his age, he shouldn't have even been playing, and he'd won the bowling. John rose and stretched his muscles, only to be faced with Blowsy doing the same.

"Here, I noticed you're in the caravan a few up from ours. We'll trot back with you, won't we, George?"

George shrugged on his coat, mute.

Having walked from the clubhouse back to the caravan, with Blowsy hanging on to John's arm for support, her stiletto heels clacking loudly against the pathway, her laugh belting out, he was relieved to climb into bed beside Irena to reassess the evening.

He had to go through it in his head and ensure he hadn't fucked up.

CHAPTER SIXTEEN

The body had been placed beside the free library phone box, on the grass, her ankle-socked heels almost touching the path. Bethany frowned. Why did she have socks on, and brand-new ones at that? They were pure white, as if fresh from the packet, apart from some soil on the soles. Catherine's feet had been bare. What was the significance there? Did teenagers still wear these sorts of socks, with the fold-over cuff and lace on the edge?

A SOCO was inside the tent with her, taking photos of the naked girl, who was filthy from streaks of dirt, her face the same as Catherine's, except one cheek had a slight circular dent it in. The makeup had to mean something, to be so garish. Or perhaps that was just the way the killer wanted to see them, in colours from the eighties—an older man now, thinking back to the girls of his youth? Her hair was in pigtails, so definitely some sort of 'thing' he had.

Bethany had already asked Rob to check missing persons, and no female teenager had been reported in the last fortnight apart from Catherine and one other who'd stayed out past her curfew, rolling in at midnight instead of ten, pissed on White Lightning, panic over. Three lads had walked out after rows with their parents. Two had since returned to the family homes, and one had opted to live with his aunt until the anger had died down.

The body had a page from a notebook on her right breast, held in place at the top by a pin used in sewing. It had been pushed in deep so the silver ball on the end was the only part of it on show. The paper ruffled in the breeze, the sound of it reminiscent of sheets flapping on a washing line.

On it, someone had written: TANYA OXBREY IS 13. SHADOWS RISE.

If Bethany hadn't visited that street on the new eco estate in the recent Raven case, she'd have thought Hoody was saying something poetic with 'shadows rise' and would have wasted time trying to work it out, as would Fran and Leona. Thankfully, that step could now be discarded, and she was waiting for Fran to get back to her on which number the house was. The team and uniforms had finished up the CCTV late last night—nothing. This morning, all owners of silver Fiestas were being contacted.

Considering this location, it was doubtful CCTV would have picked the car up which had been used to transport Tanya here, but Leona was on it anyway. All boxes had to be ticked regardless.

Bethany's phone bleeped.

Fran: NUMBER SIXTEEN. PARENTS ARE LORRAINE AND RICHARD.

Bethany: THANKS. WE'LL GO THERE IN ABOUT FIVE.

She sighed. Mike was outside the tent taking a breather with Isabelle—they'd found the pin in the breast a bit much first thing of a morning. Isabelle reckoned it'd been put there after death—no blood seeping through the paper. They'd seen many things in their time, more harrowing than the pin, yet it had got to them anyway.

Some things just did.

Bethany shivered at the sound of the camera lens zooming. She imagined what the photographer saw close up, how he'd probably be able to count the pores on Tanya's face if the makeup wasn't caked on so thick, how he'd spot the delicate fuzz of hairs on her jawline.

The tent flap opened, and Presley walked in. He gave a tight smile. "Morning. I have Catherine's post-mortem on my list today. Looks like I have another one straight after."

"Sadly, yes."

He placed his bag on an evidence step and took out his temperature gadget. "I hear you need to visit the parents, so I'll get on with this now."

She turned away, sickened by the fact Tanya was white on both ends—the socks, the face foundation. Did that mean anything, or was she looking into this too deeply?

"About ten o'clock last night," Presley said.

She spun to face him. "Did we get lucky with a feather up her nose?"

He took a small torch out and aimed the beam at her nostrils. "Not that I can see. About that pillow or quilt theory as a murder weapon… When I cleaned Catherine up last night in preparation for today, removing the makeup, there are material marks on her face, the weave of the fabric, which is a waffle effect. That seems more in keeping with a cushion cover, doesn't it? It had been pressed hard to make those indentations, and for some time, probably about five minutes after she'd died for the impressions to remain. I suspect the killer wanted to make sure she was dead."

"Or maybe they felt remorse and couldn't stand to lift the pillow and look at her."

"Hmm, seems unlikely, given that they put makeup on afterwards. They'd have to look at her then."

"True. And there was me hoping we had a killer with some sort of conscience."

"There's seeing the best in everyone, then there's hoping for a miracle," he said. "No offence."

"None taken."

Presley cleared his throat. "Back to business. Lividity appears to only be on the back of her body, so to speak—the parts on the grass. So she was placed here quite soon after death—lividity hadn't had a chance to form where she'd been killed; what I mean is, it hadn't settled in the position she was killed in, unless she was on her back. She was moved within three hours of death."

"Right. Well, we'd better get going. See the parents."

"Good luck with that. Did they report her missing?"

"No."

"Strange."

"Yep."

She left the tent and waved Mike over. A shouted goodbye to Isabelle, then they were off to the eco village. She hoped Mrs Zooblavich didn't spot them and come out for a row. She lived at number twenty-four and was the mother of one of the men in the Raven case. She didn't believe her son could have done what he'd admitted—a mum who thought the sun shone out of his arse and wouldn't let anyone tell her any different.

"Wonder why they didn't report her missing?" Mike asked.

"It's the weekend. She might have told them she'd be at a mate's, back by tonight, it being Sunday and her having school tomorrow."

"True."

She pulled up outside number sixteen and cut the engine. It was one of the local authority houses, the same as Zooblavich's, the front butted up against the pavement. Venetian blinds hung at every window, closed, the family probably still in bed. The scent of frying bacon came from somewhere, and her stomach rumbled at her thoughts of a full English. Maybe they could visit a café and have one after this.

At the front door, she knocked, her ID in hand, ready. After about a three-minute wait, a man answered, Desperate Dan stubble, his dark hair unruly. He had a T-shirt and shorts on, grey, with no socks. They must have got him out of bed, which wasn't surprising.

"Yeah?" He squinted, keeping one eye closed, and scratched the back of his head. "Bloody Godlies, are you? Not interested in that shit. If I wanted to go to church, I would. I don't need you lot badgering me on my doorstep."

Bethany held her ID up. "DI Bethany Smith and DS Mike Wilkins. Mr Richard Oxbrey, is it?"

"Shite. What's she gone and done?" He sighed and rubbed his forehead. "It'll be that new lad she has, sending her astray."

What lad? And if he's asking what she's done, was she usually a bit of a handful?

"It'd be better if we come in." Bethany smiled.

He led them down a short hallway.

They stood awkwardly in the living room, Richard adjusting his privates, hand beneath his shorts. Nice.

"Is your wife home?" Bethany asked.

"In bed. Better that you tell me first, then I can break whatever it is to her later. Lorraine gets a bit irate about shit. Stuff. Sorry."

"Can you wake her up, please. We need to speak to you together." Bethany jerked her head at the door to emphasise she meant it, no messing about.

"Oh, so it's serious."

About as serious as it gets. "I'm afraid so."

"Christ. That bloody kid. She'll be the death of us." He left the room, his footsteps loud on the stairs.

Bethany looked at Mike and whispered, "So they know about a 'lad'?"

"Maybe she told them she had a boyfriend but didn't say it was someone online," he said quietly.

The floorboards creaked above, then, "It's fucking eight-odd on a Sunday. What the hell do I need to get up for?" Lorraine, angry by the sound of it.

"The police are here about Tanya." Richard.

"I'll bloody kill her!"

"Great..." Bethany sighed.

"Might have a job on our hands here," Mike muttered.

"Might? I'd say that's certain." *Just what we need.*

Thuds, a door slamming. Footsteps.

Lorraine flew into the room and flung herself on the sofa. "Don't even *think* about speaking to me until I've had a sip of coffee and a vape. I'll need them if our Tan has done something with that fella of hers. I tell you, she needs a slap, that one."

"I'm DI Bethany Smith, and this is DS Mike Wilkins. You get on and vape. Mike will make you a coffee. Sugar? Milk?"

Lorraine grabbed her vape off a side table. "Two sweeteners, and yeah, milk."

While Lorraine stocked her body with nicotine, Mike left the room, and Bethany turned at Richard's entrance. He raised his eyebrows as if to say: *I told you she'd be like this.* Bethany shrugged—she had a job to do and news to deliver whether Lorraine was mardy or not.

Lorraine took a phone out of her dressing gown pocket and browsed. "I've had no messages from her for ages. The little cow stormed out last week, snotty mare."

Bethany's stomach rolled over. "Um, just a moment. We'll talk about this when my colleague is back so he can take notes."

"Why don't you just come out with it?" Lorraine dropped her phone on the sofa. "Then we can deal with whatever she's done and move on with the day."

Because you said you needed coffee first. "As I said, we'll chat when DS Wilkins is back."

Lorraine huffed out a long breath and stared at the fireplace. Richard sat on the edge of a chair, elbows on his spread knees, and found the carpet interesting. The central heating boiler clanked, then a radiator donked.

Bethany studied the room to see what sort of household Tanya came from. It was clean, tidy, and modern, lots of grey crushed velvet—cushions, curtains, a shade on a lamp beside the sofa, and the sofa itself. Dark laminate flooring, silver fluffy rug. A photo of Tanya, which looked like a selfie printed out, in the middle of the mantel in a pale wooden frame. To the outsider, she belonged to a nice family, but from what Bethany had experienced so far with the parents, Lorraine especially, maybe a trendy home masked secrets, although it seemed there was no secret regarding a 'lad'.

At last, Mike came in and handed Richard and Lorraine coffee in white china mugs with silver stripes around the rims. He stood by the door and took his notebook and pen out. Once Lorraine had taken two sips and said, "Ahh, heaven!", Bethany jumped in.

"When was the last time you saw Tanya before she walked out?"

Mike widened his eyes.

Bethany explained to him, "Lorraine mentioned it while you were making coffee." Then to Lorraine, "I need the day and time."

"It was Saturday," Richard butted in. "Not yesterday, the one before."

She's been gone a week? "Okay. Time?"

"About twelve," he said. "She was going to meet that lad of hers."

"Who is this lad?"

Richard shrugged. "Simon or something. Nineteen. We had a row about it, her being thirteen and seeing what amounts to a bloke. She's always been older than her years, dressing in short skirts and shit. She was meeting him at the turbine place. Wind Energy or whatever the chuff it's called."

Mike took his phone out and tapped the screen.

Nineteen. Fits the theme. Why would they want to go to Wind Energy, though? The wind farm offered tours and showed how the turbines worked. Was that something a thirteen-year-old girl would enjoy? "So was she interested in that sort of thing?"

"Apparently so." Full of sarcasm, Richard sipped his drink. "I took the piss, said she was turning into a nerd. She said no, Simon was the one interested in it, and she was getting the bus out there."

Again, Mike used his phone.

"Where did she originally meet this Simon?" Bethany asked.

Lorraine sniffed. "Online. A mutual mate."

Same MO lure. "And you were okay with her just going?"

Richard blushed. "Well, a mate's a mate, isn't it? That's what it's like these days with kids. They all know each other through someone else."

"She's thirteen," Bethany said. "And you let her go off with a male. For a week." She sighed. Why did they not see a problem with that? "Okay, so when did you last hear from her?"

"The same Saturday she walked out," Lorraine said. "Here, look at this." She woke her phone, brought up her texts, and handed it over.

3:57 p.m.
Tanya: STAYING WITH SASHA FOR A FEW DAYS.

4:01 p.m.
Lorraine: RIGHT. WHAT ABOUT YOUR SCHOOL UNIFORM?

4:03 p.m.
Tanya: SASHA HAS SPARES.

4:05 p.m.
Lorraine: WELL, DON'T PISS HER MUM ABOUT. BE GOOD.

4:07 p.m.
Tanya: YEAH, YEAH.

Bethany's eyes stung. They'd need to go and visit Sasha after this, see if she'd even had Tanya at her house, which was highly unlikely. Surely she'd have said when Bethany and Mike last spoke to her.

"Are you okay with Tanya staying at people's houses for that long—and when it's a school week? I'll need a screenshot of this message—all right if I send it to myself? And don't delete it, please. Someone will call round to collect your phone. It needs going through."

"Yeah, we are okay with her staying away." Lorraine nodded. "And yeah, send it."

Bethany did that while talking. "So that's why you weren't worried she hadn't come home?"

"I knew where she was." Lorraine sucked on her vape. "She's done it before."

"What about not hearing from her in all that time. Is that usual?"

Lorraine rolled her eyes. "Look, Tanya's a pain up the arse lately. She acts out, gobs off at us, makes us feel awkward on our own home. She went to stay with Sasha, and that was a relief, to be honest. We got a break. And what's she done anyway? Nicked a lipstick from Superdrug or something?"

"Have you been reading the recent news?" Bethany placed the phone on the sofa arm and glanced at Mike for him to arrange for an officer to pick it up.

"Nope. I avoid it. It gets me riled up."

"What about you, Richard?"

He paled, something seeming to click into place. "Oh no." He stood, putting his cup on the mantel. "That Catherine kid's missing. Are you saying…?"

"Catherine was found dead yesterday," Bethany said gently. "Please sit down."

He flopped back onto the chair. "What?"

"Who's Catherine?" Lorraine asked.

"One of Tan's mates." Richard gripped his hair. "She met up with some bloke from online, too." He stared at Lorraine. "Around the same time Tan went to meet Simon."

Lorraine blinked—her brain didn't appear to be computing the information. "Eh?"

Richard shot up again. Paced. "This Simon..."

Bethany took a deep breath. "We believe Simon is the same man who took Catherine and attempted to take another thirteen-year-old girl just yesterday. I really do need you to take a seat, Richard."

He shook his head. "No."

"Okay. I have some bad news. I'm sorry to say a body was discovered this morning. The description fits Tanya—it's the same girl in the photo on your mantel. A note was left with her, telling us her name, age, and address."

Both parents gawped at her.

"Do you understand what I've just told you?"

Richard punched the wall, a white-painted wicker love heart jumping off a hook and landing on the floor. Lorraine picked her cup up and lobbed it at the coffee table. Mike laid a hand on Richard's back, and Bethany approached Lorraine to offer the same.

"No. Don't come near me," Lorraine shouted. "I'm likely to beat the shit out of you, bringing us news like that."

"They're just doing their jobs, woman," Richard roared.

Lorraine stood. "And by doing that, they've wrecked my fucking life." She ran out, sobbing.

Richard hit the wall again. "Fuck. *Fuck*. What are we going to do? I can't... This is..."

"We'll arrange for the Family Liaison Officer to come and talk with you. She'll explain everything and answer any questions," Bethany said. "I don't think it's advisable for you to be on your own at the moment."

He faced her. "Was it...was she murdered by the same man as Catherine?"

"We believe so."

"I'll bloody kill the bastard, you wait and see." Richard nodded. "I'll find him—and end him."

CHAPTER SEVENTEEN

Sweat broke out, small rivers rolling down John's back, pooling at his trouser waistband. It was morning, and he'd just closed the caravan door on some coppers, who'd been round to question everyone on the site.

"What on earth was that all about with the police, John?" Irena, tousled-headed, sat sipping her tea at the table in the living room area.

"No idea, love. You heard as much as I did. Some woman was murdered. It's really upsetting, isn't it, when you can't even go away on holiday without a crime being committed right under your nose." He shook his head and sat beside her to sip his own tea.

"Should we go home? If there's a murderer…"

"No, don't be silly. It'll be a one-off. Can't really see a serial killer rampaging through the same holiday camp twice, can you?"

"No. I suppose you're right." She stared down at the cheap Formica table and scratched at its surface with a fingernail, clearly perturbed.

"Feeling better today?" he asked. *"Headache gone?"*

She frowned as if her mind was elsewhere. *"Yes, thank goodness. I was in tears at one point after you left last night."*

He did love her. She was so fragile. He didn't ask why she'd been crying, told himself it was because of the migraine. He didn't want to admit fully that maybe she was suspecting him of something, that his beloved wife doubted him.

"Fancy going into Barnstaple, do a bit of shopping?" he asked.

She brightened. *"Can we afford it?"*

"For this week we can."

He finished his tea with a burning gulp, patted Irena's hand, then went to their tiny bedroom, where he got the penknife from out of his jeans pocket and took it into the bathroom with him. He ran the shower, testing the heat, and stepped into the small cubicle, carefully washing the knife, then reached out across the narrow space and dropped it in the sink.

The stream of water and bubbles from the soap rinsed away the sweat of the police's visit.

John thought about the murder. The worry.

It would be okay. He was sure of it.

After browsing the shops in Barnstaple, lunch in Banbury's, then dining at the caravan park's restaurant, they went on to the clubhouse for the evening's entertainment, Edward once again off with his friend.

Unfortunately, Blowsy and George, the former having no qualms about loudly discussing the previous night's murder, joined them.

Having introduced her and George to Irena, and finding out Blowsy's real name was Rachel, John sat and suffered her colourful vocabulary for the next couple of hours.

"I was telling George that we go on bleedin' holiday to get away from killing and crime, only to have some poor cow bumped off, throat slit, right on our bloody doorstep."

Irena, to begin with, found Blowsy's choice of words startling—John could tell by the rise and fall of her eyebrows—but she relaxed as the evening wore on. They chatted animatedly, discussing everything from the murder to the merits of dishcloths versus the scouring sponge.

John struggled to find anything to discuss with George. The bloke seemed content to stare into space, taking occasional sips from his pint glass. This lack of interaction gave John time to think, until:

"Fuck me! I tell you, your missus is quite a card." Blowsy slapped John's shoulder with her chubby hand. "Having a right old laugh, we are."

"Good to hear that."

Her jelly jowls wobbled, tits heaving with her deep intake of breath. The gin had been replenished in her glass more times that he dared to count. Already three sheets to the wind, Blowsy showed no sign of actually shutting up.

Irena looked like she'd lost a pound and found a tenner, her features animated, eyes alive and dancing. She touched John's arm. "I'm so glad we took this holiday."

"Me an' all," Blowsy piped up. "Normally, when we go away, no bastard'll come and sit with us because of old dopey bollocks here." She gestured to George, almost smacking the downtrodden man on the end of his nose.

"Oh, I'm sure it isn't George's fault," Irena said.

"It bleedin' well is, ain't it, George?"

"Hmmm?" he finally responded.

"You," Blowsy continued. "The way you sit with a face like a smacked arse. Don't exactly encourage friendships, does it?"

"Suppose not." George stood, keeping his gaze on a group of small girls playing grown-up dancing.

"Mine's a G and T if you're buying, George." Blowsy laughed and slapped him on his arse.

He made his way past her, unsteady from his gimp leg. "Yes, dear."

About ten minutes passed, John half listening to the women talking.

Blowsy sighed. "Fucking hell. He's a bleedin' nutcase, I reckon. Needs his head seeing to. Sits at home, he does, at the window all day. George don't do sod all, see, what with being incapacitated an' all. It's me who runs the stall and the house. I told your John that last night, Irena. Anyway, where's he gone? Been ages, he has. Can you see him at the bar from there, mate? What's your name again...John? Forget me head if it weren't screwed on."

"No. I can't see him. Shall I go and find out where he's got to?" John asked.

"Yeah, you do that, Rick. Err, John. Me throat's as dry as a vulture's crotch."

The devil took John to the children's play area. He stood in the trees bordering the small park which was lit by Victorian-style streetlamps all around.

George was talking to a little girl. A sweet thing, she sat on the roundabout, her hair rippling in the breeze as he spun her round and around. She was giggly and happy, just as she should be for one so young.

George threw a ball across the tarmac. A dog, John assumed it was hers, bounded over to retrieve it. George stopped the roundabout.

"I had two dogs," she said. "This one's called Jasper."

George had perked up since being in the clubhouse. "I bet the other one's a good doggy, just like Jasper, eh?"

"She. It was a girl dog, but she's dead now. I always say I got two dogs 'cos I forget..." Her bottom lip popped out.

"Well, now, that's a shame. Do you think Jasper would like to take a little walk on the lead?"

"Yeah, but...me mum, she'll be here soon, and I'll get told off for talking to a stranger."

George switched to a concerned face. "Your mum's right, and you're a good girl for doing as she says. You stay and wait for her." He smiled and walked away.

"What's the time, mister?"

George stopped and looked at his watch. "Do you know what? I'm not sure. I can't tell without my glasses on." His laugh sounded forced.

She skipped over to him, eyes bright. Her ankle socks got John's attention, and he took in the length of her legs in her little denim skirt.

Like a flower growing from the soil.

"That's all right. I can tell the time. We learnt it at school." She danced closer to George until she stood next to him.

He stooped to show her his watch.

Something was amiss; George was up to no good, and John struggled with his conscience. He'd done some terrible things in his life, but this seemed different somehow. Maybe it was watching someone else doing something wrong that bothered him. It was okay for him but not for other people.

"My mum'll be here soon. She's in the clubhouse."

"Well, then..."

A sharp female voice broke the spell, and the girl's hand sprang from George's arm.

"Harriet! What have I told you?"

"Oh, I'm sorry." George turned on the charm. "We got talking about dogs, you know, and I offered to walk Jasper here, but she was a good girl, weren't you?" He glanced down at Harriet. "And she said she couldn't, because you'd told her not to talk to strangers. She was just checking the time to see when you'd be here."

Her mum's face softened. After all, if he was intent on doing wrong, who'd suspect a man who looked like George? He could be anyone's grandad.

"I'm sorry, really, but...you know, these days..." She seemed embarrassed.

"Oh, yes, I understand. No problem at all." George offered a jolly grin and turned to Harriet. "Well, young lady. Maybe I'll see Jasper again sometime, eh? If Mummy allows it, of course."

John thought about Blowsy saying George sat at their window a lot, staring into the street, and everything fell into place. Who he was. What he thought about. Who he watched.

"Are you here for much longer this evening?" the mum asked.

This question appeared to throw George. "Err, well, yes, I was just about to have a rest on that seat over there."

"Well, then, Harriet, you can stay with Mr, umm...?"

"George. George Phelps." He slipped the dog's ball in his pocket.

"Mr Phelps," she said. "Harriet, you can stay a little while then, just so you can play with Jasper. It'll save him from being cooped up in the van. Make sure you're back in the clubhouse by half past nine, do you understand?"

Harriet hopped from foot to foot. "Thanks, Mum." She threw herself at her and got a big hug in return.

"Be good. Oh, and thanks, Mr Phelps." Her mum backed away and waved at Harriet.

"That's quite all right. And it's George."

"Okay then, George. My name's Sandra."

Sandra. The stupid bitch—stupid for leaving her alone with George. Even John could see what he was about. So why didn't he say something or step out of the bushes?

Jasper's tail wagged like mad, and he strained against the lead, Harriet unsteady being tugged along. "You're pulling me!"

The dog slowed, and the tautness of Harriet's arm eased a bit.

John followed them at a distance.

"Shall we throw his ball, mister?"

"George, call me George. And yes, we can throw his ball. You go first."

He brought the ball from his coat pocket and handed it to her. Her fingers brushed his. She launched the ball, but it didn't go far, more up in the air than any great distance. It bounced down and rebounded, but Jasper waited patiently for it to come to rest.

"Your turn, mister...George." She smiled, her fists clenched in excitement, legs dancing a jig.

Adopting a cricketer's stance, the old man propelled it this time, lunging forward to ensure it went into the bushes that lined the edge of the small field next to the park.

"Aww! Look at him run, Mister George. Get it, Jasper."

The dog snuffled about in the bushes, searching.

"You got it yet, boy?" George's smile was so broad. "You reckon we should go and help him find that ball, Harriet?"

She stared up at him and put her finger to her bottom lip, frowning while she considered his question. It was Edward, Edward all over again. Did all children do this?

"Yeah, okay," she said. "I think it got lost."

She scarpered off, hair streaming out behind her. John ambled after George and Harriet, glancing at his watch. Amazingly, only seven minutes had passed.

"I can't see it, Mister George."

"Deary me. This doggy's a silly one, isn't he? Let's see where he goes."

Again, she paused, but the dog barked excitedly, enticing her to follow.

She did.

Jasper moved forward through the hedges into a small glade surrounded by trees.

"He's funny." She giggled. "Don't his nose hurt when he sniffs them bits of bark on the ground?"

"Oh, I don't think so, Harriet. That's what dogs do, isn't it? Sniff about a lot." George made a pretence of trying to look for the ball, no longer limping. "That ball must have bounced all the way over here."

"Yeah, but I reckon he'll find it, 'cos he's a clever dog, ent he, Mister George?"

George had found the ball and slipped it into his pocket. He and the girl moved farther into the bushes. There was a muffled scream, and John ran over. Why didn't he stop it? Now, before it was too late? He hid in the hedge; he'd put an end to this soon, he had to.

He couldn't make anything out through the thick bushes.

George said, "Harriet! Don't move any more, do you understand?" His voice was low.

A strangled gasp.

"Be good, and I'll let Jasper sit near you, all right?" George said.

Another gargled noise.

"Good. Just. Be. Quiet…and everything will be okay."

Harriet made noises again. Why couldn't she speak? What had he done to her?

Yet John still stayed put.

"Be quiet, Harriet, there's a good girl. I'm going to take the ball out of your mouth now. Are you going to be good and do what Mister George tells you?"

A lion, king of his jungle. John battled his emotions, his breathing ragged.

George spoke again. "Now then, I have a nice camera here."

More muffled noises, like feet shuffling in undergrowth, and Harriet mumbling.

"I want...me mum."

Oh God.

The camera clicked again.

Minutes passed, and then George said, "All right, Harriet, we're done."

She sobbed. It reminded John of the time Edward cried, when he'd heard him through the bedroom wall.

"It's time for you to have a little sleep. Are you tired? Would you like Mister George to read you a story? Well, you'll be having a sleep whether you like it or not, madam. You flinch again, and I'll..."

John felt like he had as a child, when Mum had spoken to him in that way. Vulnerable and young, unsettled and unsure.

"I want my mummy!" Harriet's wails were heartfelt and panic-stricken.

John dry-retched. Told himself to move, do something.

"Oh dear, you really ought to shut up now. Be quiet!" George sounded angry.

Fresh sobs.

"You can't have your fucking mummy, all right? Shut the fuck up, girl. Just shut it!"

More scuffling noises.

It grew quiet.

It was then John believed she was dead.

John had been gone around fifteen minutes. Back in the clubhouse, he ordered drinks and carried them to the table on a tray, dodging dancers and small diving children.

Children. Children.

The girls who'd practised the grown-up dancing were still there, minus Harriet. Even they were oblivious to her disappearance. John glanced about for Harriet's mum but didn't see her. Maybe she'd gone to the gaming room.

John handed the drinks out.

"Didn't you find the boring old fucker then?" Blowsy was redder than when he'd left her, anger probably adding to her colour.

"Um, no, I didn't. Had a good look around, couldn't see him, so got the drinks anyway. No point in us going thirsty while we wait for him."

"Too bleeding right, Steve."

This woman could recite all you needed to know about cleaning agents but couldn't remember a simple name like John. She must have had a problem with Irena's too, preferring to call her 'love' every five minutes.

"Edward popped back at all since I was gone?" John asked.

Irena claimed her drink and sipped.

Blowsy burst in with, "Yeah, wanted some more money. Going to that bowling alley he went to last night."

Irena smiled. "Are you all right, John?"

He sat, heart still overbeating.

"Course he's all right, love. Ain't ya, Sam?" Blowsy said. "Probably pissed off at having to look for that prat of a husband of mine. Know I would be if I were him."

"No. It's all right, not to worry. I'm sure George will be back soon." John had to fight to keep his tone even. "He probably just went for a walk and a bit of fresh air."

"Yeah, you're right. More like a fucking hobble than a walk, though, eh? What with his bad leg." Her laughter filled their little space.

Other guests nodded and nudged one another, smiling at the loud mad woman having a good time on her holiday.

"He'll be a while yet then, the rate he goes," she added.

George finally came back, a glint in his eye.

"Where the bleedin' hell have you been?" Blowsy shrieked even louder. "How dare you go fucking off like that. And you haven't even got the bloody drinks."

George's mouth opened and closed, and he scanned the hall, probably for signs of Sandra, the child's mum.

"Go for a walk, George? Children get a bit much for you in here, did they?" John asked.

"Err, yes. Too stuffy." George gave a dry cough, a clearing of his throat, his gaze still roving the multitude of faces.

"Don't blame you, George. I might go for a stroll myself. Take a look near the tennis courts, you know, have a look around the site a bit."

George's face paled.

"'Ere! Are you all right, cocker? You've gone all white," Blowsy said.

George shuddered. "Y-yes. I'm fine. Just off-colour."

"Want to go back to the van?" Blowsy asked.

"Yes." He stared down at his lap.

"Well, fuck off then. Quite able to get yourself off over there, aren't you?" Blowsy slapped the caravan key into his hand. "Don't lock up, though, will you? Can't get in if you do that and fall asleep before I get back."

George walked away. He glanced behind him at John with the expression of a caged animal. John wanted to follow him, to talk to him about what had happened, but Blowsy had requested yet another drink, thrusting twenty pounds at him.

"May as well make them all doubles, Ron. Swear to God the barman's watering their spirits down. Don't seem to be hitting the spot tonight, do they?"

They'd hit the spot perfectly; she was drunk.

An hour later, Irena holding Blowsy up this time, and John and Edward walking on ahead, they made their way back to the caravans.

"'Ere, help me to my van, you lot. It's fucking dark out here. What with that murder an' all, I don't fancy being number two on his list." Blowsy let out an obscene burp. Trying the handle on the door, and too gin-polluted to function properly, she failed to open it. "Fuck me. Bet he's gone and locked up, the dozy bastard."

"Here, let me." The door opened easily for John, and, leaving her teetering on the van steps, he escorted his family to their own.

The air was pierced with a sickening scream, followed by Blowsy waddle-swaying up the path behind them, ruddy faced and out of breath.

"Fucking hell's bells," she said, her eyes tear-filled, her cheeks wobbling. "He's only gone and committed another bleedin' killing, ain't he? Slit my George's throat." Blowsy fumbled in her bag for her mobile.

John stared at her. "Edward, go back to our caravan."

Edward walked away.

Blowsy sobbed. "And there was me, telling George to fuck off an' all. Poor bloke."

"Here, give me the phone," Irena said.

While waiting for the police to arrive, John knew one thing for certain. There hadn't been another murder in this instance.

George had committed suicide, too cowardly to face what he'd done.

John woke in a cold sweat. That particular dream, that memory, always got him like this. Why did that scene bother him when he'd put the past to bed? Why, out of all the things he'd done, did that affect him the most?

He hadn't done anything to save her. He'd allowed George to do what he wanted.

The devil had kept John in place, as mute as George had been prior to becoming animated once he'd met Harriet.

John got out of bed and showered to get rid of his clammy skin. He dressed and went to the kitchen and, while making coffee, he asked himself, not for the first time, how he could behave the way he did. How he'd switched it off for thirteen years during the happy patch with Irena and Edward. If he'd done it once, he could do it again, couldn't he?

He sat at the table and sipped. And a thought came then, of how he'd let George do what he had. Harriet had become Francesca in John's mind, the girl he'd never managed to persuade to be his friend, so he'd allowed George to make friends with her while John watched, pretending he was George instead.

With that explanation settling his worries, he switched his phone on and put in the PIN. A blue bar across the middle showed him Karly had sent a message, only the first line visible: *Hello? Are you there?*

Yep, he was there all right.

He opened the conversation and read the rest.

Shit. *Shit.* She'd cut him off, ended it.

That was it then, wasn't it? Decision made? Karly wasn't available. The silly girl didn't know what she was missing.

He finished his coffee and blocked her.

There was something else he could do instead, now that the police were involved with everything. While they concentrated on finding him, he'd be off in another direction. He'd seen her, a Harriet, a Francesca, and had already written out the plan.

He'd ensure he got his first crush after all.

CHAPTER EIGHTEEN

Bethany and Mike sat outside the Oxbrey house in the car, taking a couple of minutes to process things. While the parents hadn't been ideal, they'd loved their daughter, and maybe Tanya's recent behaviour had ground them down so the break Lorraine had mentioned with Tanya supposedly staying at Sasha's…well, it'd have been welcome. Who was Bethany to judge? She had no kids and couldn't possibly understand what it was like to have a teenager in your home who made you uncomfortable.

"So, he's using different names for each girl," she said.

"Probably how he keeps track. Mind association."

"Hmm. And so the other girls don't twig they're all being chatted up by the same bloke if they got nattering together about it." She sighed. "He's a sicko to target a group of friends."

"Probably gets a kick out of it."

"Yep. But I'm having trouble with the compost. What the *hell* is that about? *Why* do they have it on them?"

"It's a new one on me. No idea, unless, like we thought, the girls were kept in outdoor conditions where they got the dirt on them."

"But it's *all* over them, apart from their faces. It's even in their hair. It's as if they've been purposely smeared with it."

"Could be a shed where a bag has split?"

"That's a thought. Maybe Presley will get some fibres from the post-mortems. He said he cleaned Catherine up yesterday, so he'll have sent anything off. I didn't think to ask him when we were at Tanya's scene."

Mike shivered. "Those ankles socks…"

"I know. Creepy on a girl that age—or is that just me?"

"Nope, it's creepy. Like he wanted Tanya to be younger."

"Then why not *go* for someone younger if that's his thing?"

"Fuck knows. As for that pin stuck in her chest… Couldn't he have used tape or something, for fuck's sake?" Mike shook his head. "Ever since I saw it, I keep imagining him poking it into her. I know she was dead when he did it, but you still get a sense of the pain if she'd been alive."

"Like when Thomas Volton had his nuts chopped off in the Butcher case? You went all funny about that as well."

"Don't. That was a nasty sensation."

She laughed, regardless of the situation. Sometimes you had to for your sanity. "Well, we'd better go and see Sasha. We've given her family enough time to get up and ready. Did her mother reply again yet?"

Mike had contacted Faith Irons when they'd got in the car. He took his phone out. "Nope, so I assume she's fine with us visiting."

"Tough if she isn't. We've got a job to do."

Bethany drove them there, stuck inside her head for the whole journey. Her comment about Hoody going for a younger child was bothering her. Why choose teenagers when it was clear you wanted something else? Was there a girl in his past where certain aspects of her had stuck in his mind? The ankle socks, the pigtails as a littlun, then the teen, perhaps experimenting with makeup? Had these things come out in his selection process and how he'd left the bodies? If that were the case, who was the original girl? Was she still alive, or had he done away with her already?

She thought about the years of planning serial killers usually went through. Those times were enough for them for a while—imagining it all, the thrill of it—but later, that *wasn't* enough, and the real deal was needed to achieve the same high.

Had he done this before, the space of time between kills longer than they were now? When murder happened more frequently, signifying escalation, that was scary. Once a killer had reached this stage, there was no telling how many bodies would pile up. His plan was clear enough: speak to several girls at once and pick them off one by one. Thankfully, Elsa was safe now—or as safe as she could be. But were there others out there who weren't? Were they still chatting to him in whatever bloody name he'd thought up, excited to meet him?

She parked outside Sasha's and took a deep breath. Tomorrow, they'd go to the school and talk to the kids in assembly again. She had to make it abundantly clear that if anyone was speaking to someone they didn't actually know, who they hadn't met in person before, they must come forward or risk being killed. She hated to be so harsh, so stark in her explanation, but if she wasn't, there was a chance of more girls going missing and ending up dead.

"You okay?" Mike unclipped his seat belt.

"Just thinking how far this could go if we don't stop him soon."

"Let's hope Fran, Leona, and the uniforms get a bite from the Fiesta drivers today."

"If they don't, we'll move on to *all* colours of Fiesta—someone may have had a respray and didn't update their documents. You know how crafty these bastards can be. Right, let's get this done, then we'll go back to the station and help out there."

They left the car and walked up the path to the blue front door. Mike knocked while Bethany straightened her jacket then picked off invisible lint.

Mrs Irons opened up.

"Hi, DI Bethany Smith and DS Mike Wilkins." Bethany showed her ID.

"Come in." She waited until they were all crowded into the small hallway, then whispered, "Has that man been talking to Sasha as well?"

"As far as we're aware, no," Bethany said. "We've gathered from our chat with her last time that she's got an old head on young shoulders and wouldn't do anything like that. We're here because we need to check whether you and your daughter were aware of something—if we could just go somewhere to talk. Nothing to worry about."

Faith led them to a kitchen, the units nice and shiny, the worktops clean with minimal appliances on them, just a black toaster, kettle, and some tea, coffee, and sugar pots. Sasha sat at the dining table eating cereal. The milk had gone brown from the chocolate.

Once everyone sat, Mike remaining standing, as was his way, Bethany began.

"Thanks for speaking to us today. Now, Sasha, if I can start with you. How well do you know Tanya Oxbrey?"

"She's in our friendship circle. I don't know her as well as Elsa—me and her are best friends—but Tanya's nice enough."

"Has she ever stayed over here before? You know, for sleepovers?"

"Only once, last year for my birthday."

"So Tanya wasn't here all last week?"

Faith gasped. "What? Was she supposed to be?" She slapped a hand to her chest.

"She told her parents she was at yours from last Saturday and would borrow some of Sasha's school uniform throughout the week."

Faith shook her head. "There's no way I'd have anyone here on a school night. You just don't do that, do you?"

"I wouldn't have thought so, no." Bethany smiled at Sasha. "Is there anyone else in your friendship group that we're not aware of? So far, we have you, Elsa, Catherine, Gina, and Tanya."

"There's Karly. She's our mate as well."

"And what's her surname?" Mike asked, pen and notebook at the ready.

"Young," Sasha said. "She only lives down the road. Number ten."

"Has she mentioned speaking to an older boy recently?" Bethany prayed Hoody hadn't got to Karly.

"No." Sasha pushed her bowl away. "She wouldn't fall for anything like that."

"Back to Tanya. Did she ask you to pretend she was staying here for the week?"

Sasha's eyes widened, as if that were the most ridiculous thing. "No. I wouldn't have done that. I'd have said something."

Yet you kept it quiet about Elsa meeting Jolly19, even after we'd been to the school to talk to you all about Catherine going missing. Bethany put that to her.

"Well, that was different. I didn't know he was a man, like, a proper man, all old and fat. And I went into town, didn't I, in case Elsa needed me. Turned out she did, and it was me who told her we had to tell the police. I'm sorry I didn't say anything. It was just… Elsa was so excited and…"

"I understand. What I'm getting at really is, if you know something now, like you did with Elsa, you need to say." Bethany brushed a strand of hair back. "Because the man targeting your friends is dangerous, as you know. If he's talking to anyone else, we need to hear about it."

Faith pressed a hand to Sasha's shoulder. "Can you think of anything, love?"

"I swear, I've told you all I know."

"Didn't anyone wonder why Tanya wasn't at school all last week?" Bethany asked. "You and your friends, I mean."

"She said she was ill."

Bethany's stomach flipped. "She's been in *contact*?"

Sasha nodded and picked up her phone. She prodded the screen a few times. "Here, look."

Tanya: I'M SKIVING ALL WEEK LOL. MY FRIEND'S RINGING IN EVERY DAY TO LEAVE A MESSAGE ON THE ABSENT ANSWERPHONE. HILAR.

Sasha: WHAT ARE YOU DOING?

Tanya: CHILLING AT MY MATE'S. CAN'T BE ARSED WITH SCHOOL AT THE MINUTE.

Sasha: WHAT IF YOU GET CAUGHT?

Tanya: I WON'T. ANYWAY, CHAT SOME OTHER TIME. I'M WELL BUSY. BYE!

Had Tanya really sent that? Had she met with Hoody, didn't care he was old, and thought it was all one big bag of fun? Or had he selected Sasha from Tanya's contacts and tapped out the messages? That was more likely, wasn't it? What thirteen-year-old girl would realistically want to be with a man old enough to be her dad? Unless she had a thing about needing a father figure... If that had been the case, then he turned nasty on her, which he clearly did... God, how had the poor girl felt during her last hours?

"Okay, I'll need to have an officer come to collect this phone. You can have it back once digital forensics have been through it, all right?" Bethany handed it to Mike and took a deep breath. "I know this has been a terrible time lately, but I'm afraid I have some more bad news. Tanya has been found this morning. She wasn't with a friend. She'd been with that man."

Sasha stared. "What?"

Faith sucked in a sharp breath. "Dear God. Is she…?"

"I'm afraid she's deceased." Bethany swallowed.

Sasha crumpled. It was inevitable she would. Faith held her in a hug. Bethany got up and walked out into the hallway with Mike.

"Can you nip to number ten and speak with Karly?" she asked.

He nodded, put the phone on a shelf by the door, and left the house. Bethany returned to the kitchen, where Sasha and Faith were crying. This was too much for a teenager to handle, also for the mother of one. Faith was no doubt imagining herself in Lorraine's shoes, how she'd feel if Sasha was gone and not Tanya.

"Would you like me to put you in contact with someone to talk to?" Bethany sat again and looked at Faith. "Sasha might benefit from a therapist at this point. It's all getting a bit much, isn't it?"

Faith nodded. "It's okay. My sister-in-law's a counsellor. I'll give her a ring."

With that sorted, Bethany said her goodbyes and left, sending a message for someone from forensics to collect the phone. She stood by the car to take a moment to digest what she'd learnt. Hoody had covered Tanya's school absence well, even going so far as to ring the school absent line and report her as off ill. Had he done that with Tanya because with Catherine, there'd been a missing person's report out on her so there was no point? Had he also made out Tanya was staying with Sasha, texting Lorraine as a cover? A whole week where he could do what he wanted to Tanya, no risk of anyone searching for the girl. He must have kept Catherine and Tanya together.

He'd planned it so well.

Mike came walking up the street, taking her out of her mind and into the here and now.

"Karly's out somewhere," he said. "Her mother doesn't know where."

"You're kidding me. With all that's going on? Just Catherine's disappearance in the news is enough to lock your kids up, isn't it?"

"Faith didn't with Sasha. She was allowed into town by herself yesterday."

What was the matter with these parents? Was Bethany being too harsh here, condemning them for not taking better care of their kids? For not realising the seriousness of it all?

"Did the mother try ringing Karly?"

"Yes, no answer."

Bethany's heart sank. "What if...?"

"She texted her back, don't panic."

"Right, but what if it's Hoody doing that? What was said?"

"That she isn't speaking to any bloke—the mum asked her outright at my request."

"We still need to speak to Karly. What if she's lying? What if she's next?"

Mike nodded. "I've asked the mother to let us know when she comes home. For now, we need to get back to the nick."

At the station, Mike got on with helping the team with the Fiestas—they'd moved on to other colours as the people who'd been spoken to with grey or silver ones all had alibis, had scrapped them, or were dead. Bethany filled in the new info on the whiteboard, then read over everything to get her mind straight on it.

Catherine and Tanya had to have been held captive at the same time. Had they known the other was there, or had they been placed in separate places? Was there a building somewhere being used to harbour young girls? If so, where the hell was it?

That thought gave Bethany a road to go down. She used the computer at a spare desk and brought up a map of Shadwell and the surrounding area. She printed it off and tacked it to the board. Using small round stickers, she placed red ones where Catherine and Tanya had been found. Then she used green to show where they'd met Hoody for the first time—plus one at the courtyard where Elsa had gone. It didn't make a pattern, anything she could use as a lead. All locations were spaced apart, giving no idea where Hoody may live.

So she studied the outlying land, searching for places that were remote. There was Shadwell Hill, the old warehouse and steel mill, Wind Energy and, dotted around, some cottages that she recalled from memory.

She walked to her office and called Rob on the front desk. "Can you send some uniforms out to have a chat with everyone who owns property on the outskirts, please. I'm thinking these girls have been kept somewhere no one else would hear them if they screamed or whatever."

"I'll sort that for you now."

"Thanks."

She returned to the incident room and got stuck in, helping out with the Fiestas and phoning the owners. About two hours later, Rob called her back.

"Mostly elderly people. A couple of owners weren't in, so uniform will go back later. If there's still no answer, they'll visit again in the morning," he said.

"Got a list of occupants?"

"Yep, will email it."

"Cheers."

She slid her phone in her pocket and accessed her mail on the computer. Rob hadn't been wrong about the elderly, and most of them were couples. There were four sole occupiers, three of them men, one female. Of those who hadn't been in, one was a David Flemmish, the other a John Keagan.

She checked their stats.

David Flemmish: 48, accountant. Widower. Two children. Owns a Mazda.

John Keagan: 47, hospital porter. Divorced. One child. No vehicle registered.

Neither seemed anything to worry about, but then again, what could you tell from that sort of information? Seeing them in the flesh was better. But how was Keagan getting from his cottage to Shadwell proper without a car, unless he regularly got the bus or a taxi? She checked the scale on the map and worked out the distance from his place to town. Hmm, okay, a mile and a half. Doable. Maybe the bloke liked exercise and walked it.

She clicked on the attachment Rob had included. Driving licences. Both men looked average and nothing like Hoody. She imagined them with beards and glasses, but it still didn't bring Hoody to mind. The CCTV hadn't been clear enough, plus he'd had most of his hood covering his face.

Clutching at straws, that was what she was doing.

She got up and walked out, heading for Kribbs' office. She needed to give him an update. That would probably take a good hour, then she'd check in to see whether Karly had gone home yet. Later, she'd grab Mike and go out and see Flemmish and Keagan for herself. Men living alone in the sticks were a red flag, possibly just one she wanted to be there rather than actually existing, flapping in the wind of hope, but what else did she have?

Better to have checked it out than not. For all she knew, another girl could be held somewhere against her will. While missing persons hadn't thrown anything up, that didn't mean it wasn't happening. Look at how Tanya's disappearance had been masked.

They were dealing with a clever man.

One Bethany was determined to see locked up. For life.

CHAPTER NINETEEN

John had Irena and Blowsy as an alibi, not to mention half of the campsite had been in the clubhouse, many of whom had chatted with him or said hello in the men's or at the bar.

Of course, it was inevitable they'd find little Harriet's body, her mum having reported her child missing just minutes after Irena's call to the police about George. Stupid Sandra, leaving her kid in George's care.

Holidaymakers had gathered in clusters, talking in whispers. Sandra told the police George's name—why had he told her his real one? With a bit of luck, he'd get the blame for John's crime, too, murdering that woman who looked like Mum.

Later, news swept through the camp, and rumours of the detectives' theory: a paedophile had murdered the child discovered in the bushes, then took his own life.

The rest of the holiday was spent with Blowsy in tow, Irena consoling her. Statements given, John was cleared of any wrongdoings depending on the outcome of the forensic reports.

"Fucking hell," Blowsy said. "What a holiday I've had, eh? Me old man has seemingly topped himself after fiddling about with a kiddie. Just shows what you don't know about your other half, eh, Irena?"

"Yes," Irena agreed in a strange voice.

It bothered John, the way she'd said it.

Returning home calmed him, though. Much as he'd enjoyed the break, it was good to be back amongst the familiar, but the first night, he was unable to fall asleep. Images swirled round his head until he had to get up, make some tea with brandy in it.

Eventually, he did drop off. It must have been the police activity that brought on insomnia, the fear he'd experienced after killing that woman, whose name was Rebecca White, he'd found out before they'd left the camp, a receptionist at the site.

Something warned him he needed to beware. To stop. Go back to being normal instead of playing the game of hide-and-seek—him hiding his true feelings from the world while at the same time seeking...whatever it was he sought.

His resolve lasted two years, and then a man at a party, held at a hotel to raise funds for charity, annoyed John just a little too much that night.

He'd been a master of holding it all in, disguising what he really felt behind a happy mask. In reality, he was seething; he could've ripped off the man's face if he'd let the irritation run free. The bloke was employed by the hospital and often annoyed John there, too. Perhaps it was the way he held himself, or that he smiled at John all the time, trying to be friendly. He didn't want to be his friend, didn't want this overly happy twat in his face, and he didn't need him following him around that night. John was going to place his hand over the dickhead's face and shove him over backwards if he didn't shut his mouth and leave him alone.

He had to get away. Outside, he leant against the wrought-iron fencing that edged the terrace, elbows resting on the ledge, head hanging low. Deep breaths. Make the devil leave.

Dickhead followed him. He was invading John's space as well as his mind. If he didn't get away from him soon, something would happen.

John went inside and raced down the stairs; the confines of the lift would have driven him mental. He made it to the car park, head roaring, lungs bursting, sweat covering his face. Calmer, he strolled to a cluster of trees, leaning against one, his battle with the devil receding.

"Hey there!"

John's blood pressure rose again. Why the fuck wouldn't the man leave him be? Dickhead didn't see John's fist coming. He had no clue what he'd started, what he'd done. John had tried so hard these past two years, and now look what had happened.

Dickhead was out like a light.

John dragged him deeper into the cluster of trees and stamped on his head with both feet until he didn't move anymore. John walked across the grass, scuffing his shoes to get rid of the mess. Blood had spattered the bottoms of his trousers. When would the rage return again? Would he ever be left to live in peace?

He hoped he hadn't been seen.

As luck would have it, Irena had been unable to attend the party. She often had to work second or third shift at the hospital. Edward had stayed with Dad, so going home to an empty house was a bonus. John scraped his shoes clean and washed and dried his clothing before anyone else came home.

The next evening, the news channels reported what he'd done.

"Oh my God. Isn't that the party you went to, John?" Shocked, Irena stared at the TV then looked at him with a horrified expression.

The distrust in her eyes nearly knocked him out of his chair. How had it come to this? His wife, gawping at him like that? Had he thought he was behaving normally in front of her when, in fact, he wasn't?

"Hmm?" he said. Best to feign nonchalance.

"That murder. It happened at the hotel you were at."

"Blimey."

The news reporter stood just in front of the trees where he'd been, telling in his sombre voice of the tragedy, the horror of this senseless killing.

It was a bloody tragedy that the man had annoyed John. He'd got what he'd deserved. He wouldn't be bothering anyone again.

"I might have to start worrying about you," Irena said.

"Eh?" He broke his gaze from the telly. "Why's that then?"

"Well," she said, "every time there's a murder or someone's hurt, you know, Lucy and her mum, those holiday murders, you've been out on your own. I should be scared witless by rights."

She was smiling, joking—at least he hoped she was bloody joking—but all the same, his blood ran cold.

"What a thing to say. Makes me look awful." He got up and stepped into the kitchen, calling in a casual tone, "Do you want a coffee, love?"

"Please." There was quiet for a moment, then she said, "I was only messing about, you know."

"I know. Whoever the murderer is must have a pretty good reason to kill someone."

Irena got up and leant against the kitchen doorframe, arms crossed over her stomach. "You can't seriously mean that?"

He poured boiled water into cups. "Of course I don't mean it, I was trying to lighten the mood, that's all. Murder isn't something I'd choose to talk about."

Oh, but it was. If only there was someone out there to talk about it to. Someone he could trust and share experiences with.

"I'll agree with that," Irena said. "Anyway, this has reminded me to ring Rachel."

Irena and Blowsy spoke to one another frequently on the telephone, sometimes in whispers. Once, Irena even left the room to sit on the stairs.

John had an idea his time with her might well be up soon if he didn't sort himself out.

John cleared up the shards of cup from the hob, wrapping them in some kitchen roll and putting them in the bin. He hated living alone, lost by himself, no Irena as his rudder. Without knowing it, she'd steered his devil away for years, but shit had hit the fan, and John had ended up in the cottage, by himself, still working at that fucking hospital.

He'd be back there tomorrow, the weekend over, but maybe he'd have to ring in sick with a stomach bug or something so he could get hold of his new Francesca then sleep late in the morning.

He needed her legs to grow out of the soil.

It was amazing, really, how he'd wandered through life doing what he wanted, not getting caught. He'd piled on more weight, his comfort-eating bouts longer now, doing nothing to give him that feeling he needed—where he belonged somewhere, with someone. Even the girls hadn't given it to him. Selfish bitches, just like Mum.

He walked to the fridge and opened it. Grabbed a two-pack of cream slices. Sat at the table and licked off the icing, then stuffed half a slice in his mouth.

It beat the bread and jam he'd eaten as a kid.

CHAPTER TWENTY

Karly lounged about on the grass in the park. She'd been here for ages, just dossing, not wanting to see anyone. Her chat with Tom16 played over and over in her head, and she needed some space to work it out. What should she do? Ignoring it had ever happened was an option, but what if he got hold her of again? She'd have to tell the police then.

Mum had tried ringing, but Karly had ignored it. Then she'd texted, and Karly had to deal with it. A copper was at her house, wanting to know where she was. Mum asked whether Karly had been speaking to anyone online and said the policeman wanted to speak to her when she got home.

She didn't want to go home now.

Her phone blipped. Karly's belly went over so hard it hurt. What if it was him? It was the Messenger tone, so it was likely. Shit.

She accessed the app, relived it was Sasha getting hold of her.

Sasha: OMG, THE POLICE HAVE BEEN ROUND.

Karly: WHAT? WHY?

Sasha: BECAUSE OF TANYA THIS TIME.

Karly's stomach rolled over again, more painful this time. What was going on? She felt sick and came over all cold. A quick glance around—for all she knew, someone could be watching her. Tom16 could be that weird bloke. God, she was getting herself in a right old state.

Karly: WHAT ABOUT HER?

Sasha: SHE'S DEAD! LIKE CATHERINE.

Karly moved over onto her back, her heart hammering, and stared at the sky. Dead? Tanya? Why would the police have gone to Sasha's about it?

Karly: HOW COME THEY WERE AT YOURS?

Sasha: BECAUSE TANYA TOLD HER MUM AND DAD SHE WAS STAYING AT MINE FOR A WEEK, BUT SHE DIDN'T, AND SHE WAS FOUND DEAD THIS MORNING.

Karly: OMFG.

Sasha: I KNOW, AND GET THIS. TANYA MET SOME KID CALLED SIMON ONLINE. A MUTUAL FRIEND, APPARENTLY, SAME AS WITH CATHERINE AND ELSA.

Karly bolted upright, her pulse thudding so hard in her neck it was sore.

Karly: WHAT MUTUAL FRIEND? AND ELSA? WHAT DO YOU MEAN?

Sasha: THAT'S THE THING. NO ONE KNOWS WHO HE IS—BUT THEY THINK HE'S THE ONE WHO KILLED CATHERINE. HE FOLLOWED ELSA YESTERDAY. I SAW HIM.

Karly: THIS IS SO SCARY.

Sasha: I KNOW. THEY TOOK MY PHONE BECAUSE TANYA HAS MESSAGED ME. MUM RECKONS IT WAS REALLY THE MAN WHO TOOK HER, PRETENDING TO BE HER. I FEEL SICK.

You feel sick? What about me?

Karly sent love hearts as a response. She needed time to think about this. The mutual friend part was bothering her. Was Tom16 the same man? *Should* she tell the police?

She checked her phone, then remembered she'd deleted the conversation with him. She tried to bring his name up to write him another message, didn't even know why, but he wasn't there. Had he blocked her? Was she safe now? Or did he really know who she was—like, had he been watching her on Facebook before he'd got hold of her and knew where she lived?

Karly: I DON'T KNOW WHAT TO SAY.

Sasha: KNOW WHAT YOU MEAN. THERE'S A BLOKE OUT THERE KILLING OUR MATES. WHAT IF WE'RE NEXT?

Karly heaved then vomited on the grass. She'd have to go home, no doubt about it.

She wiped her mouth with the back of her hand, gagging at the taste sitting on her tongue. It was a struggle to get up, all the strength gone out of her, but she managed to walk across the grass towards the play area. A little girl was on a swing, going high, her hair flying, and Karly wished she was that age again. No worries, nothing to care about but when dinner was on the table and whether there'd be sweets after. She had the urge for some Smarties and rushed now, eager to be at her house. Funny, when not two minutes ago, it was the last place she wanted to be.

She'd speak to the police, tell them everything, although it wasn't much, not really. But it might help, and anyway, she hadn't said anything she wouldn't want Mum to see.

Mind made up, she ran, the little girl's squeal of delight chasing after her.

CHAPTER TWENTY-ONE

After doing what he had to for the start of the plan, John watched her from afar. She played on the swings, hair flying back in the breeze, eyes closed against the sun. He'd seen her here a few times when he'd come to find out her patterns and had learnt all he needed to know.

He'd first approached her last week, laying down the groundwork, throwing trust over her by being kind, telling her his name, because he wanted her to call him by it, and he could pretend it was Francesca. He'd gone on a swing beside her, and she'd laughed, and all the while, Catherine and Tanya had been in the cellar.

Another girl appeared, coming from the right. She seemed familiar, the sweep of her hair, the shape of her profile. John had seen it on Facebook.

Karly. What the hell was *she* doing here?

He held his breath until she'd run off, out of the park, seemingly intent on leaving.

But what if she came back?

It doesn't matter. She has no idea what you really look like.

That was true. He hadn't even got to the stage as Tom16 to send her any fake pictures. He was safe. It would be all right.

He stepped out of the bushes.

"Hey, John," the little girl said. "You coming for a swing again?"

"Yep!"

He checked his watch, and, like clockwork, the ice-cream van came by, chime jangling, parking by the railings. She looked over at it longingly.

"You want one?" he asked.

She smiled, gaps in her teeth, and then dragged her shoes on the tarmac to stop the swing's motion. "Yeah."

"Come on then."

The van had a straggle of customers. This was where he should have left it. The fact that people had seen him should have been sufficient warning. But no, unstoppable John pushed on, the urge to complete his cycle too strong to ignore.

"What're you having?" he asked.

"A cone with a Flake, please." She danced from foot to foot, excited, happy, carefree. Her hair pranced with her, blonde pigtails bouncing.

He turned to smile at her. "Same for me then."

The van owner leant over, palms down on his little counter, staring at John. He looked Greek, his wide arms strong. "What do you want?"

John ordered, then, taking the cornets, said, "Shall we walk round the outside of the park while we eat them?"

She didn't seem at all worried. "Yeah, cos by the time we're back, my mum'll be here for me. I told my mum all about you. She said you sounded nice, and she wished she could swing with me, too, but she's too busy working since my dad left."

John didn't want to hear anything about her home life, but the fact she'd told her mum gave him a frisson of fear. He didn't want to get caught, wanted to end this his own way.

"Did she?" John said. "Maybe we could get her on a swing when she comes to pick you up, eh?"

"Nah, can't do that, cos she told me not to let you near me again. Said you could be one of them nasty men, so if she sees you at the park again, she'll call the police."

Shit. "Well, your mum's right." There were strains of George's and Harriet's conversation going on here. "Tell you what, we'll carry on walking round, and then once we've got back to the park, I'll get off home so you won't get into trouble, yes?"

"Yeah, okay."

It was up ahead. The place where he'd put something. He switched sides so he saw it first. "Oh. Oh, what a shame."

"What?"

"There. Down there. Will you look at that? How sad." He went down on his haunches to get closer to it, shaking his head.

"Aww, is it all right, John?"

"I don't know. Let's see, shall we?" He knelt, checking for signs of life in the kitten.

"Is it dead?"

"I'm afraid it is, Clare."

"Should we leave it there?" She seemed worried. Her eyes watered, and her unfinished cone dropped onto the grass.

"No. That wouldn't be nice. Some other animal may come and eat it later. A badger or fox or something. Best if we bury it really." Picking up the cat, he walked along a little way.

Clare followed with her head down.

"Do you want to wait here while I find somewhere to put it?" he asked.

The black-and-white fur was warm, but it was only the heat from his hands giving the illusion of life.

"No, I'll come."

He veered off to a clump of trees where there was a small dip in the ground. "We'll put him in here, shall we?"

"Have we got time? I mean, before my mum comes?"

"Plenty of time. We can collect some small rocks and stones to cover him with. Not much else we can do as we don't have a spade."

"Will he be all right here, though, with just them stones?"

"Oh, I should think so." He placed the kitten in the hollow and turned to her. "Unless you can get out later on. You could bring a spade and cover him over."

She thought for a moment. "I can come back later, but we ent got a spade. Not got a garden neither."

"Well, that's okay. I have a spade that should do the trick. What time could you make it back here?" He put some stones, twigs, and leaves on the furry body.

"About seven. I'm allowed out until eight cos we only live over there. I could get back home in time, couldn't I?" She helped collect some debris.

"Okay then. I'll meet you back here at seven. We'll bury the poor chap, and then you can get off home. How's that sound?"

"Great!" She looked down at the pile of rubble.

"Well, then, you've got ten minutes to get yourself back on that swing over there before your mum comes."

"Okay, John." She turned, running, shouting back, "See you later then?"

"See you later, Clare."

Time passed, and Dad was getting on in years, his back a little stooped, his hair thinning, pure white now. Lively enough, though. John didn't think he had reason to worry, but still, it took him by surprise. How had he not noticed the years passing, aging Dad's skin, his eyelids drooping, his mouth turning down slightly?

John watched him on the bank, holding his fishing rod.

"Everything okay, son?" Dad kept his attention firmly on the water, probably waiting for any sign that a fish was close.

"Fine, Dad, fine. Edward's enjoying work now, and college, you know..."

"Good lad. He'll learn all he needs to know if he sticks at it. Plumbing may not be the most glamorous of apprenticeships, but there'll always be blocked drains. He'd do well to remember that. Always be a job in plumbing. Like your electrician, they're always needed. Get away with charging the earth, too, on those callouts they do."

"He knows all that, Dad." John sat next to him and fiddled with a blade of grass.

"He's a good lad, is our Edward."

"He is."

That was the last conversation they ever shared. That night, after John had walked away, going home to his family, Dad had climbed into bed and died in his sleep.

Dad's passing didn't hit John properly for a while. The part of his brain that processed hurt and sadness shut down, or maybe he didn't want to believe his hero was gone.

It wasn't until Irena and John cleared out the cottage that the grief slammed into him. Seeing things from his childhood that Dad had kept, things John had forgotten about, had him choking on tears.

Crouched in a ball on the floor, he sobbed, clutching the brass starling. Irena knelt next to him with her hand on his back, unable to soothe the pain. He didn't care about anything much after that. Not Edward or Irena, his job, or himself. Depression consumed him, so overwhelming he sometimes didn't realise a whole week had passed.

His marriage suffered. He became moody after Edward moved out to live with friends in a flat, going to college once a week and work the rest. John found it hard to believe seventeen years had gone by since his birth. Where had the time gone?

Irena stayed with Blowsy in London most weekends, her way of escaping John's bad temper and complete silences. He'd constructed an impenetrable brick wall. They'd drifted apart, and he didn't give a toss, too consumed with grief.

She rang him one Sunday afternoon to say she wasn't coming back, except to pick up some clothes and bits and pieces, moving to London near Blowsy.

He'd always hated Blowsy, but at that moment, he despised her, blamed her for luring his wife away, encouraging her to leave him during those long phone calls. He should have put a stop to it, to their friendship, and talked to Irena more.

"You've changed," she said. "You're not the same person I married." She sounded distant, hard and cold.

His world caved in. "We all change as we age, you know that. Come on. I'll stop being so moody; I'll try to be how I was. We can't just let this thing go. Please, love. Please."

But she didn't want to make it work.

The cottage was still empty, Dad having bought it from Reg many years ago, leaving it to John, so he moved there, taking what furniture would fit, using the time to heal himself within the familiar confines of those walls.

He never again visited the house he'd shared with Irena and Edward. Didn't see Irena for many years, until Edward got married. She was a new person, alien, a stranger. Re-married to a nice-looking man who appeared to worship her.

Edward visited John once a month, and they fished in the stream like Dad and John used to. It brought back painful memories, but it also helped to ease some of the ache of grief. Edward had become distant. Perhaps he, too, had noticed the change in John, who'd been too preoccupied in teaching people a lesson to see the crumbling of his family.

Still, John clung to the times Edward came to see him, their stilted conversations. It must have been hard on the lad to not mention his mum—he saw her quite often; she was a big part of his life. What a mess it had all become. John felt as lonely as the boy he used to be.

Dad and Irena were gone, and he rarely saw his son.

Perhaps he'd got what he deserved.

John had nightmares.

Out of breath, lungs bursting, he ran from an alley towards the woods, knowing it was a dream but unable to wake up.

Harriet was there, dead on the ground. He looked down at her. Leaves, curled from being brittle and dry, intertwined in her pigtails, the two tresses splayed out, muddied and unkempt. Fingers curved towards her palms, her nails broken and filled with dirt. Pink coat concertinaed to the waist.

Legs, bare.

Shoes, lost.

Snapshot images indelible on his brain, the spool of negatives stored.

Did her eyelashes flicker, or was it merely the breeze brushing over pale cheeks, her lips tinged blue?

Grey. She was grey.

Light filtered through the trees as the early sun rose.

Visions of his past deeds mixed together to make one fresh, novel experience. It gave John a new burst of energy, a reason to continue. There were girls out there who needed his form of teaching. Irena might be gone, Edward a rare visitor, but John still had things to do.

The lethargy was gone.
He was ready to begin again.

CHAPTER TWENTY-TWO

Karly burst into the house, lungs aching from her mad pelt home. As she'd reached the edge of the park, she'd got a horrible feeling—that someone was watching her. Too afraid to turn back and check, at the same time telling herself she was imagining things, what with Catherine and Tanya being taken by that bloody man, she'd kept on going, her mission to get to her house eventually eclipsing all else.

"I'm back, Mum," she called, out of breath, relieved to finally be behind closed doors. She walked into the kitchen and leant on the worktop, forearms sticking to the Formica she was that sweaty.

"Where have you been?" Mum stirred gravy in a saucepan.

Dad liked it done the old-fashioned way, none of that 'granules in water bollocks'. Roast lamb had been cut up, now piled high on a plate by the kettle, and roast potatoes sat in an oval Pyrex dish, all crispy and brown on the edges.

Karly's stomach panged from hunger. "Just at the park."

"I was about to ask you to get your arse home before you turned up. Late roast today, what with Dad doing a shift at work. He'll be here in a minute, so if there's anything you need to tell me, do it now. The police wouldn't be here for no reason." She bent and whipped some Yorkshires out of the oven, fluffy and light.

Karly wiped sweat off her forehead and walked to the doorway so she could keep an eye out for Dad. "I lied to you. There was this kid called Tom16. Said he knew me from Jessica's party. I don't remember him, but he said he recognised me."

Mum turned to look at Karly, her face pale, pausing in taking off the oven gloves. "W-what?"

"I told him I couldn't talk to him anymore." That was true. "After…after Catherine…"

"What did he talk about?" Mum grabbed a colander out of a cupboard so she could drain the veg that boiled on the hob.

Despite the news Karly had revealed, Mum still had to get the dinner sorted for as soon as Dad walked in. Things wouldn't be pretty if she didn't.

"Nothing nasty. Just chat." Karly glanced at the front door. No Dad-shaped figure through the glass.

"Show me your phone." Mum held her hand out. "Quickly!"

Karly passed it over, fumbling it in her rush. "The conversation isn't there. I deleted it, and he's blocked me."

Mum scrolled through Messenger anyway. "You didn't tell him where you live, did you? Arrange to meet, anything like that?"

"No!"

"Thank God. You'll need to tell the police all this. They want to know as soon as you're home, but we'll get dinner out of the way first else Dad'll get funny." She handed the phone back.

"He's going to go spare." Karly's stomach knotted.

Dad didn't like the police, and he certainly didn't like anyone knowing their business. If they did, they'd know he hit Mum on the regular and called Karly a little cow half the time. No wonder she'd decided to cut off chatting with Tom16. If Dad found out, he'd have a right old go at her. And if he found out she'd been to Jessica's party, he'd probably lump Mum one. He'd been working nights that weekend, and Mum had covered for Karly, lying by omission, letting her go so long as she was back before Dad got home.

"He's not going to know," Mum said. "Me and you, we're going to go round Sally's. She's having a candle party."

"Is she?"

"No, but he's not to know that, is he. We'll meet the police somewhere. Sally will make out we were at hers if he asks her."

Which he might well do. He didn't like Mum doing anything for herself and often tried to catch her out.

"Sasha got hold of me," Karly said. "Tanya was taken as well. She's dead." Tears stung her eyes.

"Fucking hell, that's awful." Mum stilled, cocking her head, alarm drenching her features. "He's back."

Both of them knew the rumble of his car off by heart.

"Act normal." Mum took three plates out and got on with dishing up.

Karly laid the table, her nerves in tatters.

Please let Dad be in a good mood, please let Dad be in a good mood...

CHAPTER TWENTY-THREE

Bethany stood on David Flemmish's path, hoping he'd open up and she'd see Hoody standing in front of her, the beard in place, the glasses, the wide girth, the short height. The man who peeled the door back, though, was clean-shaven and had a blond-grey mane sitting on top of his thin head, his shiny pink scalp visible through the sparse strands. His slender body didn't match that of Hoody either, so she was shit out of luck here. Even she didn't believe Hoody had bought a fat suit and put it on every time he went out to meet a teenager, although strange things like that did happen.

"Ah, hello, sir." She held up her ID, unsure how to proceed now it was obvious he wasn't who they were after. "DI Bethany Smith and DS Mike Wilkins. We're just here for a quick chat."

"What about?" He ran a hand through his hair, and it got caught on his wedding ring, a dull silver affair with years' worth of fine scratches on it. Maybe he couldn't bear to take it off, despite his widower status. Just because your spouse was dead, didn't mean you weren't still married, in your head and heart, at least.

She found a subject she could use as a reason for being there. "I see you're pretty isolated out here. Do you get much activity? Cars and the like? A grey Fiesta? Maybe someone walking to town on the main road?" *A man, overweight, on his way to meet young girls, the fucking bastard.*

He shook his head, detangling his hair, rubbing his whiskery chin. "I'm not much good for anything at the moment. My wife died..." He cleared his throat. "Two months ago. Life isn't the same and..." His eyes watered.

Bethany didn't know how she'd manage if she didn't have work to take her mind off personal things. She'd probably think about her late husband, Vinny, and all they could have achieved had he lived, driving herself mad with what-ifs. This man here had fully succumbed to grief. Now she took the time to really look at him, not just to see if he had Hoody's characteristics, it was clear he had no energy, no zest for anything. Dark shadows camped out beneath his eyes, and sallow, wrinkled skin hung off his face as if it were melting. Maybe he'd been a bigger person when his wife had been alive and the weight had fallen off him since.

Another thing Bethany related to. She'd been a size sixteen at one point. Now? Getting a bit skinny, same as Mr Flemmish. Cooking for one seemed a waste of time.

"Okay, sorry to have troubled you." She smiled and turned away, knowing it wasn't him they were after. Too slim, too tall, too tired to kidnap girls and murder them.

In the car, she said to Mike, "Not our bloke."

"Definitely not. Let's move on to Keagan's place."

She drove away, thinking about her earlier meeting with Kribbs, who'd been raging at another teenager being found dead. He'd said he wasn't fully up to date with it all because he'd been called out to a meeting with some bigwig or other, then went on to have lunch with him. He'd come back to the station because of the current state of affairs—he also worked weekends if a big case was ongoing so he could help the team out, not that Bethany ever asked him to. When she'd walked into his office, he had red cheeks from a whiskey or two and a blob of something on his light-grey tie. Probably custard from the sticky toffee puddings he was so partial to, something his girlfriend made him once or twice a week, apparently.

She'd updated him, and he'd suggested a press conference, one that focused on telling girls not to speak to strangers online. He'd be using the CCTV still of Hoody, asking members of the public to phone in if they'd seen him yesterday outside Lloyds. A team of officers was being set up to handle any calls. Bethany was glad she didn't have to deal with that. Cranks didn't get her in the best of moods. Those who wasted police time for a laugh, making out they'd seen or heard something, really were the worst.

Bloody prats.

Five minutes later, they stood outside a cottage. No vehicle in the drive, but then she wasn't expecting one, seeing as there wasn't a car registered in Keagan's name.

Doesn't mean he hasn't got one, though.

She scanned the drive for dirty tyre marks or oil spills. Nothing.

The garden was basic, just grass, and with no answer to her knock on the door, she wandered down the side of the property. Maybe he was out the back. The trickle of water reached her, and she peered down the end of the rear garden. A stream, a line of trees and hedges as a border on the farthest bank, and beyond that, fields, one of the estates in the distance. She scanned her brain and came up with the Heights, where many a scragend lived.

She moved to the house and stared through the glass in the door. A kitchen, the internal door closed. On the floor, a muddy pair of trainers. Dark mud. Like compost.

Her knees weakened a tad.

"Mike?" she called out, moving back a bit to inspect the patio. Nothing out of the ordinary that was immediately visible.

Mike appeared around the corner. "Yep?"

"Look in there on the floor." She pointed at the cottage, her mouth dry, an adrenaline rush coming on. "By the door."

He moved over and stared in, shielding his eyes with his hand. "Oh."

"You thinking what I'm thinking?"

He made a 'don't know' face. "It could be compost, certainly looks like it." He inspected the area. "Hang on, there are pots here with flowers in them." He walked to a row of terracotta ones bursting with various-coloured petals. "Some has been spilt." He crouched and indicated the space between two patio slabs. "Maybe he dropped the bag, trod in the compost."

"Okay. Perhaps I'm just hoping too hard." Her whole body seemed to sink.

"Maybe, but it won't hurt to come back and see if that's the case. You know, ask him if he trod in the mess."

She nodded. "Right, nothing for it but to go to the station, see what the press conference has thrown up, if it's even gone out yet."

"We could do with eating."

"Fair point." She had another nose inside the property. "It's so dated. See the state of those cupboards? They're from the eighties, I'd bet, and it's all a bit grubby."

"Maybe he hasn't got the money to do it up."

"Hmm. He's a hospital porter. Divorced." She took her phone out and rang Rob. "Hi, can you do a check on John Keagan's cottage for me? How long he's lived here, who owned it before he did, whether it's even owned by him or rented. We're off to get some food, so if you ring back, Mike might have to answer if I'm driving."

"Yep."

She drove them towards town, keeping an eye out for a man walking along the roadside. No one. Perhaps he'd gone to his son's for the day. Some families still got together on a Sunday, didn't they, although she'd say that was a dying art now.

On the retail park, she avoided looking over at Tesco and parked up outside Burger King, sodding the calories a Whopper and chilli cheese bites would add to her waistline. She could do with adding a few extra pounds anyway, so what the hell. Inside, they ordered then sat at a table in the corner.

Mike opened his cheeseburger, stopping when his phone tinkled. He glanced at the screen. "Karly's home. She has something to tell us. Her mum wants to meet us outside the house, as in, completely away from it." He raised his eyebrows.

"Maybe she doesn't want the police at her door twice in one day." Bethany shrugged and peeled back the wrapping on her Whopper. The scent of it wafted up, and her mouth watered. Dirty food, but so bloody good. It didn't hurt to indulge once in a while. "Some people are funny about that, aren't they. Makes them look bad with a couple of suits on the step. Tell her to come here if she's that bothered."

Mike replied to the text, then slid his phone in his pocket. They ate in silence for a while, Bethany gazing through the window at shoppers coming out of the big, two-storey Next opposite. Others wandered from M&S as if the cost of their shopping had given them a bit of a shock.

Should have gone to Aldi.

At the point Bethany popped the last cheese bite in her mouth, which burned from the chilli, a mint-green Renault parked directly in front of the window, two people inside.

"That's them." Mike grabbed a napkin and wiped tomato sauce off his fingers.

Together, they cleared the table sharpish, and Mike dumped it all in the bin while Bethany slid the tray on one of those holder thingies. He intercepted Mrs Young and Karly at the door and guided them over to Bethany, chatting away.

"I'll just get some drinks," he said and walked off.

Bethany held a hand out to the woman, conscious of them being sticky from her food. "DI Bethany Smith." And to Karly, "You're not in any trouble, so please don't worry."

The poor girl was shaking and pale. She settled beside her mother, hugging her arm.

"Sorry about having to meet here," Mrs Young said. "We don't want my husband to know about any of this."

Bethany didn't warn them he might have to be told if Karly *was* involved. She may well be needed in court, albeit via video link if she was too afraid of whoever the accused was. "That's fine. We'd stopped for dinner anyway."

Mike returned and placed a milkshake in front of Karly, a coffee for her mum.

"What's your first name?" Bethany asked the mother. "I don't want to keep calling you Mrs Young."

"Rosie."

"Okay, Rosie." Bethany went on to tell them about Tanya.

Neither of them appeared shocked by the news.

"Sasha told me," Karly said, "and I told Mum."

"Tell them what you said about that Tom kid," Rosie prompted. "There's something not right about it."

The short story came out, how Tom16 had got chatting to Karly, how they'd supposedly been to the same party, but Karly hadn't really believed him. She explained she'd got a funny feeling after finding out Catherine was dead so had called off the chat, telling him she couldn't speak to him anymore, then deleted the messages. Whatever, it didn't matter to Bethany. What did was Tom16 was undoubtedly Jolly19, ManBabe19, and that Simon bloke. All these girls were friends. He must have studied their social media, spotted who spoke to who, and garnered they were a group. He was risking them spilling their secrets to one another, or maybe he'd told them not to tell anyone and waited to see if they did. To see if he could trust them. To play with them.

She didn't know, but it was clear Karly and Rosie were jittery about being here. Why?

"How come you're so ill at ease with us?" Bethany asked.

Rosie coughed. Blushed. "Oh, um, it's just that we're meant to be at a candle party."

"What, and you're anxious to get off there?"

"No. Yes. I mean…" Rosie fidgeted.

"Is everything okay?" Bethany raised her eyebrows.

"Yes." Rosie nodded. "It's great, isn't it, Karly." She nudged her daughter.

Karly jumped. "Oh. Yes. Fine."

What was going on here? The tension was too thick for words. Rosie had mentioned not wanting her husband to know about this conversation. How come? Was he some kind of controlling bully? Would he go mad if he knew his young daughter had been on the verge of being lured in by a paedophile?

"Are you sure?" Bethany directed that at Karly.

The girl shrugged. "It's just Dad. He gets funny."

Bethany knew what wasn't being said. She took cards from her inside pocket and slid one each to Rosie and Karly. "If you need me, at any time, ring."

Mother and daughter looked at each other, and Bethany imagined all the words they weren't saying floating between them: *Should we tell her? What if he finds out? Will he hit you if he knows?*

Rosie broke the stare first. "Thanks. But there's nothing wrong. It's just easier if this stays between us, that's all." She stood.

"But when there *is* something wrong, when it's more than usual, you know where I am," Bethany said.

Rosie nodded, frowning, as if she thought: *How does she know?*

Years of spotting the signs, Bethany silently replied.

"We'll be going now." Rosie gave a tight smile. Forced. Fake.

"Take care." Bethany waited until they'd left, then, "Classic abused wife behaviour, or is it just me?"

"I clocked it as well."

"I hope we're wrong."

"Me, too, but a nose at the dad's file won't hurt, will it, if he even has one."

They were on the same page. It was rare they weren't.

"Right, that mess in Keagan's house is still bothering me." She pushed up from the table.

"We'll nip back there now. I need the loo first, though."

She did her business, washing her hands thoroughly to get rid of the Whopper smell. Mike was coming out of the men's at the same time she exited, so they wandered out and got in the car. She drove off, praying Keagan was in this time.

His place was still empty, although she could swear one of the dirty trainers had been moved. Or that could be her wishful thinking.

But what if it isn't?

She shrugged and drove them back to the station, going straight to the front desk to speak with Rob. "Did you manage to get that information I asked for?"

He slapped his forehead. "Bugger, I got sidetracked. I had two blokes brought in. Affray, sexual assault. Causing hassle in The Lamb Shank. Rita's in as well."

"Rita? The barmaid?"

Rob nodded. "Walloped one of the men round the head by all accounts. With a bottle of Becks."

"That's a shock. She's usually so happy."

Rob leant forward and said quietly, "He actually pinched her nipple, hence the sexual assault charge."

"Poor cow. Is she all right?"

"You know Rita. She'll bounce back. Anyway, here's the info you wanted." He drew a piece of paper towards him. "The cottage belongs to John Keagan outright. Previous owner was his father, Henry. Before that, it was owned by a Reginald

Button, who rented it out to Keagan's dad for a few years."

"Right, so no mortgage to fork out for," she muttered to herself. Probably how he could afford to live there on a porter's salary. "Thanks. Has Keagan got any previous?"

"I'd have told you that when I sent the email earlier. He's done nothing, but he was spoken to regarding a murder of a lady in Devon—a Rebecca White; Keagan was on holiday at the time—the suicide of a man named George Phelps at the same caravan site, plus an incident where a girl went missing, subsequently found strangled in the bushes."

Bethany's body flushed with cold. "What?"

"He was cleared of any involvement, just spoken to as a matter of course."

"How old was the dead girl?"

Rob inspected his notes. "Five. It's all on there. Dates and everything."

Bethany took the paper and scanned it. "Bloody hell, this is a can of worms. Could be innocent, might not be." She explained about the compost and the trainers. "There may be something in that."

Rob nodded. "Follow it up. If you don't, you might live to regret it."

She agreed.

Another hour of work, then she'd send everyone home. She'd take Mike with her back to Keagan's, and, if he still wasn't in, she'd drop Mike at his place. It had been a long weekend, and she was in dire need of a soak in the bath. After that, she'd sit down and piece everything together, point by point. You never knew, she might find something they could go on, especially now Keagan had the shadows of murder in his past.

CHAPTER TWENTY-FOUR

A while before Clare arrived, John traipsed through the park with his backpack, shovel, and rope. Three lads were in the play area, but he didn't reckon any of them took any notice of him. In the copse, he uncovered the kitten and dug a similar hole farther back in a more secluded place. And then he waited at the original burial spot for her.

Glancing at his watch, he grew nervous. It was five past seven, and she hadn't shown up yet. She had to come, couldn't let him down now he'd psyched himself up, working out how it was to be done, what he'd need to carry it all out. To have Francesca at last.

Small footsteps shuffled in the grass. She emerged through the bushes, head down, walking towards him.

"Hey, Clare," he whispered.

She jumped, as if she hadn't really expected him to be there. "I'm a bit late cos I had to help me mum with the washing up."

He wondered if the mother had called out to Clare to be careful while she was at the park. Whether she'd hugged and kissed her when she'd left or if she was so relieved to get some peace and quiet that she'd slumped down on her chair with a vodka and tonic and a cigarette, relishing the stillness around her, the very air of home soothing away the day.

"That's all right, Clare, don't you worry. Now then, let's get this kitten buried, eh?"

She looked down at the ground, confusion flitting across her pixie features, eyes narrowing as she tried to work out what was different. Realisation dawned, and her eyes sprang wide. "Where's he gone?" She stared up at him.

"Well, I've had to move him, see. While we were weren't here, an animal had been sniffing about.

Some of the stones were moved. I thought it'd be best to bury him properly. What do you reckon?"

She nodded, glancing round the clearing, shoulders hunched.

Something created a rustle in the undergrowth.

"What was that?" she asked.

"Probably that nasty little animal coming back. Come on, the sooner we bury this kitty the better. This way, just over here."

She followed. Funny how to her mind the unseen noisemaker held more of a threat than him. The simplicity of an immature mind. He thought about the differences between her and him as a child. He couldn't remember ever feeling safe unless he was with Dad, and even then, if Mum was in one of her moods, John wasn't secure. Based on that, he'd built the childhood for Edward that John had wanted, the one he'd deserved but hadn't got. He'd watched his son live without fear, pretending it was himself who existed in that carefree bubble.

Clare? Although her mother let her out at a young age by herself, the child was loved, that much was clear. Otherwise, why would her mother have said she'd call the police on John if he bothered her daughter again?

Angry at his own mother, nothing new there, he led Clare to a tree where the boughs grew low enough for him to reach up and touch when he'd tied the rope there earlier. He'd wound it around the sturdy branch so it didn't dangle and catch her attention. His bag leant against the trunk, the zip open for easy access.

"Here, look. I started with my shovel before you came. Made quite a deep hole for the kitten, see?" He was glad his voice had come out steady and with none of the pissed-off feelings he experienced tinging it.

The hole was around three feet. Clare peered down into it. Ensconced as they were within the wooded area, it really had worked out well. No one would see them here.

"Nothing will get him in there, will it?" she asked, clearly worried. "They'd have to dig for a long time to reach him, wouldn't they?" Did her mind play out that scenario, a fox coming along and scrabbling at the earth to get to the dead kitten beneath? Did she see it being eaten, ripped apart, fur flying?

"They would, so don't you worry. Once we've covered him up and stamped down the earth, he'll be safe."

While on the one hand he wanted her afraid, going through some of the upset he had as a little boy, he needed her calm. Otherwise, things wouldn't go to plan.

He moved closer to the tree, reached out for his shovel, and walked behind her. "Shall we put him in the hole then?"

"Okay." She picked up the kitten, seemingly all right with the fact that it was dead, and knelt beside the hole.

She didn't have ankle socks on but long ones that came to just below the knees.

Anger bit John. Why couldn't she be like Francesca? Why did everything in his life have to go wrong? His devil whispered that John had made it go wrong, thirteen years after marrying Irena, and John had to hold back a retort. It'd faze Clare if he spoke to his beast in the kind of voice he'd have to use. She knew him as soft-spoken, the man who went on the swings with her, not some brute.

"I can't reach to put him in, so I'll have to drop him," she said.

"I'm sure that'll be fine." He checked his watch. She had forty-three minutes left before she had to be home.

The animal's body hit the bottom of the grave, and he dug his shovel into the mound of earth next to it, lifting a good wedge of it and scattering some over the furry corpse. Clare helped by taking handfuls of and throwing it into the hole. She'd get dirt under her nails, just like Catherine and Tanya.

Life's idiosyncrasies were beautiful.

While she was busy, he rested the shovel on the trunk and went behind her. Stared at the back of her head. Itched to cave it in.

She threw in one more handful. "You gonna help me, John?" She gazed up at him over her shoulder.

The devil took over him, that thing inside him growing, and once again... He. Did. Not. Care. Francesca needed to learn she couldn't spurn him.

She needed to learn if she did that, she'd have to die.

He took the large bottle of water from his bag, doused the shovel, then threw it down, in with the kitten. He kicked the soil back into the hole, burying that wretched cat for good. Smoothed the ground with the side of his trainer. He reckoned he'd erased all of his footprints, all evidence that he was ever there.

He made his way out of the clearing, walking across the park—those three kids were gone—opening the small gate farthest from Clare's eternal swing, where she hung from a noose attached to the tree branch. Francesca had left him hanging for years, so this was only fitting. He emerged onto the path, scuffing his feet to remove the mud from the treads. He might have appeared a normal man, backpack bouncing, or could have seemed strange.

A little 'off'.

At the cottage, he sat and wondered whether doing what he'd done to Clare/Francesca would be his downfall. People didn't like kids being killed, did they, especially the small ones. Too late now, though, it was done. She'd learnt her lesson: Don't piss John off.

He made a decision. Time to shave the beard off. He'd finished his plans, so what was the point in keeping it as a disguise? He could always grow it again if he decided to let his devil push him into meeting more girls.

The electric razor dealt with it in no time, and he stared at himself in the bathroom mirror while smoothing on some of that after-a-shave stuff. Edward had bought it for him last Christmas along with some socks. Typical 'for your dad' presents. Still, John had been grateful to get anything at all.

A knock at the door startled him, but he told himself not to be so silly. It would probably be Edward—John's thoughts of him must have conjured the lad up. He usually nipped in once a month, although the next visit wasn't meant to be for a fortnight. That was why John had fitted his plans in between. Why was his son here then?

John walked to the front door, wiping the sheen of sweat off his forehead that had decided to sprout. He was still on a high from offing Francesca, so the chat with Edward would undoubtedly be a good one. Lots of bants, as the kids liked to say these days.

He swung the door open. A man and a woman stood there, him all officious and stern, her a skinny waif with hard edges to her face, as if she'd lived a shit life. Or maybe she'd been working too hard lately and needed a break. They were probably those church people, seeing as it was Sunday. Maybe the roof needed fixing—wasn't that always the way? Every church on the country seemed to have broken tiles. What was that all about?

She held up some identification, and John's legs almost went out from under him.

"DI Bethany Smith and DS Mike Wilkins," she said.

She was a bit serious for his liking. Still, he'd need to act like he had at the campsite when he'd been questioned there. Calm, innocent.

"Yes?" He frowned, as if he had no idea why they might be standing on his doorstep. Best to do that, wasn't it.

"We're talking to everyone who owns a Ford Fiesta." She pointed to Dad's on the drive.

Fuck. They had to be investigating him being caught on CCTV. He'd been so careful an' all, avoiding cameras, but not careful enough. The car was still registered to Dad but at the Churchill Road address. He never did bother changing the details.

"Particularly the old-style ones," she said.

Pushing her point. He wasn't stupid, he'd seen enough TV to know how these coppers worked. A drop of a hint here, a slip of a well-worded sentence there, thinking they were clever and criminals didn't know what they were up to. Well, he'd show her.

"That's my dad's," he said.

"I see. Can we have a word with him? Is he in?" She had the type of expression that said she was lying, that she knew Dad was dead.

That she knew all about John and his plans.

Or was that his imagination?

"He died years ago," John said. "I don't use the car. Prefer to walk."

She eyed him funny, like if he walked, he wouldn't weigh as much as he did. Cheeky cow.

"Right, so if you don't use it, why wasn't it on the drive last time we were here?"

Last time? He hadn't heard anyone knocking. Had they come when he'd been at the park? "Well, I move it every so often, but only round the back. You know, so the engine doesn't seize up."

"It wasn't parked there when we looked."

They'd been poking about? Shit.

"Are you insured to drive it?" she asked, all smug.

He'd love to drag her to the stream, shove her face beneath the water, and drown the bitch. Slice off her cheeks like Bouncy Woman. "I don't have any tax or insurance. No need when I'm not using it on the roads."

"So it'll have been registered as off the road then?"

She was getting on his nerves.

"I don't know. It's just there, on the drive."

"We noticed the number plate is dirty, which matches one we're interested in for a current case."

"Maybe someone nicked it when I was out." He shrugged. "Brought it back afterwards."

"That sounds very generous of a car thief, don't you think? To which address is the car registered?"

"Churchill Road."

"Right, is that where your dad—" She paused at the sound of her phone bleeping. "Excuse me one moment."

If John's heart didn't stop skittering, he'd have a problem on his hands. Pain punctured his chest, and his skin broke out in even more sweat.

The woman glanced at the man beside her and jerked her head. To John, she said, "We'll be coming back. There are still things we need to talk about."

They rushed off to a car and got in, speeding away.

Blimey, where was the fire?

He closed the door and leant against it, his breathing heavy. That was too close for comfort. And all Elsa's fault. If she hadn't blabbed, those coppers wouldn't have come here. Had they recognised him from the CCTV image that had been in *The Herald*? If so, why leave? Wasn't it important to them that he be arrested so he didn't do anything else? Or didn't they have enough to go on? Him owning Dad's car wasn't exactly the crime of the century, was it?

In the kitchen, he washed his face at the sink then glanced around. She'd said they'd come back. He had work to do before they did. His attention fell on the trainers by the rear door, the ones with compost on them, and also the others with mud from where he'd buried the kitten. They could bag them, take them away, and match the soil with Catherine, Tanya, and Francesca.

Quickly, he snatched the trainers up and went into the garden, dumping them in the barbecue and firing that fucker up using lighter fluid. It brought back memories of burning his gloves and mask after slicing Bouncy Woman's cheeks off, and for an eerie moment, he imagined Irena stood at the window again, watching him. He turned to check, to make sure it was all in his head.

No one there.

Next, he put on some yellow Marigold gloves, gathered some thick black bags, his spare shovel, and rushed down into the cellar. The brass starling told him to get rid of the conversations on the wall, so John ripped them down and ran back upstairs to put them in the barbecue. A return to the cellar saw him scooping up the compost, dumping it in the bags, then carrying it all upstairs. It took a few trips. He shoved them in the boot, would scatter it elsewhere later, then, in the cellar again, he used his Shark hoover to suck up all the remaining bits. Satisfied he'd got rid of the evidence, he stroked the school uniform, pressing it to his face to inhale the scents of all those who'd put it on for him.

"You're a clever man, John," the starling muttered.

John nodded. "I hope so. If not..."

"Don't think about it." The starling seemed to wink.

And then John remembered what that bird had done to Tanya's face, so he snatched it and pelted up the stairs to the kitchen, the Shark banging his backside, cumbersome in his grip. He plonked it down and took the starling to the washing-up bowl. Hot water and a good squirt of bleach would soon sort out any skin cells or blood on the beak.

Christ, the things you had to do to cover your arse.

CHAPTER TWENTY-FIVE

A body had been found, not long after a woman named Tina Hall had called the police stating her daughter, Clare, was missing. Clare was supposed to have come home at eight, going to the park to play on the swings, something she did a lot. Tina had gone there at five past, worried, and searched, although she hadn't gone in the copse, just called out from the tree line.

Clare wasn't there and, knowing something was terribly wrong, Tina phoned the police right there in the middle of the field by the play area.

Glen Underby and Tory Yates had arrived, Glen being the one to find the child hanging from a rope noose in the copse, the tree trunk bowed only slightly from her weight. He'd rung Bethany immediately, and she'd had to make the decision whether to arrest Keagan on suspicion of whatever or walk away.

What did she really have on him, though?

The compost on his trainers—but Mike had already pointed out the man had probably been potting plants.

The use of an old-style grey Fiesta—and despite what Keagan had said, he *did* drive the bloody thing. But he could be lying because of no tax and insurance.

The sight of the Fiesta in the drive when they'd turned up had been a shock, especially with the dirty plates. Was it enough to haul him in?

His body shape and size, it matched that of Hoody. His face didn't, though. No beard or glasses, but that didn't mean a thing. Beards could be shaved off or stuck on—look at Zooblavich in the Raven case. And the specs could be false.

Maybe she ought to send officers out to watch Keagan, see where he went in that Fiesta, but everyone was currently tied up at the park. Limited resources. On the way to Tina's, Mike had rung Ursula Fringwell, the nighttime desk sergeant, and requested that she look up the Fiesta registered at Churchill Road and anything else pertaining to that address—Bethany tried to recall what had been written on the whiteboard about that particular car but couldn't remember. It would have been cleared by Fran, Leona, and the uniforms, otherwise it would have been flagged. With the actual owner dead, the team probably thought that was the end of the line for that vehicle.

The information had come back from Ursula as: Owner, Henry Keagan. Ex-wife, Paula Keagan, deceased—suicide. Son, John Keagan. Paula's second son, abducted as a newborn, child or body never recovered.

It just kept getting better. The murders in John's past, then this recent knowledge. She'd get away with asking him in for a chat based on those things, but what excuse could she give that wouldn't arouse his suspicions and put him on alert? Reopening the baby's disappearance? Make out it was a cold case? With no Henry or Paula to talk to, John Keagan was the only one left—that'd work.

She'd go and see him again later, depending on how long they were here in Tina's living room, then at the park scene. It might have to wait until the morning, and seeing as no other girls were missing, to her knowledge, a few hours wouldn't hurt. If she hadn't received the emergency call on his doorstep, she'd have asked Keagan if they could go inside. His trainers had mocked her from down the hall in the kitchen, another pair right next to them, also dirty. Shame she couldn't just go in there and pick them up.

Tina Hall's flat was on the third floor of a highrise on the Heights estate, one of the better ones situated away from where the main druggies lived. Tina sat huddled on a brown, sagging corduroy sofa, her legs up, knees beneath her chin. She gripped her shins hard, the skin over her knuckles stretched and white, the bones prominent, reminding Bethany of the ends of chicken drumsticks. Alice Jacobs sat beside her, there to offer support should the woman need it.

Tina had already told them her movements since Clare hadn't come home. Now it was time for the hard questions.

"Do you know of anyone who'd want to do that to Clare?" Bethany had yet to see the body in situ—she'd made the decision to come here and find out as much as she could from the mother first.

Tina shook her head. "No."

"Is her father in the picture?"

"He left. Haven't heard from him in years. He doesn't even pay child support."

"What's his name?"

"Aemon York. He moved to Smaltern, apparently."

"The seaside?"

"Yeah."

Bethany knew the DI there, Helena Stratton. She glanced at Mike for him to get hold of her to go round to York's, see where he'd been today. Mike took his phone out and got on with it.

"Was Clare regularly allowed out by herself?" That was bothering Bethany the most. The child was five. It was only a short walk from the high-rise to the park, but all the same, there were stairwells to navigate—the lift was broken—plus the skip or run to the park about four hundred metres away. Anyone could have intercepted her on the stairs.

"Yes, she knew only to go to the park."

"Right." Bethany peered out into the darkness spotted with lights from homes and streetlamps. The brightness of the halogens at the park were visible from here. "Did you check she was there from time to time whenever she went out to play?"

"Yes. I made sure she got to the field tonight, then I had a cuppa."

"Was anyone else around?"

"Just some older kids sitting on the benches by the slide."

"Do you know them?"

"Can't see exactly who they are from this height, but it looked like that lot from number seventeen—they weren't there when I went to see where Clare was, though, only when she arrived. The place was empty later."

"Did you check again before eight o'clock?"

Fresh tears fell. "No. I...I... Oh God, I nodded off."

Alice reached out and patted the woman's arm. "It happens, love."

Yes, it happened, but the child was *five*, for Pete's sake. She was allowed to the park by herself, not even with an older kid to watch out for her. While Tina slept, Clare was being hanged.

Bethany reined in her temper. Whether Tina was charged with neglect later down the line remained to be seen. For now, all Bethany was interested in was finding the fucker who'd killed that little girl.

"Does Clare have any friends she plays with at the park?"

"No. Oh…" Tina stared at Bethany, her eyes glassy. "There was a man…"

"What?" That had popped out. Bethany hadn't meant to say anything, let alone bark it out like that. *May as well forge on*. "Which man? When?"

"He sits on the swings. Clare said he's nice and kind, funny, but I told her to stay away from him."

"Did she ever describe him?"

Tina's lips wobbled, as if she cried at hearing her daughter's voice in her head: *There's this man, Mummy, and…* "She said he had a big belly, like Mr Greedy."

Bethany's skin went cold. No, it couldn't be Hoody, could it? There were plenty of larger blokes out there, it could be any of them. Still, she asked, "Did he have a beard or glasses?"

"She didn't say." Tina shivered. "She said she'd had an ice cream earlier—she'd been to the park this afternoon as well, and she came back a bit dirty. Messing about with mud most likely."

Mud... "Go on."

"I asked her who'd bought it, and she clammed up. I warned her again that if the bloke had got it, she must never take anything from him again."

"Do you know which ice-cream van it is?"

"Gusto's. Greek bloke."

Mike sent a message on his phone.

Bethany hoped Gusto had seen Clare and the man—but he might not remember. He must get hundreds of faces at his serving window every day.

"Were you not worried about letting her go back to the park this evening after knowing a man had plied Clare with a treat?"

Tina sighed. "I was so tired. I didn't think an hour would hurt, and I looked out before she went, and he wasn't there."

But the copse is. A good place to hide.

While heaping guilt on the woman might make Bethany feel better, it wouldn't solve who the man was or whether he even had anything to do with this. She finished the interview and left, waiting until she'd reached the end of the third-floor walkway, then spoke to Mike.

"She's going to blame herself for the rest of her life." She took the stairs. "We need to visit number seventeen, see if it was those kids at the park."

Mike's message tone went off. He read them. "Okay, Gusto lives in the next block along." It beeped again. "And Helena Stratton is on her way to York's."

"You go Gusto's while I speak to the kids."

They parted ways on the second storey, Mike going downwards, Bethany moving along the walkway until she reached seventeen. She knocked on the door, and a teenage lad opened it, staring at her while scoffing a Daim. It brought back memories of the time she'd visited the local drug lord on this estate and a kid had been eating chocolate then, too.

"Yeah?" he said.

"Is your mum or dad in?" She held up her ID.

He winced. "Hang on," he managed around a mouthful of chocolate. He trudged down the hallway and disappeared into a room.

A man in a white shirt, stained at the armpits in a rather fetching shade of mustard, thumped along to meet her. "What can I do for you?"

She showed him her ID. "I just need permission to speak to your children. They're not in trouble at all." She went on to quietly explain that she needed to know if they'd seen Clare Hall at the park this evening, adding, "It's a murder inquiry."

"Oh, bugger me. Yeah, all right. Come in." He stepped back. "Poor little sod."

"Do you know the Halls well?" she asked, moving along the hallway with him.

"Nah, but I know who she is. Kids," he barked upon entering the living room. "Copper's got some questions. Answer them."

Three boys stared back at her, ranging from about nine to fifteen. All appeared frightened, but whether that was of her or their father, she couldn't tell.

"Hi," she said. "I just need to know if you saw Clare Hall at the park this evening, around seven?"

Daim Eater nodded. "Yeah, she went into the woods. We left after that. Dad wanted us home to do the washing up and hoovering."

The place did look tidy.

"Right. Can you remember if anyone else came?"

One of the younger lads nodded. "A bloke was there before Clare."

"What time was that?"

"After six because we got there then."

"Can you describe him?"

"Fat git." He giggled behind his hand as if embarrassed.

"Anything else about him?"

"He had a bag."

"I didn't see him," Daim said. "You sure you're not making it up?"

"No! He had a rucksack and a shovel."

Bethany's stomach rolled. "A shovel?"

The kid nodded. "Yeah. It was dark, not shiny, reckon it was rusty, and his bag was black. He had on some trainers and jeans."

She took her phone out and accessed the image of Hoody from outside Lloyds. "Do you know this man?"

"Nah."

Shit. "Okay. Anything else you can remember?"

"I thought it was weird that he went in the woods, then Clare did a bit later," the younger boy said.

Chills sped up Bethany's spine. Had he gone in there to wait? Why carry a rusty shovel?

The smallest kid waved, probably how he got attention in this busy household. "He had rope."

"Did he?" She crouched to be at eye level with him. "How did you see that?"

"It was hanging on his arm, round and round, like cowboys have it." He smiled shyly. "I want to be a cowboy when I grow up."

Daim laughed. "You probably didn't even see any rope, you just wished you had because you're obsessed, cowboy freak!"

"Pack it in," the father said. "What would your mother think of you, talking like that?"

Daim blushed. "Sorry."

"I should think so." The dad rubbed his forehead. "Their mother passed."

"Oh, I'm so sorry." That must have been why Daim winced when she'd asked if his mum or dad were in. She smiled at the children. "Look, you've been so helpful, you really have. Thank you for remembering all that." She stood and left the room, waiting for the father by the front door. "Good memories, those boys, to recall so much."

He nodded. "Rope…" He looked as if he'd guessed what it had been used for.

"I'm afraid so. It isn't public knowledge, although it will be soon as we'll be putting another press conference out, but if you could keep it to yourself for now. Can you give me your sons' names, for my records? Of course, they may need to be spoken to again at a later date."

He gave them and opened the door. "I'll not be telling them why you were asking about Clare. Not yet. Tomorrow is soon enough."

"Probably wise. Thanks for your time."

She walked along the balcony then down the stairs. Mike came towards her from the other tower block, and they met in the middle of the grassy area. She told him about what the lads had said.

"Rope." He shook his head. "Carrying it openly like that. And the shovel—what's that all about?"

"God knows. Did you get anything from the ice-cream man?"

"He doesn't remember any of the customers from today at the park. Says they all become a blur because he serves so many."

"As I suspected. Okay, we ought to go to the park now, much as I don't want to."

Mike sighed, and they walked there, Bethany turning back once they were on the field so she could look up at Tina's high-rise. People were at their windows on all levels, staring out, probably wondering why the police were at their local park. Was the killer a different one to the other girls, just another big bloke, not Hoody at all? Was he one of those looking down on her, seeing the outcome of what he'd done?

She shivered and walked to the SOCO van, taking protectives from a box in the back and putting them on, as did Mike. Tory stood at the opening to the copse, and Bethany signed the log to enter the scene, Mike doing the same afterwards.

"What vibe did you get from the mother when you got here?" Bethany asked her.

Tory sighed. "Absolutely distraught. She kept saying it was her fault because she'd fallen asleep. To be honest, unless Tina stood at the window the whole time Clare was here, she wouldn't necessarily have seen anything going on anyway. She's bound to have moved away, to go for a wee or whatever. And the park is so close to home. Who'd think the kid would be snatched?"

"Me." Bethany grimaced. "Clare was five. You don't let them out alone, not in this day and age where there's a paedo on every corner. Sorry, sore subject for me, and I'm tired. I don't mean to take it out on you."

"No, I get what you're saying." Tory smiled. "I suppose I'm thinking of my childhood, where it was still relatively okay to go out by yourself, especially on your own estate where everyone knows everyone else."

So she didn't get bristly and say something she'd regret, Bethany said, "Right, we'd best go and have a look then. Is Glen still in there?"

"Yes. He's found something…interesting."

"Okay." Bethany dipped beneath the cordon strung up between two trees and headed towards the tent which was lit up from inside. She bypassed the cluster of SOCOs around the hanging body and went to the tent, poking her head through the flap. "Tory said you found something?"

Glen turned from watching two SOCOs on their knees digging up dirt and placing it in large plastic containers. "Yep, disturbed ground. The mud had been smoothed over, flat. It was too fresh, recent, so we're having a look now to see what's there."

"Shovel," one of the SOCOs said, gently taking it out of the hole.

It was rusty.

"Oh, and what's this?" the other one said. "Ah, shit." He tucked his gloved hands beneath something and lifted it.

An animal. Black-and-white fur.

If it wasn't for that little kid mentioning the rope, Bethany would have thought the man had just come here to bury his pet. He could have dumped the shovel as well, unable to bear taking it home knowing it had been used to dig the grave. Some people had quirks like that, associating things with events.

"Water bottle, empty." The first SOCO held that in one hand and the shovel in the other. "Mud's stuck to the shovel, so maybe the water was used to clean it?"

"Someone hiding evidence," Bethany said. "But why is there a kitten here? It *is* a kitten, isn't it?" It was hard to tell with mud all over it.

"Yep."

Bethany let out a puff of air behind her face mask. What the hell did the kitten have to do with anything? Was it even linked?

Of course it is. The kid said the man had a shovel.

She nodded to herself. The animal was a puzzle for later. At the moment, she had another small body to view. She left the tent and joined Mike, who stood in front of the tree in question. So she didn't have to see Clare at the minute, she told him what was in the tent.

"Okay, it could have been a mistake, killing Clare," he said.

"What do you mean?"

"Man comes here to torture the kitten—say he planned to hang it from the tree and watch it die. Plausible, there are some sick fuckers out there. Clare comes in, sees what he's doing, and the bloke panics. Grabs her, hangs her. Buries the kitten. Leaves."

"Not a bad assumption, except the rope would be too thick to do much to a kitten, considering how small its neck is."

She ripped her attention from Mike and pointed it at Clare.

And her heart broke. Oh God, how it broke.

CHAPTER TWENTY-SIX

With the starling soaking in the bleach water, John had kept busy. He'd been cleaning the whole cottage while the scent of burning trainers and paper filtered in. He'd hoovered, then filled a bucket with lemon Flash and boiled water from the kettle, mopping the floors. He used disinfectant spray to clean all the surfaces and door handles, anywhere the girls might have touched, and lastly, he sanitised the indoor alley, glad he had because he found a fair bit of compost on the floor that must have fallen off them when they'd wedged themselves down at the end. The walls had smears on them, so the green scrubbing side of a kitchen sponge got rid of that.

All this because Elsa had opened her big mouth.

Pleased with his efforts, he boiled the kettle again and made a cup of tea, putting a nip of brandy in it, same as he had when they'd come back from their holiday in Devon. He experienced a similar set of feelings as he had then. The time periods were much the same. Three deaths each. Rebecca White, George Phelps, Harriet. Catherine, Tanya, Francesca.

The parallels were a comfort. He'd got away scot-free then, even with the police sniffing around like they were now, so he'd be free again this time.

He'd make sure of it.

His earlier thought that Francesca would be his downfall came along, swirling inside his head while he drank his tea. Two hours had passed since he'd embarked on his manic cleaning spree, and the coppers still hadn't come back. That was a good sign.

He fished out an old pair of shoes. He'd have to buy some new trainers, what with his two pairs being charred. In the garden, he put the stuff from the barbecue in a metal baking tray, the deep kind you used for turkeys at Christmas.

The drive to Shadwell Hill didn't take long. He slowed along the track inside the woods, parking halfway down. With the black bags containing the compost in his tight fists, the shovel wedged between his side and one arm, he walked to the outer edge where a ditch ran around the perimeter. A quick dump of the bags, then he returned to the car and took out the baking tray, the contents tossed into the ditch with the compost.

He dithered on whether to leave the tray or take it home.

He threw it on top of the other stuff.

Then he got to it, digging up some earth, covering the evidence with it. Back-breaking work, that, but it needed to be done. He was tired from his time with Francesca, the cleaning, now this, but sleep was for shitheads anyway. He'd definitely ring in sick tomorrow. He could catch up then.

The journey home was fraught with him expecting coppers to be sitting on the verges in the darkness, watching for him to come past, waiting for the moment they could prove he *did* drive Dad's car, *and* without insurance or tax.

He hadn't thought that through properly, had he. It was only a matter of time before the car would be flagged on that ANPR thing, so why hadn't he factored it in?

John didn't bother flicking his indicator switch to turn into the driveway at the cottage. It wasn't like anyone used this road much, and no one was behind him. He did an emergency stop at the sight of another vehicle parked in front of the property, and his frazzled brain told him it was those coppers, come back to finish their chat. Then he recognised the make, and Edward stepped out of the shadows down the side, into John's headlight beams, his skin stark white.

What was he doing here so late? It had to be about eleven o'clock now, surely.

John swerved so he could leave the Fiesta in the front garden. He got out, no longer able to see Edward, what with the lights being off now. He walked towards where he'd last seen him, spotting his shape in the gloom.

"Everything all right, son?" John asked.

"We ought to go inside really."

John let them in, worry clouding his head and flickering in his chest. Edward hadn't sounded right, tense, not his usual self. Something was up, especially for him to visit at this time of night, but what?

In the kitchen, John put the kettle on, unease slithering all over him. He imagined his son had wrestled with his thoughts all day and had come here to tell John he didn't want to know him anymore.

Edward came in and stood by the dining table. "I won't be staying, so no tea for me."

John turned. Now he got a good look at him, Edward appeared to have been crying.

"What's the matter?" John's voice wobbled.

"It's Mum."

"What about her?"

"She died this morning."

John staggered against the cooker, all the wind knocked out of him. All right, they'd been divorced for years, but it didn't change how he felt about her. Irena would always be the woman who'd steadied him for a time, showing him what family life *should* be like. She'd loved him like no other, his raft on the sea, and allowed him to live with an inner peace until his devil had become more powerful and tuned her out. Although she'd remarried, John still held a candle to her.

"What?" he managed, heart banging.

"She didn't want me saying anything while she was ill. Asked me to keep it quiet until she'd gone." Edward let out a shuddery breath.

"Ill?"

"Cancer."

"Oh." That wasn't a way to go, not for anyone, but especially not for Irena. She didn't deserve that. She was good and kind and… Fuck. "I'm so sorry." Whether he'd said that to Edward, to Irena, or to himself, he wasn't sure.

"I'll let you know when the funeral is," Edward said. "Her husband doesn't mind you coming. Said you were married once, you know, and were a big part of her life. You need to grieve as well."

That man, that new fella she'd married, was a better man than John.

Everyone was a better man than John. Seemed Mum was right there. He was a waste of space who shouldn't have been born. Why had Irena ever loved him? He should have declined that first date in The Blue Star, let her meet someone else instead, not tainting her with his presence.

"I'm going to get off now," Edward said.

No hug. No need for a cuddle off his old man.

It had gone drastically wrong somewhere down the line. John's depressive episode had well and truly pushed his wife and son away, to the point his own kid didn't have it in him to offer more than just the words he'd spoken, and those had been stilted, like Edward had to work hard to get them out.

He walked away, a stranger.

John shut his eyes at the click of the front door closing. He didn't think Edward would come here again—maybe a sixth sense, but John reckoned the next and last time he'd see him was at Irena's funeral.

Anger seemed to sweep up from his feet, right to the top of his head, giving him the hug Edward hadn't. It was welcome, that rage. It would fuel him to do what he should have done yesterday.

A day late wouldn't hurt. So long as it got done, that was all that mattered. If he did this, it'd take his mind off Irena, how she must have suffered. The image of her in a coffin loomed in his head, though, the poor woman ravaged by disease, her hands clasped over her chest. Did she have hair come the end? Had it vanished from chemo? Did she have a wig on?

Bizarrely, John remembered he'd shaved his beard off. Rather than it being a problem, it was probably better this way. He wouldn't be recognised as the bloke outside Lloyds. He'd keep the fake glasses off, too.

After a change of clothes—he put all black on so he wouldn't be seen well in the dark—he collected his cushion and stuffed it in his backpack. It was the only weapon he needed for this one, but he had his penknife in his pocket anyway. He went outside to the end of the drive and scanned the road, checking for cars hidden beside bushes. The risk of the police catching him now was high if they intended on coming back. He got in the car and drove away, heading for a street that was probably quiet by now, the majority of residents in bed.

If they weren't, he'd wait.

He parked on the other side of the street and checked the clock. Quarter to twelve. He stared across at the house. A downstairs light was on, maybe a lamp, seeing as it was only concentrated in one area. A bit of a pest that they were awake, but patience, he had plenty of it. While he waited, he entertained the past, and that other murder he'd committed. God, there had been so many, it was a wonder he remembered them all.

John had pulled himself fully out of the deep, dark depression he'd immersed himself in after Irena had left, taking precious Edward with her. It had taken some effort, but you had to move on, didn't you. His devil told him that often, along with: If you just let me run free, you'll feel better.

One day, leaving work, John was almost jaunty for once. He only had himself to answer to now, could just get up and do things on a whim, not think about it too much. There were plus sides to being alone, although he missed that family feeling when they were all together watching TV or chatting.

How easily he'd let it all slip away.

Jung worked in the hospital cafeteria. The woman irritated him constantly, the hairs on John's neck standing on end every time he saw her. Everyone else seemed to find her lovely, and he didn't understand why when the bloody woman was always asking questions.

"You want chips with that?"

"You want some ketchup?"

"You want a yoghurt for pudding?"

No, he wanted her to leave him alone, to order his own chips, pick up the tomato sauce bottle without her prompting, take a fucking yoghurt out of the fridge himself. Some days he managed to ignore her, pretended she hadn't spoken. But the most grating thing of all? Why did she smile at him as if she cared for him, was concerned about him?

The only person he'd truly wanted to do that was Mum.

Jung's shift ended half an hour after John's. She'd go and eat some leftover sandwiches in the park by the duck pond, as was her habit, her back to the bushes as she sat tossing bread to the mallards. He knew this because he'd watched her.

John had collected his heavy bag, slung it over his shoulder, and made his way to those bushes to wait for her. The conscious decision had been cemented in the early hours while he'd stared at the ceiling, thinking of what he could do to cheer himself up even more.

She came along then, settled herself on the bench, the moon casting its image on the lake's surface. They'd both worked the afternoon shifts today, and evening had come along while they'd been toiling away. Her black, short hair sprang up in tufts, and he had the urge to jump out from the bush and pull it, but he held back. The act itself would come in time.

The bushes he'd hidden in had a small clearing inside, large enough to do what he wanted. It was a similar scene to when George had killed Harriet. Higher than a six-foot man, the hedges created a canopy, the moonlight filtering through enough so John could see what he was doing.

He shifted his weight a little, winced as the leaves rustled somewhat. She turned her head, registering the sound, shrugging it off as a night animal or bird behind her.

Stupid girl.

Adrenaline pumped then. She threw the bread to the ducks, who seemed oblivious to her even being there, most of them nesting somewhere on the island in the centre of the lake.

Water plopped, fishes coming up for the spoils.

A twig cracked beneath John's foot.

Again, her head turned, and again, she shrugged.

John lunged.

She screamed at him yanking her hair. He stuffed an old sock into her open mouth. Grabbing her by the tops of her arms, he shoved her backwards towards the bush. Her legs scrabbled for purchase on the gravely pathway, feet digging into the damp earth in the small clearing, hands clawing at his.

He pushed her down on the ground, picked up his mallet, and smacked her on the head with it. She landed, faceup, legs bent at the knees, her arms upwards, face blood-smeared, eyes glazed and unseeing.

A quick death, but John didn't care. He hadn't finished yet.

He peered down at the cadaver, reaching for his axe. He raised it above his head with both hands, bringing it down in one swift motion, trying to sever her leg at the thigh. It took several more hacks before he got through just the muscle. The force within had woken, taking over his everyday senses, urging him to strike this body anywhere, everywhere.

So he did.

Once he'd got bored, he was covered in blood. It brought home how lax he'd been, how he should have put a boiler suit on or something. Next time he planned a kill, he'd do it properly, writing it all down from start to finish until it was ingrained in his head, then he'd burn his notes and act it out.

He thought of Lucy Berry, and an idea sprouted. It might take years before he pulled it off, but he'd do it. The planning stages would give him something to do after work, a focus while he got used to being alone in life.

Females, they were such pests, weren't they? All the ones in his life had hurt him.

So it was about time he hurt them back.

John waited half an hour after the downstairs light had gone off, then another twenty minutes once the bedroom one clicked off. He had an idea where the mum and dad's room was from the description the girl had given him. He'd made out they should do a virtual tour of their homes so they could imagine the other in them, another way to get closer to each other. The stupid cow had fallen for it. She'd done a good job of telling him which room was where, so he basically had a mental map he could follow.

He reached to the back seat for one of his many balaclavas, and his guts rolled. Had that woman copper peered inside the car and spotted them? No, it was okay. They just looked like pairs of thick, balled-up black socks. You couldn't tell what they were.

John pulled it down over his face, a sense of peace enveloping him. He was strong behind the mask, a force to be reckoned with. His features being hidden gave him courage. He'd reveal them to her soon; he wanted to see her reaction. Would she like what she saw or recoil like Catherine and Tanya?

He put on gloves, got out, and shrugged his backpack on. In one of the pockets was a tool he'd use to gain entry. He closed the door quietly, leaving it unlocked so he didn't have to fumble with keys if he needed a speedy getaway. They dangled in the ignition. He doubted anyone would be awake and want to nick a clapped-out Fiesta, so he strode across the street, watching for signs of life. For people looking out at him.

No one.

He dipped down the side of the house and opened the gate, something that wasn't bolted, so she'd said. She hadn't lied, and the hinge didn't creak—she'd put WD40 on it like he'd suggested.

Gullible bitch.

He shut the gate and walked into the middle of the garden, peering up at the windows. She had light-pink curtains, she'd told him that, but there was no glow behind them from her watching TV in the dark or being on her phone.

Good.

John crept to the back door and inserted the tool. It took a couple of fiddles, then the keeper sprang across, creating a bit of a clunk, one he could have done without, to be honest. He waited, breath held, and listened for sounds of anyone coming.

Nothing.

He turned the handle and entered, the aroma of the house coming through the wool of his mask—the hanging-around smell of what they'd had for dinner, something with fish; the spray used to mask it, rose-scented; possible damp lurking in corners, musty and cloying. Altogether, it was a revolting miasma.

John closed the door quietly and brought the mind map to the forefront. This was the kitchen. He thought about what he wanted to do, how he'd only brought his cushion and penknife with him, when he needed a better weapon for the others. A knife block sat on the worktop, and he selected the largest one.

He crept to the hallway, the door to the living room on his left, the stairs to the right, and beside the front door was a toilet.

There had been a conversation, when he'd told her to WD40 the gate, where she'd said the fourth stair groaned if you stood on it. He went up, bypassing it, his breathing getting more laboured the higher he went. His weight was a problem, his lungs unable to cope with too much exertion. He was unfit from all the comfort-eating, from not exercising, and wasn't that just stupid, considering what he'd been doing recently, and what he was doing now? If the dad came out onto the landing and tackled him, John wouldn't stand a chance.

He should be quick then. Get things moving.

He stood outside the parents' door, ear close to it. Someone snored inside, loud and grating, and it reminded him of Mum when she conked out on the sofa after a session with the gin. Dead to the world, so the saying went.

Fitting.

John thought about what came next. To get to *her*, to do what he wanted with her, he needed to sort the mum and dad first. He couldn't risk them waking, interrupting, trying to save the little cow.

He twisted the handle. Pushed the door. Stood in the frame, surveying what was in front of him. A double bed, the shapes of cabinets either side, both with lamps on top. A window to the right, an ottoman beneath. Wardrobe to the left, spanning the entire wall.

The dad should go first.

John stepped inside, taking it slow, levelling his breathing out, although his heart rate sped. He wanted to hack the bloke up, like Jung, but the mother would rouse, and *her*, and then where would they all be?

He stood beside the bed and stared down at the man, who was on his back, mouth open. The snores belonged to him and soughed out, the bottom lip wobbling with every exhalation. John glanced at the mum. She rested on her side, her back facing her husband. Orange earbuds—maybe she couldn't sleep without silence, or this bloke's snores kept her awake.

John plunged the knife into the man's mouth, the tip meeting the back of his throat, then going farther. The victim opened his eyes, and a terrible noise burped out around the blade. John yanked it out and sliced the fucker's throat to shut him up, the father jerking as if having a fit. It didn't wake the mother. Maybe her illness meant she slept through a hurricane.

Blood seeped from the gaping wound, and John watched it for a moment in the semi-darkness, the grey-like surroundings, that blood a deep black, and he imagined it red, what it looked like on the sheets with the light on.

He moved around to the other side and, in sharp and swift moves, he pushed her onto her back, sliced her throat, and wiped the knife on the quilt. He stabbed it into her throat, and it jutted proudly, Excalibur, a sword in the stone.

The stench of blood fuelled his fire, but he needed to be calm now. He stood by the door, inhaling deeply, exhaling steadily, until his nerves had lost their serrated edges. He left the room, closing the door, and went to the next one along. It was ajar, and he smiled at that. Some kids had to have it open, to see what was coming, the monster of the night who broke in and hurt them.

She'd see what was coming all right, but not until it was too late to do anything about it.

In he went, stepping over a book, the open pages brighter than the gloom surrounding them. He lowered his backpack to the floor and removed his cushion, placing it at the foot of the bed. She didn't stir.

John opened the top drawer beside her bed and fumbled for what he needed. A sock, his gag of choice. He pressed her chin so her mouth opened, and while she batted at him in her sleep, he shoved the sock deep, right to the back of her throat. A hoarse wheeze, and she tried to get up, but his body blocked her.

"Hello, Elsa."

CHAPTER TWENTY-SEVEN

Clare's tongue, bulbous and purple, bulged out of her blue-lipped mouth. Her jaw had clamped shut on it, and mucous had dried on her lips and pale skin. A foam-like substance was present, although it had a deflated look. Petechiae dotted her cheeks and below the eyes, the whites of which were red. Her head lolled to the right, the knot of the noose to the left. Her clothing at the groin, damp, needed no explanation, and her hands, at her sides, had squeezed into tight fists.

Presley must have seen Bethany staring at them. "That's called 'posturing', the fists. Happens at the point of the brain dying. Prior to that, when the effects of suffocation take over, even after consciousness is lost, a hanging victim will automatically clutch at the throat to get the noose off, even though, in most cases, they want to die. It's a natural reaction for the body."

"So why hasn't she got scratch marks on her neck?" Bethany asked.

Isabelle sighed. "Christ. I don't think I can take much more today."

Murmurs of agreement went round.

"Look at her wrists." Presley pointed at them. "They've been held down with a hard grip—see the bruising coming out? Even a small child like Clare would thrash about violently, so the killer was lucky if he didn't get clipped by her legs moving—another product of hanging; people kick out, usually scrabbling to find the chair they so recently knocked away, although in this case, no chair."

The thought of a man deliberately preventing this child from reaching for the noose sickened her. Had he stood in front of her, staring, fascinated at how she'd died? Did he watch the light fade from her eyes? Why hang her? If this *was* Hoody, the change in MO made no sense. Why hadn't he put makeup on Clare? Why did she still have all her clothes on?

Clare's socks were odd. At first glance they were ankle versions, but now Bethany studied them, they were long but had been folded over to create an illusion.

"Would it have been quick?" she asked.

"Losing consciousness, yes. Anywhere from twenty seconds to a minute. As the brain needs a continuous flow of blood, when this is stopped, it takes from one to six minutes to actually die. She'd have possibly had flashes in front of her eyes, a roaring in her ears—some who have come out the other side of this have mentioned it's like being near a rushing stream or brook. Others say it's a ringing. Those few seconds where she'd have wanted to release the noose would be the only time she was aware, alert, then she'd have been out of it."

That was something then, but the terror she may have suffered prior to this, him putting her head through the loop, her understanding what he was about to do—even at such a young age she'd have known, wouldn't she? It was beyond awful.

Isabelle walked around the body. "Considering her time of death"—she looked at Bethany—"which was between seven and half past—Pres did the temp before you came in—and the time she arrived at the field, according to the mother, there was a window of minutes where Clare would have been alive with the killer. As her body shows no evidence of hurt other than her bruised wrists and her being hanged, do we assume he didn't hurt her in some other way prior to the murder?"

Presley lifted Clare's top and inspected her torso. "No bruising. I noted there isn't any on her head either, so no knocking her out before applying the noose. Is the photographer finished? I'd like to ger her down now."

Isabelle nodded.

Bethany turned away while it was done. Any death was hard, but a child's was more so. Innocence and the knowledge of a life lost so young, one where the little one could have gone on to do anything and everything, living a good and happy existence, now snatched away because a man with a rusty shovel and a coil of rope had decided it would be so.

The crackle of plastic sheeting told Bethany some had been laid out to place Clare on it. She faced the tree, the body on the ground, the noose removed. A deep, red furrow marred part of her neck, the indentations of the plait-like fibres leaving their mark.

"Did..." Bethany took a deep breath. "Did her neck break?"

Presley felt it. "I'll need to do an x-ray to be sure, but it feels like only the hyoid has been snapped. She may have fractures elsewhere in the neck, though. So, to answer your next question, she died of asphyxiation."

"Can you explain that foamy stuff around her mouth?"

"It's from an excess of saliva mixed with air which creates a froth. I doubt very much she was poisoned, it's a classic occurrence with hanging, but of course, I'll do her tox and see if she was given anything."

Bethany glanced at her watch. Where the hell had the time gone? She'd spent longer with Tina than she'd thought, and God knew what the father of the three lads had thought with her turning up so late—and how come they weren't in bed when she'd arrived?

None of your business. God, she was getting a right old busybody as she aged.

She'd been here for ages, too, leaving the area after her first glimpse of Clare so she could gather her emotions. She'd busied herself helping to inspect the park itself, the field, and then nipped to the tent to see if anything else had been dug up from the hole. Then she'd found the courage to go back to Clare, and now, it was past midnight.

"We should go and have that chat with Keagan," she decided.

Mike sighed. "It's late."

"I don't care. Look at her socks. Strains of Tanya there. And one of those lads said the man who did this was fat. Keagan is fat. I want to rule him out now, so I can actually get some sleep tonight. I don't want to be tossing and turning, thinking about it until morning. If he has nothing to hide, he won't care if we call round now."

They said goodbye to everyone and walked to the car.

"Do *you* think it's him? There's no denying the description fits," Bethany said.

"Hmm." Mike scrubbed his chin. "Something else also fits."

"What's that?"

"Remember we were talking about Hoody taking teenagers, and the ankle socks didn't make sense, so we wondered whether he wanted younger girls really..."

Bethany's heart stalled. "Clare is younger."

"Exactly."

"Fucking hell..."

They stripped off their protectives, put it all in an evidence bag from the boot, and Bethany handed it over to Tory. In the car, Mike's phone went off. He read the message.

"Helena Stratton has been to see Clare's dad. He was at the pub from six until closing."

"Right. Well, we know it isn't him anyway."

She drove them out into the sticks, her heart thundering and adrenaline swooshing.

"I need to get calm," she said. "If we're going to talk to him, I don't want to give away the fact we suspect him. I want him to slip up, and even if he doesn't, with the Fiesta and those dirty trainers, surely we'll get a warrant so we can seize those things."

"It's likely. We have nothing else except suspicion."

She nodded and swerved onto the cottage driveway, then stopped short. "The car's gone." She thumped the steering wheel. "So much for him not using it." She leapt out and, using her torch, ran down the side to the back. The car wasn't there either. She peered through into the kitchen. The trainers were gone, and the whole room had been cleaned since she'd last seen it.

Bethany ran back to Mike, who peered through into the living room. She joined him. There were stripes on the carpet where it had been hoovered.

"Seems someone's had a mad spree with cleaning products," she said. "And why the fuck is he out at this time of night?" She rang the front desk. "Ursula, it's me. I need a CCTV check doing on the Fiesta belonging to Henry Keagan. I'm not holding my breath, but if the man who's driving it has panicked, he might fuck up somewhere and drive by cameras."

"Okay, will do. Got to go. A call has come in."

"Right, just text me any sightings."

She looked at Mike. "Why the need to clean once we'd been? Sorry, but something's off here. I'm going to message Kribbs now and ask him to sort a warrant." She did that, explaining why they needed one.

Kribbs: BIT LATE IN THE DAY, BUT YES, WILL DO THAT NOW. BEAR IN MIND, YOU MAY NEED TO WAIT UNTIL THE MORNING FOR IT TO BE ISSUED.

Bethany: I KNOW.

Her phone rang. Ursula's name was on the screen. "Yep?"

"Just had a call from patrol—as you probably know, some officers returned to normal duty once the child's body was found. They've done their trip down Elsa Masters' street, and there's a grey Fiesta parked opposite their house. They knocked on the door and had no response, would have walked away had they not seen a scuff on blood on the front doorframe."

"And?" Bethany held her breath.

"They broke in. Gary and Beverley Masters are dead, and Elsa is missing."

"Oh, fucking Nora! We're on our way—what's the bloody address again?"

Ursula gave it, then Bethany stuffed her phone in her pocket.

"You're not going to believe this." She jabbed a finger at the cottage. "That fucker who lives here, and it's got to be him, has only gone and murdered Elsa's mother and father—and she's missing." She gripped her hair. "Fuck it. Shit!"

They dashed to the car, and while Mike organised for Fran and Leona to get to the incident room as soon as possible, and for Ursula to keep them abreast of everything going on with regards to searching for Elsa, Bethany sped towards the Masters' address.

"His Fiesta is there," she said, "in the street, so if Elsa's gone, where the hell has he taken her, and how?" She thought about him saying he preferred to walk, but that was ridiculous when you had a teenager with you, one who may know her mum and dad were dead, one who was hysterical—unless he'd knocked her out and carried her away.

A thought occurred.

The clever bastard.

"Get on to Ursula again. I want to know what car Gary Masters drives. If it isn't at the address, then the fucker took it. He knows we're on the lookout for a Fiesta."

Mike did that, and she also asked him to message Kribbs for her, explaining that things had escalated and Keagan was definitely their suspect—was it possible for him to get that warrant pushed through before the morning?

"He'll grumble, but I really think we need to get into Keagan's cottage sooner rather than later, even though he's gone through it with a good clean." She pulled up outside the Masters' place, behind the police car.

Out on the path, while she put gloves on, she stared over at the Fiesta and messaged Ursula to arrange for it to be collected. God only knew how much evidence was inside it. She strolled across to it and, using her torch, peeked in through the driver's-side window.

They keys were in the ignition. So had he planned to use it to escape with Elsa and then changed his mind? Or had he always intended to leave it here?

Further examination showed nothing out of the ordinary, just some balled-up socks on the back seat, so she opened the door and popped the lock for the boot. She'd explain her need to do this on looking for Elsa. She lifted the lid, and her heart thudded hard.

Grains of compost on the light-grey carpet.

She closed the lid and ran across the road, asking PC Nicola Eccles, who stood at the front door with the log, to keep an eye on the Fiesta as there was evidence inside.

"It's being picked up, so hopefully you won't have to watch it for long."

Mike got out of the car—his messages had probably ended up with him answering them, hence the delay. He glanced down the street. "Ah, SOCO are here."

"Wonder if Isabelle's sent one of her other teams, seeing as she's with Clare." Bethany walked out onto the pavement and waited for the van to park.

Isabelle jumped out. "Pres is dealing with Clare now, so I opted to lead this one. And there was me saying I couldn't take much more today." She jerked her head at the house. "I'm wide awake anyway, second wind, so might as well. Two bodies, yes?"

Bethany nodded. "Gary and Beverly Masters. Their daughter, Elsa, is missing. She's one of the girls, the one who spoke to Jolly19."

"Oh shit." Isabelle sighed. "Let's hope we don't get to see that child dead then." She walked to the back of the van and spoke to her colleagues while handing out protectives.

Bethany and Mike snagged a set each and got dressed. Isabelle and her team went inside first, then Bethany followed, tailed by Mike. While SOCO moved into various parts of the house, Isabelle and two others went upstairs. Bethany and Mike also took that route, except Bethany led them into the back bedroom rather than the murder scene at the front.

She switched the light on, her glove sticking on the plastic plate. A book on the floor appeared to be one from school, some manual or other, an English one as Coordinating Conjunctions was at the top of the left page as a thick-fonted header, followed by: An easy way to remember them all—FANBOYS. For, And, Nor, But, Or, Yet, So.

Bethany couldn't recall being taught that. It seemed Elsa had been studying before bed, perhaps lying on the floor on her tummy, legs bent at the knees, and maybe she swayed them from side to side as she read.

Images such as those were Bethany's imagination supplying possible facts, giving her an idea of what had happened before someone had come in, killed her parents, then took her. A setting of the scene. Nothing was out of place or seemed suspect. The quilt was rumpled, but that was to be expected if she'd been woken up. Her phone was on the bedside chest of drawers, the top one open, as if something had recently been taken out. She peered inside—neat rows of socks at one end and rolled-up knickers at the other. Sports bras were in the middle, again, rolled, their straps giving away their identity.

"Doesn't appear to have been a struggle," Mike said.

"I thought that." Bethany sighed. "Suppose we'd better go next door then. A quick look, then I want to—"

Mike's phone chirruped. He undid his suit zip and took it out. "Ursula. The Masters own a Mazda, royal blue. She's got Fran, who's just turned up, on CCTV to see if it's been spotted."

"Right. We'll see the parents now then." She walked out onto the landing and poked her head into the other bedroom.

So much blood. Both bodies were on their backs, their throats slit, although the man had a lot of claret on the lower half of his face.

"Stabbed in the mouth," Isabelle said and pointed to Gary's. "Bit of a mess inside there."

"Why the hell did he do that?" Bethany said, not expecting an answer.

She thought of how nice Gary had been when she'd interviewed Elsa, how he was more bothered about the girls than what his daughter had said during the chats. With him and his wife in bed, whoever had come in—*it's Keagan, for God's sake*—hadn't woken them, so his entry had been silent.

"Mike, I think we should go back to Keagan's. Standing here isn't going to do any good. We can come back if he's not there."

He nodded. "Yep."

Downstairs, she snagged a SOCO's attention in the kitchen. "Any sign of forced entry from in here? The front's obviously a bust because our lot came in."

He shook his head. "No, but the door's unlocked, so maybe he came in this way and exited via the front, what with the scuff of blood there."

"Thanks."

With that, she signed out of the log, stripped her protectives off, leaving them with Nicola, and got in her car just as the recovery lorry arrived. She sat in the driver's seat and took out her buzzing phone.

Kribbs: WARRANT ISSUED.

Bethany: THANK YOU. ON THE WAY TO KEAGAN'S COTTAGE NOW. SEEING IF HE'S TAKEN ELSA THERE.

She drove that way, Mike updating Fran, and, almost at his place, she slowed. The front corner of a car poked out of the hedges, the royal blue bright in her headlight beam.

"Shit! Call for backup." She drove past it, coasting to a stop with her beams and engine off. She didn't want the noise alerting Keagan that they were there.

Mike finished his call, then they got out, Bethany grabbing her little torch and stuffing it in her pocket. They walked up the road. Where the hedge had a gap for the driveway, she took in a long breath to steady her nerves, then peered around the corner. The hallway light was on behind the front door, but everywhere else was in darkness.

"Okay, that wasn't on when we were last here," she whispered to Mike while beckoning him to have a look.

"Hmm. And where else would he go out here anyway—the Mazda shows he's come home."

"What do you want to do, get in there somehow or wait for backup?" she asked.

"We should wait, but if Elsa's there, alive…"

"I know. Okay, we'll play it by ear."

She crept up the drive in a crouch, going down the side of the cottage. If there was a chance they could get to Elsa sooner, she would. Minutes lost waiting for backup could mean losing a life, and she wasn't prepared to do it, no matter what protocol dictated.

CHAPTER TWENTY-EIGHT

Elsa hid behind the sofa, trying not to breathe loudly. He'd said if he didn't find her, he'd set her free. Her heart throbbed painfully, and she worried he'd hear it, which was stupid, but she wasn't rational at the minute.

When she'd woken in bed at home, a wedge of something in her mouth, she'd all but choked, her scream cut off by the material. Then she'd seen him looming over her, but just his eyes and mouth, a balaclava covering the rest of his face, and oh God, it was him, Jolly19, she knew it.

"Get up and walk out of here calmly," he'd said. "Quietly. If you don't, I'll kill your mum and dad, got it?"

Fear had streamed into her, and she'd nodded, doing everything he'd said, stumbling down the stairs behind him, his hand tight on her wrist, the skin pinching.

By the front door, he'd paused, as if he hadn't known whether to go out that way. "Where's the car keys?"

She'd pointed to the hallway table, and he'd snatched them up. He pulled the chain across the door, undid the bolt at the top, and opened up to reveal the sleeping street with the darkness punctuated by the orange fuzz from lampposts. No glows from behind windows. No one staggering down the street, drunk from the pub.

She'd had the urge to scream.

"Don't even think about it, bitch." He'd squeezed her wrist harder.

The pain burned.

She shook off the memories and thought of Mum and Dad. How long before they realised she was gone? Mum slept with earplugs in, so she wouldn't have heard them leaving the house, but Dad, wouldn't he have picked up on them going down the stairs? J had stepped on the fourth one, and it had created its usual groan, and then she'd wondered, was this even J? She'd told him about the step. What if this was someone else, an abductor, totally unrelated to him? Maybe Dad thought Elsa was just getting up for a drink.

"Coming, ready or not!" he shouted.

She shivered. He'd told her who he was after he'd got her out of the boot by his cottage, where he'd parked in a field, then dragged her through a hedge, muttering something about it being just like Tanya. He'd shoved her along the road, her bare feet hurting on the loose stones on the tarmac. But she already knew who he was, despite trying to convince herself it wasn't him, and had known he'd come for her, regardless of the police checking the street every so often. It was a sixth sense, perhaps, that whispered he wasn't going to let her get away, not after they'd chatted for so long. He'd wanted them to meet, she'd fucked that up by running away, and he'd come to get what was his.

Elsa released a shaky breath, her rear pushed against the wall, her front pressed to the sofa. The back of it curved, so she hadn't had to move it to shuffle backwards inside the gap, and if it was still in place, he might not look there.

Footsteps.

She imagined him coming up from that horrible cellar he'd first taken her to, where he'd forced her to put a school uniform on while he jabbed a brass bird at her, one he'd grabbed from the kitchen sink when they'd arrived. He'd spoken in a weird voice, in third person.

"She's worth the hassle, John."

"She's a beauty, John."

She'd had to strip in front of him, removing her pyjamas, and he'd stared, the pervert, at her bare skin. The uniform had Velcro on it, and it had a musty smell, as if it hadn't been washed in years.

That scent was strong in this tight space.

Was he coming through that weird little cupboard at the top of the cellar stairs, the one with all the coats and shoes in it?

The footsteps grew louder.

Closer.

"I'm coming to find you!" he called, singsong.

She held back a gasp, tears spilling. Her whole body shook, and she had to press her toes to the floor to stop them drumming and making a noise.

Please don't find me, please don't find me.

He crashed around, maybe in the kitchen, as the noise was like pots and pans being moved. There was a big cupboard in there, one of those old-fashioned larders. He must have thought she was in it, hiding on a shelf. Was he stupid? She wouldn't fit—she'd looked and seen it for herself while searching for somewhere to hide. And what was that strange space between the kitchen and living room? It was just there, a narrow passage that didn't lead anywhere. What did he use it for?

"Where are you, you fucking little cow?"

She stared ahead, waiting for his feet and legs to appear in the shaft of light coming in from the hallway.

The carpet had lines on it from a hoover. It reminded her of home, how on cleaning days, she loved creating the stripes.

A lump clogged her throat.

Mum, I want my mum.

Was that a car engine? Was someone coming past? Could she get out in time to wave at the window, get their attention? The rumble stopped, so whoever it was must have driven by. Hadn't they seen Dad's car poking out of the bushes? If they had, didn't they think it was odd?

"I can smell you," he said.

Elsa bit back a whimper.

"Ripe for the taking, isn't she, John?"

Oh shit, he was talking funny again. Had he brought the creepy bird with him?

"Yes, she is. And she's mine."

"You deserve her, John. You deserve love."

She almost let her bladder empty.

There was a loud crash, maybe from the kitchen.

"Shit!" he said.

He was in the room, his voice near.

"Get out from behind there, bitch. Now."

His hand reached in and grabbed her hair. He dragged her out, yanking her along with him, into the hallway. She glanced through to the kitchen, and a woman stood at the back door. Oh God, it was that detective. Bethany.

Elsa screamed. "Help me!"

Bethany's partner appeared and threw a plant pot at the glass in the back door.

"Fucking bastards," John said, then manhandled her into the coat cupboard.

He gave her a shove to the floor. She fell on stinky shoes, gagging at the smell. Scrabbling to her feet to the sound of him turning a key in the lock, she screamed again.

"Shut your stupid mouth." He jabbed the brass bird at her face, lighting his up with a slim torch, his balaclava looming in the surrounding darkness. "If you know what's good for you, keep your gob zipped, or this bird here, it'll peck a hole in your cheek. Now, get down those stairs before I push you down."

She lunged forward, bashing into him, then past him, hammering her fists on the door. "I'm in here. Help me! Please, help me!"

He snatched at her hair again and spun her around, her back to the door, his fat body flush to hers, his breath in her face. "I lied to you."

She stared into his lit-up eyes. Yes, he'd lied to her. For months. He wasn't J, the nineteen-year-old. He was a maniac pervert.

"Your parents are already dead." He paused for a second. "I slit their fucking throats before I came to get you. So, maybe now you'll do as you're told." Then, "The devil won't like it if she doesn't, John."

Banging came from the other side of the door. "Open up, John. It's the police."

Elsa was still processing what he'd said, her mind sluggish, desperate to catch up. Mum and Dad, dead? "W-what? No, please, no..."

"Piss off," he shouted, staring at the door to the right of her head. "And as for you…"

He hauled her behind him down the stairs by her hair. She clunked on each step, losing her balance, ending up on his back with him carrying her to the bottom. His grip on her hair was too tight to get loose, despite her reaching up to prise his fingers off it. He dropped her on the floor and kicked the door shut, using another key to lock it.

The door was silver. Steel?

"Probably got about five minutes, John." He moved the starling from side to side. "Hmm." He pointed the bird to the back of the room. "Get over there, Heaven13. No messing me about."

Elsa scrabbled on her hands and knees, desperate for the police to come down and save her. She pressed her back to the cold stone wall.

"On your back. Legs open," he demanded.

And she knew then, what he intended.

He stared at the bird and smiled. "Do as John says, Elsa, or you'll regret it."

CHAPTER TWENTY-NINE

Mike managed to shoulder-barge a panel of the hallway door in, reaching in to twist the key in the lock. He entered the space, Bethany following close behind, accosted by loads of stale-smelling coats hanging from hooks on the walls, the floor covered in shoes, boots, and even a pair of ratty grey flip-flops. Mike seemed to be going downwards, and it took her a moment to realise there were stairs to the left, her mind jolting at the oddity. She followed him, turning on a square landing, then descending once more.

A steel door was at the bottom.

"Fuck," Mike said. He tried the handle. "We're not getting through that."

Bethany couldn't breathe. The tension was too much, knowing what might be happening behind that steel. She ran back up, out into the hallway, then rushed around the house in search of some kind of power tool they could use to cut out the lock. Failing that task, she rang in to request the fire brigade.

Then she searched for keys, thinking there'd be spares somewhere. She rooted through drawers, cupboards, went into the bedrooms and checked there. All the while, a pounding echo filtered up, poor Mike trying to get inside the basement.

As she rummaged through the kitchen once again, in case she'd missed something the first time around, she jumped at Armed Response officers entering the kitchen from the back of the house.

"Steel door downstairs—he's taken her there," she said. "Fire brigade en route."

She showed the lead officer the odd little coat cupboard, and he disappeared inside. Unable to stand around doing nothing, she rushed out into the rear garden and checked for any ground-level windows. There weren't any, so she couldn't even get down on her knees and look at what was going on below.

What was Elsa going through?

What depraved act was John committing right this second?

She felt sick at the thought.

CHAPTER THIRTY

She was just like Catherine and Tanya, behaving wrong in the uniform. What was up with these girls? Why didn't they like him, love him?

He got off her and stormed over to the shelf. The starling sat there beside the packet of ankle socks and the makeup he'd forgotten to burn. He was glad he hadn't got rid of them now, because the cow needed a pair of socks on, and the makeup, although she didn't look right down there on the floor without compost dirtying her skin. How was she meant to grow out of the soil?

"But you didn't expect to bring anyone else back here after you tidied up, John."

He stared at the bird. "No, I didn't."

Elsa cried behind him, and it got right on his nerves. She ought to shut up before he turned on her and did something she wouldn't live to regret.

John rushed over to his backpack by the door, ignoring whoever it was hammering on the other side. They could go and do one. He pulled out the cushion, hugging it to his belly, and stared over at her.

She sobbed. "I want my mum…"

"You can't have her. John told you, she's dead."

He nodded at the starling as a thank you for reminding her—he was too angry to do it himself.

With the cushion held beneath one arm, he took the makeup off the shelf and walked over to her. She didn't have her wrists tied as he didn't have any strips of material down here, and it'd be too difficult to put the makeup on her while she was awake. She'd already scratched the shit out of his face while he'd tried to get her laughing like Mum had in her bedroom with the men. Elsa had struggled and kicked and slapped.

A fighter, but not for much longer.

John placed the makeup beside her on the floor, straddled her, pinning her arms by her sides, his knees keeping them in place, and rested the cushion over her face.

She screamed.

John pushed down on it, and she soon shut up.

She thrashed, she bucked.

She died.

He removed the cushion and stared at her. Perfect. So still.

The makeup went on well, despite him having to rush. A machine had started up out there, likely some kind of electric saw. They'd be in here soon, coming to get him, and all this…all this would come to an end. The only way he could make it continue was to imagine what things would have been like in the future, had he not been caught. He'd spend time in a cell, staring at the ceiling, pretending he was killing.

So much to look forward to still.

The sound of screeching, grinding, harsh to his ears.

He slid socks on her, annoyed her legs weren't filthy. This was wrong, so not what he'd planned. Angry, he stripped the uniform off then hung it on the wall. He took the starling from the shelf and went to sit beside her, his back against the wall, and faced the door. He'd watch it swing open, them bursting in, faces stretched into aghast expressions upon seeing her naked, dead, so very dead. They'd read him his rights, take him away, happy they'd caught him but distraught that yet another girl had died.

But that was the way of it, how it was always meant to be.

John had searched for love and hadn't found it after Irena, and it was clear now, sitting there with the cold of the floor seeping through his trousers, that he never would.

No one except your father will ever love you, John. Mum, ever the one to say it how it was.

But she was right.

And John hated that.

CHAPTER THIRTY-ONE

In the kitchen, Bethany stared at the pink baseball caps she'd found in a bedroom while she'd waited for the steel door to be opened. She'd find out at some point whether they were Catherine's and Tanya's.

She looked at the door in the hallway, waiting for Keagan to be brought through. And there he was, shoved out of the coat cupboard, into the room with her. Mike and another officer, one of the Armed Response blokes, held him tight and pushed him towards her, coming to a stop by the dining table.

She stared at John Keagan, with his face all ruined from scratches, some of them bleeding, and she knew, without having to go downstairs, that Elsa had fought him. She glanced at Mike, who shook his head, his skin ashen.

So Elsa was gone then, like the others.

A lump formed in her throat, and her eyes stung. She wanted to cry, to scream, to rail at how unfair this was but wouldn't give this piece of scum the satisfaction of seeing her so upset. He'd probably revel in the fact he was the one to get her feeling this way.

He didn't deserve to see her tears. He deserved nothing but contempt.

"John Keagan, I am arresting you for the murders of Catherine Noble, Tanya Oxbrey, Clare Hall, Elsa Masters, Gary Masters, and Beverley Masters. You do not have to say anything, but it may harm your defence if you do not mention when questioned something which you later rely on in court. Anything you do say may be given in evidence."

Another AR officer stepped in and relieved Mike of the burden of holding a killer's arm. Mike came to stand beside her, the pair of them glaring into the murderer's eyes.

"Is there anything you wish to say?" She swallowed.

"Clare is Francesca, you know." He blinked, his stare boring right into her.

She suppressed a shiver. "Who is Francesca?"

"She'd love to know, John." He laughed, sounding like birdsong. "Are you going to tell her?" He shook his head. "Maybe, maybe not."

Bethany gritted her teeth, unable to deal with a player at the moment. It was clear he saw this as a game, something to torment her with. Of *course* she wanted to know who Francesca was. It could be another girl out there, held captive, waiting for John to come back. "Is she in danger?"

John shrugged. "No idea. Haven't seen her for years. Ask her, when you find her, whether she even remembers John Keagan. It'd be nice if she did."

"Please take him away from me," she said to AR men and walked into the kitchen area, her back to the despicable bastard. She'd gleaned, from what he'd said, that Francesca was alive—if she wasn't, Bethany wouldn't be able to ask her a thing. So, someone from his past then?

They'd sift through that tomorrow.

She sighed and, once the shuffle of footsteps receded, turned to Mike. "Are you okay?"

He shook his head. "She's…"

"I gathered."

"He used a cushion. Waffle material, like Presley said." Mike shivered. "It had the imprint of makeup on it, where he'd…"

"I'll go and have a look."

She walked out into the garden, taking protectives out of a box by the door. She entered the coat space, then went down the stairs. The damaged door was open, and she took in the stone floor, the walls, a shelf with an ornament on it, what looked like some brand-new ankle socks in a pile. Her stomach rolled over at that. He'd bought them especially. Several pairs, knowing he'd take several girls.

All planned, premeditated.

And then she looked at Elsa, her face covered in that hideous makeup, her naked body, those fucking socks. Except she wasn't filthy like the others, and she didn't have pigtails.

Bethany crouched and smoothed her gloved hand over one of the flagstones. She lifted her arm and examined her fingertips.

Faint compost residue.

"I'm so sorry," she whispered to Elsa, uncaring that SOCO had come in. They'd understand why she was saying it. Bethany had failed this girl. Failed to keep her safe.

And she'd carry that burden for the rest of her life.

CHAPTER THIRTY-TWO

John had spent the remainder of the night in a holding cell, the mattress thin and uncomfortable. Now, he sat on a cheap, grey plastic chair. The walls were bare except for the many finger marks and grubby patches, from equally grubby people, he imagined. A table, chipped and scarred, had witnessed many humiliations, he reckoned, and it sat in the centre of the room. A recorder, ears of the righteous, was there immortalising his voice, as was a camera up in the corner, watching him with its single eye.

He belonged in here, some would say, but his devil thought otherwise. That devil whispered to him that there were so many opportunities in the future, many men in prison he could kill. After all, lots of them would get on his nerves. Lots would need teaching a lesson.

The solicitor, some bloke called Tabian, had come for a briefing before John had to speak to the police.

"John, tell me everything, from the beginning."

"The beginning?" He gave a nervous laugh. "Right from the start? That would take too long."

Tabian levelled him with an unwavering stare. "We've got an hour or so. Give me the main points so I know what I'm dealing with."

Retrieving the images from his mind was like flicking through a much-handled photo album. John knew who belonged on which page. He offered a quick list of his kills, explaining that they deserved it for bugging him, not really any real reason other than that. He stalled at the death of Mum and purposely left out the baby falling in the canal. Mind film whizzed past his line of vision; he saw it all as if it were yesterday, everyone he'd dealt with prior to the recent girls.

Tabian wanted to know about the child, the one in the park. Her name.

John sighed. "Clare."

"Was she the only child you killed?"

"No."

"Why are you smiling, John?"

He didn't know why.

"What happened when Clare came to meet you at the park?"

"I don't want to talk about it."

"Come on now. I've got to represent you; therefore, I need the facts as you see them. You can't expect not to tell me what I need to know."

"I killed her, all right? I killed her. There, try and get me out of the shit on that one."

The images were as sharp as when he'd stored them. Kodak fresh. Clare swinging once he'd let her go, spinning one way, then the other, until she came to a stop.

"What happened at the park?"

"What do you think? You're the solicitor, you tell me." John was tired, so tired. He hadn't had much sleep lately, what with all the fun he'd been having.

"Well, you're accused of taking children, holding them hostage, then killing them. You also took another child, Clare Hall, and hanged her from a tree. What I don't know is why. Or how many other kids you may have got your hands on before them."

"I put that noose around her neck, and she kicked out at me, pissed herself, and I got angry because Francesca had kicked me at school, too, so for her to do it again…"

"Francesca? Who's that?"

"None of your business."

"Are you going to cooperate with the police and tell them what you've told me?"

John shrugged. "Haven't made my mind up yet." God, he fancied one of those cream slices.

"Well, you need to make it up." Tabian checked his watch. "Because your interview is in five minutes."

CHAPTER THIRTY-THREE

Bethany had said all she needed to for the recording and stared at John who sat opposite beside his solicitor. Mike was next to her, and Jack Moller stood by the door in his uniform. All present and correct, probably all of them, bar John, wondering whether he'd tell all. Or maybe he wondered the same, too. She couldn't tell, couldn't read him. His face was blank, although somewhere down the line, the duty doctor had cleaned up those scratches. The distinct smell of disinfectant lingered.

"As you know, John, you have been arrested for murder." She rubbed her sweaty palms on her trousers beneath the table. "Can you please confirm, for the recording, that the following names belong to those you murdered." She reeled them off.

John seemed to think about that for a moment, cocking his head, perhaps debating whether to admit everything or keep it to himself. It didn't matter whether he confessed, they had enough evidence, and the CPS were happy to prosecute, but it *did* matter really, to the families, to those who were left behind. Some kind of answer was needed.

"There are more," he said.

Her stomach rolled. "Are you talking about more girls?"

"No. People. I did lots of things to lots of people."

"You killed them?"

"Most of them. Others…I just scared them a bit."

"What do you mean by scaring them?"

He shrugged. "I followed a girl once, in my balaclava, you know, to shit her up. Lucy Berry. She'd upset my son…"

As if that were a perfectly valid excuse.

"What did you do to her?" Bethany's pulse throbbed at the side of her neck.

"Shoved her against the fence. Threatened to kill her. She pissed herself."

Oh, the poor kid. "How old was she at the time?"

"Teenager."

"Is that why you have a thing about thirteen-year-old girls?"

"Probably." He smiled a creepy smile. "John has his reasons."

She started at his strange tone, his voice sounding bird-like. "What are those reasons?"

"Not sure I'm ready to tell you yet."

"Who else did you scare?"

"Bouncy Woman."

"Pardon?"

"Bouncy Woman. Sliced her cheeks off for being rude to my kid. Suggestive, she was. Foul."

Mike used his phone.

"What about the other murders."

John smiled wider. "If you can kill someone by telling them to slice their arm, you could say I did my mum in. If you can kill someone by dropping them in a canal, you could say I got rid of my half-brother. Then there's that woman from the campsite, a receptionist. She looked like Mum, see, that was the problem. And George, he strangled Harriet, and I let him know in so many words that I knew he'd done it. He slit his own throat, so maybe I killed him as well. There's a man at a charity function, too, and Jung, the bitch who worked in the cafeteria."

Bethany had had a chance to read the files relating to John's holiday in Devon so many years ago. The cases had been closed, one stating George Phelps had killed Harriet Wirrel and Rebecca White, the site receptionist, then had committed suicide. It had been noted that John presented as a compassionate man while being questioned and dismissed as having nothing to do with it.

There had been no file on a Lucy Berry.

"What is Bouncy Woman's real name?" she asked while drawing a pad towards her and writing a note to Mike on it.

"Jane Berry." John laughed. "She was in hospital for ages afterwards. Skin grafts, the lot. And d'you know what's funny? She thought she was so sexy, but I showed her she wasn't. Ugly for the rest of her fucking life, that one."

Revolted, she showed the pad to Mike: *Message Fran to find out who Lucy and Jane Berry are.*

Mike nodded.

"Can you explain to me why you felt it was okay to hurt and kill people because they upset you?" She rested the pad on her lap. "Because it seems that's all it was. Do you feel it's your right to do those things?"

"You don't understand what it's like to be upset all your life. It's all Mum's fault. She made me like this."

"Right. So you had no choice in the matter, is that what you're saying?"

"The devil made me do it."

How she didn't roll her eyes was anyone's guess. "That chestnut is spouted a lot. It doesn't wash with me."

"It's true. You wait until you piece it together. Thirteen years I was good. Thirteen. Then that devil came back."

"How old were you when you put the baby in the canal?"

"A kid. Ten, eleven, dunno."

"You do know."

"I can't think straight."

"I don't believe you. I bet you have everything in your head and you revisit it, think about it, get all pleased with yourself over what you've done. If you started young, I put it to you that those memories were enough to sustain you for those thirteen years, no other reason. You were happy, with Irena and Edward, loved them to distraction, and then one day, Lucy Berry upset your son, and a switch was flipped."

"That's it, that's exactly what happened."

"What I don't understand is, why take those girls? Why talk to Catherine, Tanya, Elsa, and Karly? What were you looking for?"

"I don't want to talk about that."

"What was the purpose of holding them in that cellar?"

"I wanted them to grow out of the soil."

"Excuse me?" She frowned.

"I wanted them to like the uniform and what happened when they had it on. I wanted them to be Mum, the happy one, not the mean one."

"Are you saying you wanted the girls because you wanted them to be your mother? That you have a thing about her?"

"Too painful." He stared at the ceiling. "I wonder if Mrs Drayton is still alive. She'll tell you a few stories about me. I used to kill animals, sling them over her fence, and she *hated* it." He chuckled. "Silly old cow and her Murray Mints."

He was off in his head, travelling down Memory Lane, so she let him waffle on, let him spill all the things he'd done. The part where he'd taken his half-brother out of the pram then threw him in the canal was particularly sickening, heartbreaking, and she watched his face with every explanation, how it lit up when it got to the gory parts. During the telling, drinks were replenished, sandwiches brought in, as it seemed he didn't want to stop. His earlier claim of not wanting to talk about it had gone by the wayside now he had a captive audience. People listening.

And that was the thing she got from his account. No one had really listened to him until Irena came along. Henry Keagan had been too busy with work, and too tired once he got home to really give John much attention apart from them going fishing, while his mother—if John's version of her was to be believed—was a pisshead who cared more about gin and sex than anything else. Irena and Edward, they'd steadied him for a time, John thinking he'd found the pot of gold at the end of his rainbow.

How sad that the messed-up child he'd been had found his utopia, only to ruin it in his misguided idea that hurting and killing because those he loved had been upset was the right way to go. And he'd done it for himself, too, murdering to stop those people ever hurting him again.

All in all, a fucked-up tale by a fucked-up man.

"What did you do between killing Jung and the girls?" she asked. "Were you quiet then? Had your devil gone?"

"I had the plans. They kept me busy."

"The plans?"

"On how to get the girls."

"What made you act out those plans? Why now? Why not last year or the one before?"

"I thought of Francesca a lot. It was the right time."

"Who is she, John?"

And he explained, that as a little lad, he'd become obsessed with a girl in his class, associating her with his mother—the school uniform had merged them together in his head. Bethany put two and two together. Here was a boy, desperate for his mum to love him. As he'd grown into a man, he'd become confused—Lucy Berry had represented something to him, and coupled with Francesca, he'd created a way to bring them together—he wanted Catherine, Tanya, Elsa, and Karly in ankle socks, the uniform, and to be his mother, smiling and laughing while he had sex with them.

"Except they hadn't, they hated it, hated me, just like her." He slapped his palm on the table. "They're all the same, these women."

She called a halt to the interview. It had been three hours, and they all needed rest. The soil issue was still unanswered, him using the compost, and a few other things just didn't make sense, but perhaps later today, or tomorrow, he'd explain the loose ends. Whatever they were, they weren't a good enough reason to kill. There was a tiny part of her that felt sorry for the boy he'd been, a child who'd had to learn how to feed himself, who'd released stress by harming small animals, thinking if they hurt, it would take his pain away. Transference. She suspected the animals were no longer enough. He'd progressed to people.

She left Jack Moller to return Keagan to his cell and walked with Mike up to the incident room. Fran and Leona were hard at work, heads bent at their desks.

"Anything on Lucy Berry and her mother?" She flopped into a chair.

Fran nodded. "Only the mother. She'd been followed across Southbourne, attacked in the stream, her cheeks removed and placed in her hands."

Oh. John hadn't mentioned he'd done that.

"Okay... Do they still live in Shadwell?"

Fran waved a sheet of paper. "I've got the address here. Hubert Lane. John used to live opposite."

"Hmm. I think we'll pay her a visit, see if John's telling the truth when he said he'd scared Lucy." She explained what he'd told them. "If he *did* do this, why wasn't it reported? I just don't get that at all."

"Maybe Lucy didn't tell her mum it happened," Leona said. "Sounds like he scared her shitless."

"You could be right." Bethany sighed. "We've got one hell of a lot of cases to sift through. He's being vague about the dates at the moment, but we have names to go on, which will create hits when we search the database. Anything else new?"

"Catherine's and Tanya's clothes were found on a verge along with their phones and an iPad," Fran said.

"And a baby's blanket had been stuffed inside the cushion cover," Leona supplied.

Had it belonged to John's half-brother? He'd kept it all this time?

Christ, this had turned into one hell of a Monday, what with their early morning visit to Elsa's grandparents, informing them that three of their family had been wiped out. Then there had been the interview, and there was still so much to do, but they'd plod on, as always, until it had all been wrapped up.

She planned to ask John next time about the starling and why it was on the shelf in the cellar. She suspected the reason for the ankle socks, but she wanted to hear it from him just the same. The makeup, too, and its relevance. Also, why was there a strange alleyway inside the cottage? Maybe he didn't even know.

And there was Francesca to find, a woman now, the same age as John. Old school records would help there. It would be interesting to see whether she even remembered John, or if, as he would probably admit, he was as invisible to her as John had been to his mother most of the time. Just a boy, no one worth bothering with.

No one worth loving.

And that, Bethany thought, was the crux of it.

She sighed, feeling grimy from listening to John's account. Maybe she could nip home for a shower, seeing as she'd been up half the night and had done a weekend of overtime. They were all knackered.

She looked around at her team: Mike, Fran, Leona. And at Talitia's empty desk. They needed another member really, now Talitia was back in Oxfordshire. Maybe Jack Moller fancied taking her place. She'd ask him when she got the chance.

For now, it was nose to the grindstone. Deep breaths and take one step at a time.

There was light at the end of the harrowing tunnel.

Something to be thankful for.

Printed in Great Britain
by Amazon